Operation Tonic

Robert Cubitt

Carter's Commandos – Book 5

© 2021

Having purchased this eBook, it is for your personal use only. It may not be copied, reproduced, printed or used in any way, other than in its intended format.

Published by Selfishgenie Publishing of, Northamptonshire, England.

This novel is entirely a work of fiction. All the names characters, incidents, dialogue, events portrayed and opinions expressed in it are either purely the product of the author's imagination or they are used entirely fictitiously and not to be construed as real. Any resemblance to actual persons, living or dead, events or localities is entirely coincidental. Nothing is intended or should be interpreted as representing or expressing the views and policies of any department or agency of any government or other body.

All trademarks used are the property of their respective owners. All trademarks are recognised.

The right of Robert Cubitt to be identified as the author of this work has been asserted in accordance with sections 77 and 78 of the Copyright Designs and Patents Act 1988.

Other titles by Robert Cubitt

Fiction

The Deputy Prime Minister
The Inconvenience Store
The Charity Thieves

Warriors Series

The Warriors: The Girl I Left Behind Me
The Warriors: Mirror Man

The Magi Series

The Magi
Genghis Kant (The Magi Book 2)
New Earth (The Magi Book 3)
Cloning Around (The Magi Book 4)
Timeslip (The Magi Book 5)
The Return Of Su Mali (The Magi Book 6)
Robinson Kohli (The Magi Book 7)
Parallel Lines (The Magi Book 8)
Restoration (The Magi Book 9)

Carter's Commandos Series

Operation Absalom (Carter's Commandos Book 1)
Operation Tightrope (Carter's Commandos Book 2)
Operation Dagger (Carter's Commandos Book 3)
Operation Carthage (Carter's Commandos Book 4)

Non-Fiction

A Commando's Story
I'm So Glad You Asked Me That
I Want That Job

In memory of all the Commandos of World War II
and in memory of one commando in particular. The truth of what they did is often stranger than any fiction that can be written.

Contents

Author's Note On The Language Used In This Book		9
1.	El Atacka	11
2.	Q Ship	27
3.	Alsourah	45
4.	Night Raid	69
5.	Operation Husky	89
6.	Agony	123
7.	The Bridge	149
8.	Every Man For Himself	175
9.	*Kommandobefehl*	193
10.	Montgomery	211
Historical Notes		253
Preview – Operation Terminus		263
And Now		287

Author's Note On The Language Used In This Book

This is a story about soldiers and to maintain authenticity the language used reflects that. There is a use of swear words of the strongest kind. It is not my intention to cause offence, but only to reflect the language that was and still is used by soldiers. Apart from the swearing there is other language used that may cause offence. I don't condone the use of that language, but it reflects the period in which the story is set. While we may live in more enlightened times and would never consider using such words, the 1940s were different and the language used is contemporary for the period. We cannot change the past, we can only change the present and the future and I'm glad that our language has changed and become more sensitive to the feelings of others but we must never forget our past. We should, however, seek not to repeat it.

Abbreviations of rank used in this book (in descending order of seniority):

<u>Army Ranks</u>

Lt Col – Lieutenant Colonel (often referred to simply as Colonel by their own subordinates)
Maj – Major
Capt – Captain
Lt – Lieutenant
2Lt – Second Lieutenant
RSM – Regimental Sergeant Major (Warrant Office Class 1)
CSM – Company Sergeant major (Warrant Officer Class 2)
TSM – Troop Sergeant Major (Warrant Officer Class 2) as used by the commandos.
SMjr – Sergeant Major (generic)
CSgt – Colour Sergeant

SSgt – Staff Sergeant
Sgt - Sergeant
LSgt – Lance Sergeant; a Brigade of Guards rank, but sometimes used by the commandos instead of Corporal.
Cpl – Corporal
LCpl – Lance Corporal
Pvt – Private
Tpr – Trooper, a cavalry rank equivalent to Private but used by the commandos.

Cdo – the abbreviation used when naming a specific commando, eg 15 Cdo.

Royal Navy ranks

Lt Cdr – Lieutenant Commander, equivalent to a Major.
Lt – Lieutenant, equivalent to its Army counterpart
SLt – Sub Lieutenant – equivalent to a Second Lieutenant in the Army.
CPO – Chief Petty Officer – equivalent to Warrant Officer Second Class in the Army.

Other military terminology is explained within the text where the narrative allows, or is explained in footnotes.

1 – El Ataka

Even after nearly two weeks of travel, the camp was a less than welcoming sight. Rows of dun coloured tents stretched away in parallel lines, a larger tent with a chimney sticking up behind it indicating where the mess tent was. A wooden hut that looked as though it might have been made from packing cases, served as a guardroom, a wooden pole, striped red and white, resting across a couple of white painted oil drums was the sole barrier against intruders.

Behind the camp, at a distance of about three miles across a flat plain, some low rocky hills rose to form a backdrop. The intervening ground, Carter was to discover, was called the El Ataka Plain.

A sentry snapped to attention as the commando was called to a halt on the road. His shoulder tabs bore the legend 'South Africa'. He was from one of the African Auxiliary Pioneer Corps[1] (AAPC) units that were raised from the tribal lands. Carter had seen them several times on their journey south from Port Said.

Standing next to the nearest sentry was a Captain, wearing the shoulder flashes of the Royal Army Service Corps, acting as a one-man reception committee. The sentry raised the pole and the officer marched out to salute the 2IC, who was leading the commando in the absence of the CO.

After a short conversation, accompanied by some pointing, the commando was permitted to enter the camp. At this point the NCOs took over, detailing the commandos to their tents. Twelve men to a tent, five tents per troop. Senior NCOs had their own shared tents, as did the officers. Slightly less crowded, but not by much. There was no haste. It would be a while before the rear party arrived with the trucks carrying their kit bags, ammunition and other stores.

The 2IC and Quarter Master were closeted with the RASC Captain for some while, being briefed on the arrangements for the supply of food, water and other essential consumables. The rest of the officers would be briefed later.

The heat was oppressive, the humidity worse. Sunshine glistened off the Gulf of Suez, a short distance from the camp gate. It looked welcoming but the troops knew that there were jellyfish in there that could inflict a nasty sting. Someone had suggested there were sharks as well, but that hadn't been confirmed. Out in the gulf, a dozen merchant ships sat at anchor, waiting their turn to make the one hundred and twenty mile journey through the Suez Canal to the Mediterranean Sea at Port Said. An Ack-Ack[2] ship bristled with guns, standing guard against air attack.

As the sun set over southern Egypt, a metallic clanging summoned the soldiers to their first hot meal in a week. It was 'anonymous stew', but after so much bully beef they welcomed it. The AAPC cooks also made a pretty good cup of tea, they discovered.

Fed and watered, the men stretched out on their camp beds, resting as the heat of the day ebbed away.

15 Commando had arrived at El Ataka.

[1] African Auxiliary Pioneer Corps (AAPC) – When World War II broke out, the Kings of the High Commission Territories in South Africa, the self-governing tribal lands, wished to show their loyalty to Britain. They allowed their men to volunteer for service with the British Army. In some cases the volunteering part was a little more compulsory than in others. Men from Swaziland (also called Eswatini), Basutoland (now Lesotho) and Bechuanaland (now Botswana) formed labour pools which were employed in Egypt to replace Cypriots and Palestinians who had been killed in the defence of Greece. Their main work was as labour for building roads and airfields, but they also provided guards for stores depots and tented camps. Later in the war, manpower shortages led to them being used to man coastal artillery and anti-aircraft batteries. They also followed the British 8th Army into Sicily and Italy. The AAPC grew to

approximately 36,000 strong before being demobilised in 1946. They suffered 816 casualties during the war, including 600 men of the 618th Basoto Pioneer Company that were killed when the SS Erinpura was sunk by German bombers off Benghazi..

[2] Ack-Ack – anti-aircraft. The words are taken from the word assigned for the letter A in a form of phonetic alphabet used during World War I.

* * *

"In terms of security," The 2IC said, "Our greatest risk is theft. As we discovered in Algiers, anything not nailed down is liable to go walkies. Apparently, it's even worse here. The average Egyptian is an honest, hardworking sort, but Suez is a port city and they always attract the wrong types, looking for easy pickings.

"You can say that again." One of the other officers said. "I'm from Liverpool and half the houses in our street were kept fed by stuff that had fallen off the back of a lorry leaving the docks." That brought a laugh from the assembled officers.

"Precisely. We can expect thieves to try to get through the perimeter fence at night, according to Captain Reynolds." Carter assumed that Reynolds was the RASC Captain. "The AAPC guards do carry out patrols, but there's too few of them to protect the whole perimeter twenty four hours a day. So we will do what we did in Algiers and mount our own patrols outside the wire. It worked in Algiers so I dare say it will work here. Word will soon get out not to mess with us." There was a threat implied by the words and Carter knew what injuries could be inflicted with the wooden handle of a trenching tool. He didn't approve of the action but knew that telling commandos to exercise restraint would fall on deaf ears.

One of the Tilley lamps[1] guttered as the pressure started to drop and someone gave it a couple of pumps to restore it.

A hand went up. "Any idea how long we'll be here, Sir?"

"Not a clue. Hopefully the CO will get some indication while he's in Cairo. He's due here at the end of the week.

"We seem to be a long way from anywhere we're likely to be needed." Someone else commented.

"We were a long way away when we were in Scotland" The 2IC reminded them, "but that didn't stop us doing our jobs. Even though the war in North Africa is over, the airborne threat still exists. The Luftwaffe are only a couple of hours flying time away in Crete, so the powers that be are keen to keep the army spread out, so we make a harder target. I'm sure that you saw some of the other camps as we came down here."

There had, indeed, been plenty of camps to be seen. The whole approach into the city of Suez seemed to be one vast sea of dun coloured tents. Much of the 8th Army had been withdrawn back into Egypt to shorten their supply lines, leaving garrison troops to protect the towns and cities of Libya and Tunisia.

"The men want to know if they can go into town, Sir." Carter chipped in.

"Not yet, Steven. First, we have to get the camp organised, then I want us to do some navigation exercises to get to know the area. We're here to train for our next operation, so we've got to find the right sort of locations for landing and assaults. The CO will tell us more about that when he gets here, I'm sure.

[1] Tilley lamp – A paraffin fuelled camping lamp that uses air pressure to force a fine mist of paraffin through a heated element to provide a much brighter light than could be produced by burning a wick. The lamp needed 'pumping up' from time to time to maintain the air pressure. Largely replaced by bottled gas fuelled or battery powered lamps these days. The Tilley company still exists and still manufactures its eponymous lamps.

* * *

The Officers' Club was busy even in the middle of the week. Junior officers jostled for space around the bar, while more senior figures made use of the tables for games of cards or backgammon. Carter squeezed himself into a gap that opened up briefly next to a Royal Navy Lieutenant Commander who sat nursing his drink at the bar.

The buzz of dozens of conversations was such that Carter had to raise his voice to order a glass of whisky. When the Egyptian barman went to drop ice into the drink, Carter held his hand over the top of his glass and said 'no thanks'.

"It's OK to take the ice, old chap." The naval officer said. "The water's from a safe source."

When they had arrived at the transit camp in Port Said they had been given lectures on health and hygiene by a Royal Army Medical Corps doctor. "I can't stress this enough, gentlemen." He had said. "Don't drink the water unless it has been boiled for at least five minutes or has been treated with water purifying tablets. Your weak British tummies just can't handle the local bacteria. The most common mistake people make is to put ice in their drinks or eat salad vegetables that have been washed in untreated water. You'll end up with gyppie tummy[1]. It won't kill you, but it will probably make you wish you were dead." He said, as his audience gave an appreciative chuckle.

It was a hard lesson to get across to some of the men, who thought they were strong enough to resist a few bacteria. They were wrong, of course. Two men had to be left behind in Port Said because they were unfit to travel and another had to be taken off the train as they travelled south.

"If you're sure." Carter said.

The man raised his glass and gave it a swirl, the ice cubes clinking against the side. "It's good enough for my G&T."

Carter removed his hand and nodded to the barman. Two cubes splashed into the glass and the barman hastened to the far end of the bar where empty glasses were being waved to try to attract his attention.

"Peter Curshaw." The man offered his hand.

"Steven Carter, Sir." Carter replied.

"First names only in the club, old chap. Unless there's braid on the peak of the cap." Gold braid on the peak of the cap indicated an officer of senior rank. It would be unseemly for a junior officer to address anyone of that seniority by their first name, even in a social setting such as this.

"Thanks for the tip."

Curshaw spotted the Commando flashes on the sleeves of Carter's shirt. "You lot are new in town."

"Yes, just arrived last week." Having been Duty Officer the night before, Carter had been granted 'shore leave' to visit the Officer's Club, along with the men who had just finished a week of night patrols around the camp. They had travelled in a three ton truck, the men being dropped outside the Salvation Army Club, with warnings not to stray too far. Carter knew the warning was a waste of time. The men were keen to explore the dubious delights of Suez and no warnings would be heeded, no matter how strongly worded. Carter just hoped that they would remember the other warning they had been given, to stay in groups of four. Those and the dire warnings of the medical officer in Port Said.

The truck had dropped Carter off at the Officers' Club, agreeing to return at twenty two hundred hours to collect him and however many of the men that made it back to the Sally Army.

"I won't ask what you're doing here. I know you can't say."

"It's probably the worst kept secret in Egypt." Carter replied with a grin. "You'll see us around a lot. We've got landing craft arriving in a few days and it's a bit hard to miss them. Presumably you're on convoy escort duties."

"No, actually. I've got command of a flotilla of fast Motor Launches. We're on anti-pirate patrols."

"What, 'yo-ho-ho and a bottle of rum' and all that? Sounds a bit old fashioned."

"You'd be surprised. It's a big problem."

"You mean against convoys guarded by destroyers and corvettes." Carter sounded dubious.

"Oh no. They're too well armed to be bothered. No, these are locals looking for easy pickings. They attack trading dhows."

"There can't be much money in that."

"You'd be surprised. That coffee you had for breakfast was probably made from beans grown in Ethiopia and brought up the Red Sea in dhows. The spices that hide the fact that the meat in the stew is on the turn, are traded in Aden and Muscat. Going the other way is cotton, either in bales or as made up cloth. Also, there's manufactured goods from Europe, most of it's channelled through Turkey these days so it can't be traced back to the German occupied countries, but once it arrives in Suez it's shipped on in dhows, just as it always has been. Your average dhow will carry a cargo worth tens of thousands of pounds. Then there's the people doing the pilgrimage to Mecca, travelling from Sudan, Ethiopia, Egypt and along the coast from Yemen and further afield; they're ripe to be robbed. Some are taken as slaves, especially the women."

"Slavery as well. Who'd have thought it." Carter finished his drink and signalled to the barman for another. He nodded at the Navy man's empty glass and it was pushed across for a refill.

"It never really went away in this part of the world. It's just better hidden."

"But what's this got to do with us?"

"The Egyptian Navy is quite small and is too stretched in the Red Sea and they're not well equipped for inshore work, so we're helping out as a favour. We carry Egyptian police officers who actually make any arrests, just to keep things legitimate."

"Are you having much success?"

"Not really. We have to be very lucky to intercept any of their boats. Most of the dhows don't carry radios, so they can't call for help if they're attacked. We think the pirates are based on the Saudi Arabian Peninsula and we can't encroach into their waters without risking a serious diplomatic incident. His Majesty King Saud is too busy with his internal political problems to pay much attention to a few pirates at the extreme northern end of his Kingdom. He does get a bit upset when pilgrims are kidnapped, so most of his naval activity is centred around Jiddah, which is the port nearest to Mecca."

"So where do the local pirates hide?"

"On the far side of the Gulf of Aqaba. That's the waterway that leads from the Red Sea up to Transjordan and Palestine[2]. The Saudi coastline is very sparsely populated. Mainly small fishing villages and a few palm groves where there's water. We think they may be using one of those as a base."

"Can't you lie off shore and wait for them."

"We've tried that, but they seem to have good intelligence. They always seem to know we're coming and don't venture out, or they sneak past us in the dark, or they send their boats out before we even arrive. I've got three boats and they have to be refuelled and re-victualled at regular intervals. I can't cover the amount of sea that needs to be patrolled."

"I know what I'd do." Carter said.

"I'd welcome any suggestions."

"First set a trap. Train your men to sail a dhow and then go out and wait to be attacked. I'd put a few commandos on board, maybe a dozen, just to make sure that there was enough firepower."

"What we call a Q Ship[3]." Curshaw said, looking thoughtful. "A lion dressed up like a lamb. But they never all attack at once. Some would be bound to get away and warn the others."

"You follow them. Find out where they go. Then you mount a commando raid to clean out their nest. Commandos could get in and out without anyone even knowing they'd been there."

"Sounds intriguing. Do you really think that the Saudi's would never be any the wiser?"

"Only if they actually saw you with their own eyes. Given what you've said that's probably unlikely. But any competent commando would do a recce first, just to make sure there weren't any army, navy or police around. Do the Saudi's have an air force?"

"I've never seen any planes other than ours and Jerry's. I have to say it's an intriguing idea. It certainly beats cruising around in circles hoping to stumble across them at sea."

"What sort of boats do they use?"

"Quite modern now. When they first started up they used old fishing boats or dhows of their own, but they were slow and clumsy. Since then they've stolen enough cargoes to be able to trade up to skiffs powered by outboard motors. Each boat holds four or five men. They're still not fast enough to get away from my boats, but they can outpace the dhows they attack."

"What do they do when they capture a dhow. Do they unload the cargo?"

"No. According to the ones we've arrested, they take the dhow to a safe location and let it be known they have it, what the cargo is and what price they're looking for. Potential buyers come along, view the cargo and make them an offer. Once a price has been agreed the new owner takes it to one of the ports that's not too fussy about checking ownership. There's plenty of those along the African coast and in the Persian Gulf. They sell the cargo then sell the dhow and a few weeks later it's probably back in Suez with a fresh coat of paint and a new name. It's very hard to prove ownership of a dhow."

"OK, as I see it, you have two different problems. The first is to take the pirates prisoner, the second is to find out where their base is so it can be attacked. The first part we've already covered. The second part means letting one or more of the boats escape, then follow them ashore with a boat of your own. You'd have to have a boat in the water already, something small but also capable of keeping up with them."

"I think they'd rumble us if they saw a boat in the water. It wouldn't look right to them and they'd break off the attack. I think we'd have to capture one of their boats, but that might be possible if we're using a Q boat."

"How well are they armed?"

"At first all they had was World War I vintage rifles and handguns left behind by the Turks. But they've got more modern weapons now, mainly Lee Enfields stolen from us and Italian rifles left behind after the Abyssinian campaign. There's an extensive black market for weaponry in the region. The police interrogate the prisoners we catch and we've heard tell of automatic weapons, but we haven't seen any direct evidence of those yet."

"How do they find about about the dhows they're going to attack?"

"We suspect that they've got informers in the native port, where the dhows tie up. Let's face it, the Jerries are running plenty of local agents, so it's no stretch to presume that the pirates can do the same. For north bound traffic they probably have spotters along the coast. The dhows tend to keep inshore. It's easier to navigate that way and they can find shelter quicker if the weather turns nasty."

"You'd need to put a story round the port about your dhow then. Make it sound like a nice juicy target."

"You make it sound like we're actually going to do it." Curshaw laughed.

"It's worth giving some serious consideration. The only thing stopping you, really, is the diplomatic ramifications of mounting an operation on Saudi Arabian soil. The part with the dhow you could do tomorrow if you had the resources."

"True. That itself would be success and we've had damn few of those."

Curshaw bought Carter 'one for the road' and they chatted some more, then Carter had to leave to catch his truck. Curshaw rose from his bar stool as well.

"Good luck." Carter said as he left the club, Curshaw climbing into a taxi to take him back to his boats. "If you go ahead with the idea, let me know how you get on."

[1] Gyppie tummy – a corruption of 'Egyptian tummy', an illness that had been suffered by British soldiers in Egypt since before the

days of Kitchener. Differences between the way water is treated in northern Europe and elsewhere results in bacteria remaining in the water that visitors can't tolerate. In India it was referred to as 'Delhi belly'. For the most part the water isn't dirty, it's just different. British and other European travellers still suffer from these ailments today, which is why bottled water is so popular in hot climates.

[2] These were the names given to the British protectorates that we now know as the countries Jordan and Israel. The port city of Aqaba gives its name to the gulf that gives Jordan it's only access to the sea. On one side it shares a border with Saudi Arabia and on the other a border with Israel at the neighbouring city of Eilat.

[3] A Q Ship could be a naval vessel disguised as a merchant ship to fool the enemy, or a merchant ship which carried concealed armaments. They were used to lull enemy vessels into a false sense of security before attacking them. The first recorded use of a Q Ship or boat was in the 1670s when a specially designed Royal Navy cutter, HMS Kingfisher, was used against Algerian pirates. In World War II the Germans used 13 Q Ships. The Atlantis, an auxiliary cruiser (a naval vessel that looked like a merchant ship) which they had named *Goldenfels* which was disguised as a Dutch merchant vessel, was responsible for the sinking of 145,000 tons of Allied shipping. Britain used nine Q ships with the intention of entrapping German U Boats, all but one of which were converted merchantmen. HMS Chatsgrove was a converted Royal Navy P-class sloop built in 1918. Two of those Q Ships were sunk in 1940 and the remainder were decommissioned in 1941 without having recorded any successes.

* * *

The arrival of the landing ship Prince Leopold, a former Belgian cross channel steamer, signalled the start of the commando's more intensive training. They still had no idea what their objective was to be. All they knew was that it was in the Mediterranean Sea and the landings would take place in high summer, probably July.

"To be honest with you." Lt Col Vernon had told them on his arrival from Cairo, "I'm not sure Monty knows what to do with us. Colonel Bob Laycock[1] is on his planning staff and, as you know, he's an experienced commando, but the planners don't seem to be listening to him that well. I'm sure they'll find us a suitable objective but, in the meantime, we just have to train for any eventuality."

So, the commandos built simulated defences along the rocky shore of the Gulf of Suez and started attacking them from the sea, both by day and by night. They then built strongpoints further inland and simulated raids deeper into enemy territory. All the attacks started before dawn, meaning they had to board the Prince Leopold the night before, steam out into the gulf and then turn back to board their landing craft before the assaults. It was tiring work and the three months between their operation in Tunis and their arrival in Suez had left them with lower fitness standards than those in which they took such great pride. So they now worked extra hard to regain that edge that made them, in their not so humble opinion, the best soldiers in the world.

Out on the plain beyond their camp they constructed a firing range and all day and often into the night, the crack and rattle of small arms fire echoed over the tents. Ammunition trucks, manned by more of the AAPC, were frequent arrivals at the camp gates to replace the thousands of bullets that the commandos expended on the range. As for the native population, after a few night-time encounters with the commando patrols, they learned to give the camp a wide berth.

Each afternoon, between three and five pm, the commandos took refuge in their tents, the side walls lowered and the flaps tied down as tightly as physically possible. Not only was it the hottest part of the day, but a vicious wind blew up across the plain, sending dust flying through the camp to coat anything that wasn't covered up. It got into the food and water supplies, it got into men's eyes, mouths and up their noses. It caked their weapons that they kept so scrupulously clean. It attacked their stomachs when it was ingested and, all in all, made life a misery. The men's only defence was to wrap their neck clothes around their faces and hope to get a little sleep inside the heat and darkness of their tents. After the wind died away the men were allowed to swim, all thoughts of jellyfish or sharks forgotten as they tried to clean the thick dust from their bodies, before they headed into the port to board the Prince Leopold for yet another assault on the shores of the Gulf of Suez.

Lt Col Vernon disappeared up to Cairo again and when he returned the mocked up installations they were attacking were modified. A new installation was built some distance inland, made to look like an artillery battery, using lengths of metal scaffolding pole to represent the guns. Troops took turns acting as defenders while the remainder of the commando carried out the assaults, the sounds of blank ammunition and pyrotechnics shattering the dawn. Barriers were erected for them to negotiate. They were told they were drystone walls, though a lack of materials made them appear more like heaps of brown desert soil topped with some of the smaller boulders taken from the beach.

For recreation, games of football and rugby were organised against neighbouring units but the commando's competitiveness and physical aggression soon meant opponents were hard to find. The RAF refused to play them on reputation alone, the CO of the nearest RAF base having encountered the commandos once before back in England. His technicians and aircrew were too valuable for him to risk broken limbs playing sports against the commandos. If there was no unit that would play them, the troops played against each other, making the rivalry even more intense.

Carter was making his way back from the firing ranges, wiping grime from his face with his neck cloth. He hadn't had a good morning, having hit the static targets with only half his shots and missing the moving targets completely. Although he usually carried a Tommy gun when on operations, all the officers kept their hand in with three-oh-threes as well.

He was still puzzling over his uncharacteristically poor performance when one of the Headquarters clerks intercepted him on the way to the officers' tents. "CO's compliments, Sir. Could you join him in his office." Carter suppressed a smile; the CO's 'office' was a curtained off end of the HQ tent.

"Thank you, Ecclestone. Tell the CO I'll be there as soon as I've cleaned myself up a bit."

Carter entered his tent and grabbed his washing kit. No time for a shower; etiquette dictated that he refilled the elevated water tank for the next person who wanted to use the facility and he didn't have time for that. A lick and a promise, to remove the worst of the grime, would have to do. Fortunately, the laundry truck hadn't delivered that week so he wouldn't be expected to be in a completely clean uniform. He sorted out the cleanest of his already used shirts and shorts and smartened himself up as best he could.

Still hot and bothered, he hurried to the HQ tent, coughed loudly in front of the CO's curtain to announce his presence and stuck his head around the open end.

"Ah, Steven. I understand you've met Lt Cdr Curshaw."

[1] In 1941 Col Robert Laycock took a force of three commandos, 7, 8 and 11, to the Mediterranean for the purpose of carrying out harassing and disrupting operations against the Germans and the Italians. On arrival he absorbed the three small Middle East commandos, 50, 51 and 52, into his command. As he wasn't a Brigadier, his force couldn't be called a Brigade, so it was referred to as Layforce. They provided men for the siege of Tobruk, carried out an operation on the Litani river in in Syria, a major raid on Bardia in Libya and aided in the defence of Crete, where they suffered heavy losses. A small force from 11 Cdo also carried out an audacious raid to try to kidnap General Erwin Rommel, but it failed as he wasn't at his reported location. He had left there several weeks before the raid.

Suffering heavy losses and a lack of reinforcements, Layforce was eventually forced to disband. With the remaining commandos being absorbed into organisations such as the Long Range Desert Group. One of 8 Cdo's officers, Major David Sterling, formed the unit that would one day become famous as the Special Air Service Regiment. Laycock was later promoted to Brigadier and given command of 2nd Special Service Brigade, which would evolve into 2nd Commando Brigade, operating in Italy, Yugoslavia and Albania.

2 – Q Ship

"Well, what brings you to our humble abode?" Carter asked as he shook Curshaw's hand. Out of the corner of his eye Carter noted that the CO's uniform was in pristine condition, making him feel even scruffier. The CO had a batman, of course, who probably washed and ironed the CO's clothes each night. None of the other officers had personal servants, but it was justified in the CO's case as he seemed to work nineteen hours a day. His energy was boundless and the whole commando was in awe of it.

Washing their own clothes wasn't allowed because of restrictions on the use of water. With about thirty thousand soldiers of XIII Corps camped in and around Suez, the strain on the water supply was evident, so the communal laundries run by the Pioneer Corps and AAPC had to be used. But even they were cracking under the strain. Their promise of a three-day turnaround was nothing but a joke, as everyone knew.

But Curshaw wasn't there to discuss the problems with laundry, that much Carter knew.

"I understand that you and Lt Cdr Curshaw had an interesting chat about pirates." The CO focused Carter's mind on the purpose of Curshaw's visit.

"Something of an academic exercise on my part, Sir." Carter explained himself. "Every problem has a solution. Sometimes you just have to come at it from a different angle. As a soldier and a commando, I'd like to think I was able to do that."

"Yes, Peter explained your idea to me. I have to say, it's probably the sort of suggestion that I might have made."

"I took your idea up to Commander Litton, who commands the Red Sea Inshore Squadron." Curshaw continued. "He liked it as well. Reminded him of his days chasing Chinese Pirates around the South China Sea before the war. So he took it to Fleet HQ. This morning I got the OK for the first part of it, the use of a dhow as a Q

Ship. So I trotted over here to see if you would be interested in giving us a helping hand."

"What about the second part, the raid on wherever they're using as a base." Carter asked.

"That's gone to London for Foreign Office input. But it's gone with the Admiral's letter of recommendation. Everyone's terribly impressed and I made sure you got full credit for coming up the scheme."

Carter wasn't sure that was a good thing. He knew from hard won experience what effect a reputation could have on life expectancy. The pitcher that goes often to the well will be broken at last, as the old proverb had it. His nickname in the commando was 'Lucky', but as any gambler knew, luck ran out eventually.

But Carter couldn't be seen to be ungrateful. "Thanks for that. But I'm afraid that we're right in the middle of training for our big op, so now wouldn't be …"

"Nonsense, Steven." Vernon cut across him. "I think a little break from the routine is just what the men need. How many would you need, Peter?"

"Well, you'd need to take a look at the dhow when we get it, but I think that you originally said a dozen or so, didn't you Steven?"

Silently cursing his own chattiness in the Officers' Club, Carter nodded his head. "Yes, a dozen seemed to be about right. Though you'd need a lot more if you actually wanted to carry out a raid."

"One step at a time, Steven." Vernon advised. "I think I could lend you an officer and a dozen men, Peter. When would you want them?"

"We've already identified a dhow. Its owner is also its captain and he lost a second vessel to pirates a while back, so he's willing to help us, at a price. I've been promised money to lease the dhow and the owner will train my men to sail it. I've got an officer who was a regular sailor before the war and a dhow isn't much different from a yacht. If I can get the lease sorted this week then I would guess I could have it standing offshore for you to take a look at by the end of next week. The pirates usually attack just before sunset, so they can use the darkness to make their getaway. I'd like to carry out the operation under a full moon so that we have enough light to follow them back to their base, so that would mean mounting the operation the following week."

"What do you think, Steven?"

"I think that would be enough time. The men would need only a couple of days to become acclimatised to the dhow and how best to ambush the pirates after they've boarded. They can do that while we're in transit. Who have you in mind to lead it? I think Arthur Murray would be quite keen …"

"Your idea Steven, so I think you should lead it, don't you?" Vernon was smiling, but Carter knew it wasn't just a suggestion. His plan –his operation.

It wasn't that Carter didn't want to lead the operation. After all, he was a commando and thrived on action. It was more that arresting a few pirates just wasn't that exciting a prospect. He was a fighting soldier, not a policeman. But the CO had spoken, which meant that Carter's name would go on the operation.

"As you wish, Sir. I'll ask my troop for volunteers …"

"Actually, your men have had more than their fair share of glory, so I'd like to spread it around the whole commando. Two men from each troop, if you please."

"With me that makes it thirteen, Sir. Can I make it three men from one of the troops?"

"You mean your troop, of course. I have no doubt who the three men will be. But OK. I know how superstitious the men can be. Though I didn't think you were, Steven."

"I'm not, Sir. I'm just thinking of the men." Carter lied. Anyone who believed in luck was superstitious and Carter believed in his own luck at least.

"OK, that's settled then. I'll leave you and Peter to sort out the details. I'll need to see the final plan before I give the go-ahead and I wouldn't mind taking a look at the dhow, so keep me informed of progress.

* * *

There was little Carter could do to prepare for this new operation until Curshaw returned with the dhow. He canvassed the commando to find his volunteers and was inundated with men who were looking to escape the tedium of the training regime.

He chose a good sniper from 1 Troop, along with a Sergeant who would act as his second in command. From 2 Troop came a couple of men known for their ability to hold their own in a scrap. His friend Andrew Fraser advised him on which two men to take from 3 Troop. The men from 5 and 6 Troops also came with the recommendations of their troop commanders, two of whom were chosen because they were skilled in the use of small boats that were powered by outboard motors. From his own troop he could have taken any of his men, but he knew he would end up with Green, Glass and O'Driscoll so he didn't spend too much time making his selection.

After explaining the operation to the men, there was little they could do by way of training. They would be hidden on board the dhow until the pirates attacked, they would rush out of cover to arrest them when they boarded and, hopefully, that would be that. They would practice once they were aboard ship, but in the meantime the most likely skill they would need would be unarmed combat, so they spent some time throwing each other around on the coconut matting that the QM had managed to scrounge for the purpose. Where he had found coconut matting in Suez was something of a mystery, but those men that landed face down on it suggested it smelt of stale beer.

The dhow arrived off the shore of the camp the following Friday, just as Curshaw had promised. Carter, the CO and Sgt Brody, Carter's 2IC for the operation, paddled a Goatley boat out to greet it.

A scramble net had been slung over its low side to allow them to board.

"It's bigger than I imagined." Vernon observed. The dhow was about eighty feet long and twenty feet at its widest. One mast stood just forward of midships supporting a long boom, attached to which was furled a sail, a second, smaller mast was further back, closer to the taffrail[1]. The front of the booms were pointed downwards while the backs rose high above the tops of the masts.

At the aft end of the boat a canvas awning had been rigged to keep the sun off the crew that would tend the tiller, which was connected directly to the top of the rudder. At the bows another awning covered a cooking area, the metal firepit standing on an asbestos base to prevent it from setting fire to the deck.

"They come in various sizes." Curshaw answered. "I don't think there's any sort of standard pattern. This one is at the smaller end of the scale."

"I see you still have the native crew on board." Vernon cast his eye over the rough looking crowd of half a dozen sailors that were gathered near the long arm of the tiller.

Curshaw laughed. "It seems your disguises work." He called to the men. "Sub Lieutenant McLean, would you care to join us."

A figure detached himself from the group and made his way towards them. He wore a ragged turban around his head and a typical Egyptian gallabiyah, a long robe that covered him from neck to ankle. Around his middle he wore a tightly tied sash into which was thrust a knife with an elaborately jewelled handle and scabbard. The other men were similarly dressed, but their knives were more modest, with plain handles and leather sheaths.

McLean came to attention in front of the more senior officers but didn't salute. "Angus McLean, Sir." He introduced himself. "Skipper of the Jolly Roger, as we've called her."

"We found a vegetable die that we mixed with water to colour the skin the right shade of brown." Curshaw explained. "Angus, show the Colonel your arm."

Pushing up his sleeve, McLean revealed that his brown skin stopped at his elbow and everything above that was a white so bright that it threatened snow blindness. On closer inspection Mclean's pale, Nordic blue eyes would also give away his origins. They had to hope that the pirates didn't get close enough to spot that detail before the commandos were able to restrain them.

"I only hope it comes off." McLean grinned. "They're not really used to brown people in Oban." His Scottish accent was the softer type that Carter had come to associate with the Highlands when he had been in training at Achnacarry.

"I have to say it's very convincing." Carter said. "Will my men need to die themselves and dress in that get-up?"

"Not if you accept my plan. The skin colour is only for the benefit of the dock workers and I don't intend for your men to board the dhow in the port itself. Perhaps if I can explain the plan, things will become a little clearer."

"Please, go ahead."

"We've already started a disinformation campaign around the docks. We've paid some of Kalif's sailors, he's the owner of the dhow, to spread the story that you'll be carrying a whole load of wireless spares. The wireless was very much a status symbol in this part of the world before the war, especially ones that could pick up shortwave broadcasts from Europe, but there aren't any spares available since the war broke out; valves[2] are worth their weight in gold right now. So, if it was real. the cargo would be highly valued. We've tracked down some old German packing crates taken from the *Afrika Korps* and overpainted them with Turkish labels, leaving just enough German visible to suggest they've been smuggled out of Axis[3] territory. We've also added the Turkish words for 'fragile' and 'handle with care' and a few broken glass symbols. They'll actually contain the weapons for Angus's crew and your own men, Steven, along with any other equipment you want to bring on board."

"Are you sure the bait will work?" Carter asked.

"We're pretty sure. We've already had a few strange looking characters sniffing around the dhow. Kalif even had one asking if he could join the crew. The pirates do sometimes try to get a man on board ahead of sailing time.

Angus will set sail before dawn and then come along the coast to here. It would be useful if you could have some landing craft in the water, one of your rehearsals for your big operation. Then, when you detach one to intercept the dhow, it will look like you're trying to warn it off. The landing craft carrying your men, Steven, will slip around the back of the dhow so it can't be seen from the shore and your men will climb up the scramble net which we'll have in place. That's why I want your weapons and equipment to be loaded in the port, so it won't take you so long to board. With a bit of luck, the landing craft will only be out of sight for a minute or so and the delay won't be noticed by anyone watching. The dhow will then change course, as though obeying your order to go away. Any questions so far?"

"Will you be coming with us?"

"No. I'd like to, but to have an officer of my seniority would be seen to be a bit over the top. Delegation and all that."

Carter could see his point. Sending a Captain like himself was a little bit over the top for a team of twelve. A competent Sergeant could probably have led them, even though the operation was a little bit out of the ordinary. But Commando officers lead from the front, so he would have been going if only one other rank (OR) was involved. "What course will we be taking?"

"We suspect that the pirates are using a location a little bit south of the two islands that sit in the mouth of the gulf of Aqaba, so we've let it be known that your first port of call is going to be Gayal. It's a small port, more the size of a village, just on the other side of the entrance to the gulf. It will be assumed that you're picking up more cargo from there, dates or something. But that route will force you to pass close enough inshore to be a tempting target. So, from here you'll cross to the eastern shore and follow the coast down to the tip of Sinai and across the mouth of the Gulf of Aqaba, close to the islands of Tiran and Sanafir. That will take the best part of thirty hours of sailing, depending on the wind direction. If you get a southerly wind you can double that. Angus will time your journey so it's heading towards sunset as you get into the area. If he needs an extra day to do that, then you'll have to take the extra day. If the pirates leave it any later than sunset to attack they risk missing you in the dark and you'll be way past them by morning. If that happens you'll have to turn around and come back to Suez."

"Where will my men hide?"

"In plain sight, really. You'll just sit under the awnings at the bow and stern, tight against the sides of the dhow and keeping your heads down. By the time the pirates see you it will be too late. They'll try to board in the middle because it's the lowest point on the hull and you just rush them as they climb over the side rails. That's when we expect the men in the boats to let go of the ropes attached to the grappling irons and make a run for it."

"How do we get a man into one of the boats so that we can follow them?"

"Ah, that's going to be tricky. As you heave to, one or two of your men will have to go over the stern and let himself down on a rope. He'll then have to swim around the side, grab the man in the boat and pull him overboard. Then he can clamber in himself and take over control. All he has to do is hang around for a few seconds so that the other boats get far enough ahead so they don't realise that your man isn't one of theirs. You can fish the pirate out of the water when everyone has pushed off."

"Can you rig a rope around the waterline for a man to hang onto? It will be easier for them to pull themselves around than to try and swim."

"Yes, that shouldn't be a problem. Dhows often seem to have ropes hanging over the side. They aren't always the tidiest of sailors. Now, when your man is certain where the pirates are heading, he should turn back and head out to sea again. I'll have one of my

Motor Launches following him at a safe distance, so he doesn't have to come all the way back to the dhow. Chances are he'd end up running out of fuel and drifting. We know the boats carry spare fuel, but we don't know how much they might have used getting into position. Then the Motor Launch will come and find you and you head back up to Suez. Angus will drop you off back here on the way."

"You make it all sound very straightforward." Vernon said dryly. "But no plan survives first contact with the enemy. What if things go wrong?"

"As I said, I'll have one of my Motor Launches following behind you. He'll stay back below the horizon so he can't be seen, but he'll be able to see the tops of your masts. Now, you see those three tubes secured against the taffrail?" Curshaw pointed to the objects, three foot long lengths of metal pipe. "They will each have a Royal Navy issue signal rocket in them. If you need any help, Angus will fire those. They go up to about three thousand feet, so the Motor Launch can't miss them and they'll come to your rescue at full speed. After dark they'll close with the dhow to make sure everything went to plan, then they'll follow your man in to shore as I described earlier. They'll keep a light on their bow so that your man can find them in the dark."

"Final question." Carter said. "When do we go?"

"Bright and early Monday morning, if your men are ready."

"We're ready." Carter said. "Are you happy with that, Sir?" Carter asked his CO.

"You're the man in charge, Steven, so your decision, but I'm happy with the plan."

---

[1] Taffrail – the guard rail that runs around the aft end of a boat. On European sailing ships of the 16th to 19th centuries they were often decorated and painted gold.

² The thermionic valve was the integrated circuit of its day. Their basic construction was an anode to which a positive voltage, usually about 200 volts, was applied which attracted electrons from a cathode. A heating element was used to agitate the electrons in the cathode and release them from the plate, hence the name 'thermionic'. Mesh screens, called grids, were inserted between the cathode and the anode to which voltages could be applied to vary the flow of electrons. In that way small variations of voltage at the grid could be amplified at the anode. The valve needed a vacuum to work efficiently so it was encased in glass, much like a light bulb. Valves were essential for the functioning of all electronic equipment prior to the invention of the semiconductor transistor in 1947, which paved the way for the development of modern electronic components. As a technician in the RAF the author worked on equipment that used valves that were three feet high, steam cooled (yes it does work) and which could amplify shortwave (HF) radio signals to 200kw of power, but the vast majority of valves were smaller than a domestic lightbulb.

³ The alliance between Germany, Italy, Japan and a range of smaller European countries was called the Axis. The term was first used in 1936 by the Italian leader Benito Mussolini to refer to a treaty of alliance agreed between himself and Adolf Hitler.

* * *

The raiding party was excused duties for the weekend, to make sure they were well rested. They made use of the break to visit the Sally Army club; or at least they said that was where they were going. Carter decided he didn't want to know what they really got up to. He was just grateful that they came back without the assistance of the Redcaps[1].

For his own part he made use of the small library in the Officers' Club to write letters, catch up on the weeks old newspapers from back home and to try to read a book. It was by chance that he came across a book about piracy in the Mediterranean and the fate that awaited those that were captured on the Barbary Coast[2]. He shuddered to think that the same fate might occur several centuries later if he was the one that was captured, rather than the pirates.

Monday morning saw Carter's raiding party on board the last landing craft in a flotilla of a dozen others, making yet another approach towards the El Ataka plain. They found their route blocked by a dhow, which was sailing sedately through their exercise area.

Sirens were sounded to warn the intruder off, but the boat just kept on going, so one of the landing craft broke off and approached the craft to try to take more direct action. The craft disappeared out of sight from the distant shore, but re-appeared moments later, turning across the stern of the dhow and making its way back to join the flotilla. The dhow changed direction, arcing smoothly away towards the centre of the channel. Passing the merchant ships waiting to enter the Suez Canal, the dhow was soon lost to sight over the horizon.

Carter was the first to roll over the dhow's railing and land on the deck. He scuttled away to the far side where he wouldn't hamper those following him. The scramble net was a dozen feet long, so it allowed several men to climb at once. It was something that commandos were used to doing as they boarded their landing craft or returned to a ship after another rehearsal for a raid. Sure footed and strong in the arm, they swarmed over the rail, dropped to the deck and scuttled to the aft end to take shelter under the awning, sitting on the deck with their backs to the wooden bulwarks, out of sight of any prying eyes.

None of the dhow's crew seemed to react to the new arrivals. They went about their business of steering the ship or pulling on ropes, but words of welcome were muttered from the sides of the mouth.

Once the dhow was out of sight of both the merchant ships and the land, the commandos were allowed to stand up and stretch their cramped limbs. Gathering around the fake cargo crates they collected their weapons, each man checking his for damage or dirt. To the commando his weapon was as precious as a family member; more precious in some cases.

They positioned the four empty crates at the front and the rear of the deck on either side, so they would provide some concealment for the commandos as the pirates boarded. The deck would be in deep shadow by that time of day, but every little bit of advantage had to be extracted from the situation; it was the commando way.

"Surely four crates of wireless spares can't be worth that much." Prof Green observed.

"You'd be surprised." Petty Officer Malloy, Mclean's second in command replied. "If those crates were full, that quantity of valves and other spares would be worth about two to three thousand pounds[3] in the right market. That's about a fifty percent mark-up on what would have been paid in Port Said or Alexandria. Take that cash to Massawa[4] or Djibouti and you can fill the hold with the best Ethiopian coffee beans and still have change left over. Bring the coffee back to Suez and you'd sell it for half that again. After paying off the crew the skipper would have more than enough left to buy a new cargo and start the process over. You don't see many poor dhow owners when they retire."

"I think I'm in the wrong job." Danny Glass chuckled.

"It's all capitalism." Green said, with scorn. "The peasants that grow the coffee get paid almost nothing."

"There's no denying that," The PO replied, "but when stuff is in short supply, you can set your own price."

"There's no pockets in a shroud." O'Driscoll chipped in.

"True, but being a dhow skipper is a risky business. If it wasn't, we wouldn't be here right now. Where there's risk, there is also reward. It's the only reason for investing money. If there was no reward you might as well keep your money under the mattress."

"Stand by to change course!" McLean shouted from his position alongside the steersman, effectively ending the conversation. The crew ran to their stations, untying ropes ready to swing the heavy boom across so that the sail could catch the wind from its new direction.

Carter exercised his men, putting them into hiding then having them break cover and threaten imaginary pirates as they arrived on deck. Spare sail canvass was brought up from the hold to provide additional concealment, arranged casually along the bulwarks as though it had been discarded there.

After resting through the heat of the afternoon he repeated the exercises as the sun sank towards the Egyptian desert on the far side of the gulf. The conditions were much more like those that they would have to work in when the pirates attacked and the men learnt where to put their feet in order to avoid the hazards on the deck, such as the raised edges of the gratings that covered the cargo hold.

The commandos were dressed in their normal uniforms, but two had to change into turbans and gallabiyahs. Troopers Appleby and Webster, from 5 Troop, were detailed to climb over the aft rail and lower themselves into the water to capture one of the pirates' boats and follow them to shore. That part of the operation had yet to be practised. It wasn't safe to do so while the dhow was underway, but McLean assured Carter that they would have time for that before they reached the area where they expected the pirates to attack.

Darkness came suddenly, as it always did in those latitudes and the crew settled down for the night. The sailors operated their usual four-on-four-off watch keeping routine and Carter set sentries to match that. Although a pirate attack by night was unlikely, he wasn't taking any chances. Besides, it showed the sailors that the commandos weren't afraid of work.

As dawn broke the lookout raised the alarm. There was debris floating in the water ahead of them. McLean ordered them to reduce sail to slow the dhow down. They soon found that it wasn't debris, as they thought. It was bodies. Half a dozen of them, about the correct number to be the crew of a dhow the size of theirs. From the bullet wounds it was obvious they had been shot.

"We've got nowhere to keep the bodies." Mclean said in response to suggestions that they should recover them. "In this heat they'll go off in hours and the smell will be awful."

But they couldn't be left for the fish. The dead men were hauled on board, wrapped in sail cloth with ballast taken from the hold to weight them and given a burial at sea.

Constable Masry said a Muslim prayer over the dead men, then they raised the sail again and moved on.

When they were off duty, the police in Suez spent a lot of their time in the tea and coffee houses, putting the world to rights and gossiping. Curshaw had decided that it was too much of a security risk for local police to be used for the operation. They may not mean to, but there was a risk of something being revealed that needed to be kept secret. So Constable Tarek Masry had been dispatched from the police unit at Ismailia, half way along the Suez canal, to take part in the operation. To prevent him, too, becoming a security risk he was collected from the railway station and driven straight to the dhow. He hadn't been told anything about his involvement until Mclean had briefed him after they sailed.

"That's what we're dealing with." McLean said to Carter. "It isn't the first lot of bodies we've found. I guess they were attacked last evening."

"The sooner we catch them the better then." Carter said.

"We're well on our way. Come with me."

Mclean led the way aft to where an Admiralty chart was laid out on a low table, anchored at the corners with tins of food. "We're about here;" he tapped the chart about three quarters of the way along the Gulf of Suez "I'll get a firmer fix when I take the noon sightings. This westerly wind has allowed us to sail on a beam reach[5], which is about the fastest any sailing boat can travel. Allowing for a short stop this afternoon to give your two men time to rehearse their part, that means we'll be passing the tip of the Sinai Peninsula in the late afternoon. I expect the pirates to attack before we get to the channel that separates Sharm el-Sheikh from the two islands."

"Where will you stop?"

"The Sinai Peninsula actually ends in another peninsula, like a little bit of land hanging off the southern end." He tapped the place. "It shows up better on the larger scale chart, which I'll get out later. The approach is quite shallow, lots of sandbanks, but there are navigable channels. At the southern end there's an island, separated from the mainland by what's called the Mangrove Channel, because there's mangroves growing along the sides. We'll anchor in the northern end of that channel. It's highly unlikely that we'll be observed there. If the pirates have any observers posted, it's more likely that they'd be on the very tip of the peninsula.

Once you've finished your training, we'll up anchor and sail past the tip and we'll be crossing what's called the Tiran Straight, named after the bigger of those two islands." He tapped the map again. "We'll continue to benefit from this wind direction so we'll be moving quite quickly for a dhow, which I'm sure the pirates will anticipate. If they want to attack us before dark. they'll only have about an hour spare."

"Can I suggest a slight change in plan?"

"If I can accommodate it and it doesn't place the operation at risk."

"Did Lt Cdr Curshaw mention phase two of the operation?"

"Attacking the pirate's base. Yes, he did."

"If we're going to do that, I need to do a recce first. If we go back to Suez it would mean wasting maybe a four-day round trip to come back again and do the recce. It would save a lot of time if I could do it while we're here."

"That makes sense. What are you suggesting? I don't really fancy keeping the dhow in the area with a whole load of prisoners to feed and water. Our supplies are quite limited."

"I agree, but you've also got the Motor Launch. After it picks up my two men, it could take me close inshore, I can go ashore by dinghy and the Motor Launch can withdraw out of sight. I'll do my recce during daylight, the boat comes back for me again after dark then we head back up to Suez as planned. I assume that the Motor Launch is considerably faster than this old thing, so we probably won't get back much after you."

McLean considered the idea, then nodded his head. "Look, I can't commit the Motor Launch, because it isn't my command. But I'll back you up if you suggest it to Justin; that's Justin Phillips the skipper. How about that?"

"Is he likely to agree?"

"Probably. We're all sick of these pirates running rings around us. This operation could be the solution and we're all in favour of that."

As the day wore on, Mclean took the dhow closer and closer inshore. The commandos and Constable Masry were forced to conceal themselves behind the bulwarks to escape any prying eyes that might be watching for them. To Carter's eyes the coastline was desolate, a uniform dun colour with no obvious signs of habitation. Rocky hills climbed away towards the interior.

"Don't be fooled." PO Malloy advised, speaking to Carter while appearing to be just leaning on the rail. He was an old hand on the anti-piracy patrols. "There are little fishing communities all along this coast. They come down from Suez or across from one of the towns on the western shore, spend a few months fishing, drying and salting their catch, then they go back home again. I'd be surprised if the pirates haven't got a few of them on the payroll. Or they just intimidate them into co-operation."

"How do they communicate? I don't see any telephone wires."

"Heliographs." He replied. "Mirrors that flash a signal. They've been in use for centuries around here. They're visible for miles, so it's not difficult to establish a chain of repeaters."

Carter felt a bit of a fool for not working that out for himself. He'd used the same method himself during the commando's raid on Honfleur the previous year and army signallers had used the system for over a hundred years, long before Samuel Morse had invented his code to allow whole sentences to be sent by flashing dots and dashes[6].

"There's a coast road as well. You can hardly see it except when it gets very close to the shore, but I doubt they'd send vehicles with messages. It would take too long. Maybe a motorbike could do it in few hours in an emergency."

Bored with just sitting, Carter crawled forward past the galley area so that he could peer through the hawse pipes, where the anchor cables passed through the bulwarks. Glimpses of brilliant white beneath the surface of the crystal-clear water showed where the shallows were. Occasionally the sand would break the surface, where resting gulls rose protesting at being disturbed by the dhow. Carter felt he could stretch out a hand to touch the sand. At one point the silhouette of a small shark crossed his eyeline, sending a glittering shoal of smaller fish into a panic.

The not too distant land curved away from them, then straightened out as it formed the narrow neck of land that connected a larger bit of land to the Sinai. Carter had expected to see the bulk of Mount Sinai, where Moses was supposed to have received the Ten Commandments from God, but he had no real idea where that was. He would have been surprised to find out that it was well inland and, at only three thousand feet high, it wouldn't have been distinguishable from the surrounding high ground.

At the mouth of the Mangrove Channel McLean took down the sails and dropped the twin anchors. The dhows own small boat was lowered over the side and Prof Green sat in the rear pretending to be the pirate who was operating an outboard motor, while Appleby and Webster carried out a number of practices of their mission to capture on of the pirate's boats, Carter gave permission for the rest of his men to strip off and have a swim to cool down.

Satisfied that Appleby and Webster would be able to do their job within the narrow window of time they expected to be offered, Carter nodded to McLean, the rowing boat was lifted out of the water and the swimmers scrambled back on board as the dhow's anchors were raised once again.

An hour later they changed course to pass the southernmost tip of the Sinai and cross the entrance to the Gulf of Aqaba.

[1] Redcaps – Royal Military Police. So called for the red covering to their peaked caps.

[2] Barbary Pirates, named after the Barbary Coast and corrupted from the name of the Berber tribespeople, operated off the coast of Morocco, Algeria, Tunisia and Libya for several centuries, preying on shipping passing through the Straights of Gibraltar and southern Mediterranean. Their presence was often tolerated by the Sultans that ruled the coastline, presumably in exchange for a share of the profits. The Royal Navy was largely responsible for their eventual suppression and when Gibraltar was captured by the British in 1704 it effectively put an end to piracy in that area.

[3] The equivalent of between £100k and £150k today

[4] Massawa – a port on the Red Sea in Eritrea. In 1943 Eritrea was still part of Ethiopia.

[5] Beam reach – the point of sail on a yacht where the wind is coming from the side. The sail starts to act like an aerofoil, similar to an aircraft's wing, generating 'lift' which allows the craft to travel faster than the actual speed of the wind. Contrary to the intuitive, the boat sails faster than if the wind was coming from directly behind. Some modern racing yachts have replaced one or more sails with aerofoils to maximise their speed.

[6] Morse code, just one of many that were developed around the same time to exploit new developments in electro-magnetism, was first used in 1844.

3 – Alsourah

The shadows grew longer across the deck of the dhow, the aft sail plunging the centre of the deck almost into darkness. The wind had dropped as the sun set. Ropes were pulled tighter to catch every ounce of breeze and keep the dhow moving.

It was at this point that Carter realised that his two men, Appleby and Webster, would have to go over the aft railing while the dhow was still moving. They had only practised whilst it was anchored. The prospect didn't seem to phase them.

"Always fancied a bit of water-skiing." Was Webster's cheeky response. "I've only ever seen it on the films."

The two men hunkered down next to the tiller, ready to move as soon as the pirates started to board the dhow.

Mclean appeared next to Carter, apparently scanning the horizon but really there to talk. "Can you go forward and look through the hawse pipes?" he asked.

"I could if I knew what a hawse pipe was." Carter the landlubber replied.

"It's the hole near the bow the anchor cable goes through. There are boats ahead. I think it might be them." He didn't need to say who 'them' was. They all knew why they were there.

Carter scuttled along the deck, his thigh and calf muscles screaming in protest. He threw himself onto his belly next to the starboard hawse pipe. Ahead he saw four boats, seemingly unrelated to each other. But Carter spotted that they formed a loose box formation to either side of the dhow's course. The left and right hand sides of the box were about a mile apart, leaving plenty of room for the dhow to pass between them. The short sides, where the boats were one ahead of the other, were about three hundred yards in length.

The boats were long and narrow, flat at the end where an outboard motor was mounted but narrowing to pointed bows. The four man crew were unable to sit side by side, though there was plenty of room in front. If they were really fishermen, that was where the catch would be landed. Carter suspected that the boats were flat bottomed, so that they could get close inshore to unload fish straight onto the beach.

In the nearest boat one of the crew stood up and cast a net out onto the water. A nice bit of theatre, he thought. "Don't concern yourself with us" they seemed to be saying. "Nothing here to see except some simple fishermen casting their nets."

As they closed on the four boats he lost sight of the ones on the port side, so he crawled across to see what they were up to. Like the others, they were play acting. Two of the crew stood and hauled a net in arm over arm, fish glittering as they caught the rays of the setting sun. Carter peered to starboard and saw that the great orange disc was almost touching the azure blue sea to the west. It would be dark within the half hour. He turned his attention back to the four boats.

With the net now inboard, the man next to the outboard motor started pulling on its starter chord, jerking it into life. They were about to make their move.

Carter scuttled back to the rear of the dhow, warning his men as he passed them. "Cock your weapons; stand by." He repeated several times.

"It's about to start." He called in a loud whisper to McLean, who had returned to the Captain's position by the tiller. He saw that the sailors were already armed with Sten guns, but as he said his warning, they cocked them, the sounds seeming loud to Carter's ears. His own men had been more subtle, pulling the bolts of their rifles back slowly and pushing them forward with just enough force to drive a bullet into the barrel, making hardly any noise.

Carter was no longer able to watch the pirates, so he had to rely on Mclean to act as his eyes and ears. The first clue that the pirates were getting close was the sound of their outboard motors. At such a slow speed they were making a putt-putting, but it was clearly audible above the creaking of the ropes that held the sails in place and the rush of the sea along the length of the dhow's hull.

A grappling iron sailed over the bulwark and thudded onto the deck, before it was pulled backwards to grip the rail. A second, third and fourth followed. McLean was shouting at the top of his voice, total gibberish but loud and panicked enough for the pirates to think he was either telling the pirates to get lost or ordering his own men to defend the dhow.

A head appeared above the port rail, followed by the rest of the man and then he was over and on the deck. He didn't waste any time. He sprinted for the afterdeck, unslinging a rifle from over his shoulder, his job clearly to try and take control of the tiller and turn the dhow's head into the wind, bringing it to a stop. Carter stuck out a leg, felt a foot slam into his ankle, then the man was sprawling and sliding along the deck. He came to a stop with his rifle feet away from his grasping hands and staring into the nine millimetre hole in the front of PO Malloy's Sten gun. The shock on the man's face was apparent. Dhow crews hardly ever fought back and those that did regretted it.

More men were pouring over the railing on both sides, as the rest of the pirates started to board. Carter anticipated eight men, so he had to hold his men back until they were all on deck. As they arrived, they raised their weapons and started firing into the air to intimidate the crew. Four men, then five, now six and finally seven.

"Now!" Carter yelled at the top of his voice. His men stood and levelled their weapons at the pirates, who were stunned to see them rise apparently out of the solid planks. In their apparent victory the pirates hadn't re-cocked their weapons, so they were defenceless against the new threat. One man reacted quicker than the other. Dropping his rifle he leapt over the rail, seeming to rise vertically from the deck. He disappeared from sight, but a splash threw a spout of water as high as the railing. But Carter's men were pushing forward, filling the space between the pirates and the railings, encircling them and giving them nowhere to go.

One man, braver than the rest perhaps, attempted to cock his ancient rifle, but the nearest commando fired a shot between his feet and he let go of the weapon instead. It seemed to break the spell cast when the commandos had appeared. Rifles and handguns thudded to the deck as the pirates surrendered.

The twilight was shattered by a scream from the same side as the single pirate had leapt. Carter instinctively thought of Applebey and Webster, then remembered that they were making their way around the starboard side. Time to worry about that later, Carter decided.

There was the sound of the outboard motors, the revs increasing as they made their escape; rats deserting a metaphorically sinking ship. Carter could clearly hear two boats on the left-hand side, or port as the sailors would have said. Was that one or two on the right? He couldn't be sure. Another mystery that would have to wait.

Constable Masry stepped forward, his police issue revolver pointing the way. He shouted commands in Arabic and the men obeyed, getting onto their knees and holding their hands above their heads.

Half of Carter's men handed their weapons to the other half to hold, the receivers hanging the straps over their shoulders and pushing the surplus weapons around behind them, out of the way. The unarmed men stepped forward to start searching the prisoners. They removed hidden knives and smaller guns, making a heap under the port side railing.

"That went pretty smoothly." McLean said, arriving at Carter's shoulder.

"What the dickens was that you were shouting just now?" Carter grinned.

"No idea, old chap. But the Ayrabs didn't seem to pay me any attention anyway."

He gave the signal to turn the dhow into wind and heave to. Men untied ropes and the dhow's great sails were lowered and furled tight against the booms, before the booms were lifted out of the way again. Carter ran through the priorities in his head. The pirates, at least those on board, were secure, but there was probably at least one in the water. And there had been that blood curdling scream; that didn't bode well.

"Can we get a boat over the side?" Carter asked. "There's men in the water."

"We'd better be quick, then." Mclean responded. "It'll be full dark within minutes." The PO had heard the request and was already hurrying to where the boat was stowed, forward of the hold. His men lifted it bodily and carried it to the starboard rail before tipping it upright and lowering it on the end of the ropes that were already attached to the bow and stern. Beneath the rail the scramble net was already neatly tied off, so all they had to do was lift it and tip it over the rail to let gravity unroll it.

"Green, Glass." Carter snapped. "Get into the boat and see if you can find anyone. They'll be behind us if anywhere." Out of the twilight they heard a voice calling, the words indistinguishable. "That will be one of them, but I think there may be another." The scream still lingered in his head. Someone had to be in a lot of pain to make that sort of noise.

Darkness fell as though someone had flicked a switch. Sailors hurried to light lamps and position them around the deck so that everyone could see what they were doing. They lifted the gratings off the hatches that gave access to the hold and ushered the prisoners down a ladder and into darkness. There could be no lamps down there, in case the prisoners set fire to the boat in an attempt to escape. Once the pirates were below deck the gratings were replaced and a couple of burly commandos were stationed on top of them to stand guard. The gratings were the only way of getting out of the hold. Even if the pirates made a concerted attempt to break out, the guards could be reinforced within seconds. But the prisoners had seemed docile enough. Carter didn't expect any trouble from them.

"They'll be alright down there." McLean said. "There's a barrel of water and tin mugs to drink from. We'll bring them up here in pairs to feed them. Which reminds me, it's time to get supper on."

Charlesworth! What's culinary delights have you got for us tonight?" Mclean called to the sailor who had done all the cooking since they had arrived on board.

"Stew, Sir." A voice came from the darkness.

"Would you care to elaborate?"

"Says beef on the tins, Sir."

Turning to Carter, Mclean spoke again. "We deliberately brought stuff the prisoners couldn't object to. You know what these people are like about pork and bacon."

"Considerate of you." Carter replied. He hadn't given much thought to rations other than to eat what the crew had served him. Stew, bully beef sandwiches and porridge had been the mainstays so far.

"We're back." A voice sounded from below the rail.

"What did you find?" Carter called down.

"Two men. One of them's badly injured. I think he must have got caught up in the propeller of one of the boats. The other one's fine though. He's looking a bit damp, but otherwise he's ranting and raving. I have no idea what he's saying."

"He say he just innocent fisherman." Constable Masry supplied. As the prisoners had been searched, Masry had formally arrested them in the name of the Egyptian government. "Next they will say they in Saudi Arabian waters and I no can arrest. They always say that."

"They can say what they like." Mclean grunted. "Thanks to the compass bearings I've been able to take, I've got our position pinpointed to within a few yards. We're almost a mile inside Egyptian waters."

"It make no difference." Masry grinned, his teeth white in the darkness. "Once in Egyptian prison, they no walk out again."

After the chatty man had been brought on board and sent down to join his comrades in the hold, the sailors conjured up a Robinson stretcher[1] from somewhere and the injured man was brought aboard more gently.

The medical orderly, or Sick Bay Attendant as the Navy called them, bent over the casualty and examined him by the light of an electric torch. "His leg is badly cut up." he reported. "I can bandage him up, but it looks like he's lost a lot of blood while he was in the water. I don't think he'll last the night."

"Make him as comfortable as you can." Carter ordered. If the boot had been on the other foot, the man might well have put a bullet in Carter's brain rather than offer any medical treatment. But that was what the difference was between themselves and the pirates. "Sgt Brody," Carter called his second in command, "make sure he's guarded. Just because he's injured doesn't mean he doesn't pose a threat."

"Boat ahoy." A call came from the tiller.

"That will be the Launch." Mclean said. Carter and he walked to the side to watch the boat approaching.

"Quite fast." Carter observed, seeing the white bone of the bow wave.

"Not bad. Twenty knots with a tailwind." McLean responded. As he spoke the bow wave diminished as the power was cut until the boat was almost stationary. It drifted in, to bump against the side of the dhow under its own momentum. Crewmen fore and aft grabbed a hold with boat hooks before throwing ropes across to allow it to be secured to the dhow's side. A tall figure jumped across and grabbed the rail of the dhow before hauling himself inboard.

"How was it, Gus?"

Beside him Carter thought he felt McLean flinch. It hadn't occurred to Carter that the young Scotsman's name might have been shortened in any way. He certainly hadn't asked Carter to call him Gus, which suggested he didn't like the nickname.

"It went pretty much to plan. We've got seven of them secured in the hold and another one injured. No casualties of our own; not so much as a splinter."

"In that case, I won't hang around. Capt Carter, I presume?" The naval officer offered his hand.

"Yes. Call me Lucky."

"And I'm Justin Phillips, Justin to my pals. Will you be coming with us?"

"Actually, I'd like a change to the plan, if it's OK with you." Carter explained what he had in mind, just as he had to McLean.

"Sounds fine to me. Once I've dropped you off I can motor across to Sharm el-Sheikh and wait there till tomorrow night."

"Is it a nice place to wait?"

"Absolute armpit, old boy. It's barely more than a fishing village. The Egyptian's are using it to resupply their soldiers on Tiran and Sanafir islands, but the port facilities aren't good. I had to put in there for engine repairs once. Longest three days of my life waiting for the parts to be driven down from Suez. But it will do for a temporary refuge while we wait for you."

"The locals mustn't find out why you're in the area." Carter counselled.

"No problem. My men will fend off any inquiries. There's nothing like a grumpy sailor armed with a rifle and bayonet to deter the curious."

"I'll take two of my men with me. I take it you've got a dinghy that will get us close inshore."

"Why not take the boat your two men are in? It's made for that sort of close in work."

Once again Carter had been made to feel slightly foolish by the Navy. But, then again, boats were their thing rather than the Army's.

"Can we get there before first light?" he asked, focusing on a sensible question.

"No problem, providing your men find us in the dark. We don't know where exactly they've gone to, or even if they headed right across the gulf to the mainland, so we'll position ourselves to the north and let them come to us. Once they're on board we can work out where they've been from, their travelling time and the compass bearings they took. They have been told to take compass bearings, haven't they?"

"Yes." Carter snapped, a little tetchily. He decided he wasn't too keen on Lt Justin Phillips. But he had to remain civil. His life might depend on the man. "They've also been told to make notes about how long they travelled on each bearing."

"Good. We'll be able to work out approximately where they went from that, if they can't offer any sort of recognisable description. Now, which way did they head off?" Phillips directed his question to McLean.

"The boats headed due south from here."

"That would take them towards the Arabian Peninsula. That may have been just to put us off the scent. So, they may have changed course as soon as it got dark. No matter. It's all just geometry and maths if we're given the right information."

Carter didn't need any lectures on navigation. The sea may not offer any decent landmarks to look for, but the basics of time, distance and direction didn't vary on land or sea.

"I'll get my kit and my men and we'll be ready to go in a few minutes."

"No rush, old boy. Your men won't be on their way back for a while yet, even if they went towards the nearest bit of land."

Prof Green was one of the two men Carter would take with him. It wasn't favouritism, he just knew that, no matter what, Green could be relied upon. The other man would be Tpr Wishaw, the sniper from 1 Troop. He didn't anticipate the sniper having to shoot, but the snipers were the most skilled in concealment and the three of them had to lie up on a hostile shore for the day, so it would be best if they were well concealed.

[1] A stretcher designed for use on board ships. It holds the patient tightly within its reinforced canvass sides so they can be lifted and lowered through the narrow twists and turns that might have to be negotiated aboard a warship. It can also be slung on a rope and passed from ship to ship. Invented in 1907. It is based on the design of a Japanese hammock that the Royal Navy had bought specifically

with medical use in mind. Although the stretcher bears the name of Neil Robinson, it was likely to have been a collaborative development involving other Royal Navy personnel.

* * *

MTB's, which Carter had travelled in a couple of times, were cramped, but compared to motor launches they were the epitome of spaciousness. Not even the Captain was afforded any privacy. One communal lounge-come-dining room, if it could be called that, served the whole sixteen man crew.

Green and Wishaw sat on one side, fashioning crude ghillie suits[1] out of sail canvass taken from the dhow, attaching it to their webbing in thin strips. Carter studied the naval chart of the area by the red light that was all that illuminated the cabin. Crew members shuffled past on their way to and from various hidden parts of the boat, muttering apologies to their passengers. How did they managed to work in such conditions without losing their tempers, Carter wondered.

A rating stuck his head through the hatch that led from the upper deck. "I think we've found your boat, Sir."

"I'll come up." Carter replied.

"Over there." The rating pointed. The man's eyes must have been sharp, Carter concluded, as he searched the sea of any sign of life. There, almost directly off the launch's beam, was that a sliver of white bow wave? As he watched it grew in size, the putt-putt of an outboard motor also becoming audible as the small boat drew near. At last it was alongside and hands were stretched down to help the two men aboard.

"Well done, Appleby. Well done, Webster." Carter slapped both men on the shoulder as they were hauled aboard.

"Piece of cake, Sir. I don't think they even realised we were behind them."

"I assume you saw where they went."

"Oh, yeah. No bother. Their wakes were quite clear. All we had to do was follow along behind. They went straight south for a while, then turned more easterly. We could see land ahead and they disappeared behind a headland. We followed them in and realised it was some sort of bay, so we did a quick about turn and came back, looking for you. It was quite a distance. We had to refuel once. By the way, the fuel cans they're using are British army flimsies[2]."

That was an interesting tid-bit of information, suggesting access to the black market in Suez. But that was something that could wait until they got back to port. "Good. Can you go with Lt Phillips. He'll want the compass bearings you took, so he can plot your course."

The two did as instructed, while Carter returned to the lounge. Phillips found him there a few minutes later.

"It's pretty clear they went a place called Alsourah." He reported. "The bay your men saw is one of many along that stretch of coastline." He pointed at the chart Carter had been examining and tapped his finger on the area to the south of the Gulf of Aqaba. "It's a couple of hundred yards or so deep and provides plenty of shelter for small boats. It's the sort of place any self-respecting sailor would choose as a shore base. Sand banks and reefs prevent larger craft from approaching."

"Have you got a larger scale map. One that shows the shoreline a bit more clearly."

"No. As it's in Saudi Arabia, we have no cause to patrol close in. But these small bays are all much alike. Do you want to land on the beach inside the bay?"

"No. I think it would be too easy to spot us approaching if they've set a guard. I think I'd like to land on the outside of the southern headland that forms the bay. We can circle inland and find a spot to hide up for the day and keep the area under observation. I assume they've got some sort of village there. Huts or something to live in."

"That looks OK to me. There's plenty of clear water along that bit of the coast. I can get you to within half a mile of shore and that skiff you captured will get you in close. The shoreline is shallow, but you can always wade the last bit if necessary. Just don't take your boots off. There's poisonous sea urchins, not to mention the stone fish."

"What's a stone fish?" Carter asked.

"Nasty little beggar that looks like a lump of rock, with a row of poisonous spines down its back. It burrows into the sand to hide and wait for prey. If you stand on one, you'll probably be dead before I could get you to anywhere capable of treating you. They're an Indian Ocean fish really. They're not common in the Red Sea, but the odd one has been found here, usually by someone who is no longer around to tell the tale."

"Well, thanks for the warning. We've had a couple of sea urchin injuries already; they're bad enough."

"Right. Now we know where you're going, I'd better get us underway." Phillips clambered back up through the hatch and a few minutes later the mounting volume of the launch's engines announced they were moving.

[1] The name given to a type of camouflage suit that snipers wear. Supposedly modelled on clothing worn by ghillies (gamekeepers) on Scottish estates, who wore them when stalking deer. It is made of strips of green, brown and black cloth, typically cut from sandbags or canvass, sewn onto regular clothing. The variations in colour and texture make it hard to pick out against a background of grass, trees and bushes. Carter's men would have used beige and brown colours to conceal them against rock and sand. First used in the military by Lovat's Scouts, a Highland Yeomanry unit founded by the 14th Lord Lovat, during the Second Boer War (1899-1902). During World War I, the Scouts became the first specialist sniper unit in the British Army. The 15th Lord Lovat was the CO of 4 Cdo in 1943 (he would go on to become a Brigadier). He was such a well-known commander that Hitler placed a bounty on his head of 100,00 Reichsmarks, a pre-war value of approximately £100,000.

² Flimsies – the nickname given to the rectangular fuel containers used by the British Army to carry fuel and water. The name says much about its construction. Their crimped and soldered seams split as the sides of the containers flexed and caused leakage, making them far inferior to the German jerricans. Up to half the fuel could be lost in leakage from a flimsy. Fuel lorries reeked of petrol and represented a significant fire hazard. From 1943 onwards the British started to manufacture jerricans of their own, based on the German design, much to the relief of hard-pressed quartermasters throughout the British Army. The only good use soldiers ever had for the flimsy was to cut it in half, fill it with petrol-soaked sand and setting the mixture on fire to boil their water.

* * *

The silence that fell as the naval rating cut the outboard motor was eerie, so silent that even the sea seemed to fall quiet. The three commandos raised the paddles and dipped them into the water, pulling hard to keep the skiff moving forward. Letting go of the motor's handgrip, the rating, too, picked up a paddle and added his own strength.

True to his word, Phillips had brought them to within a half mile of the shore before they had to clamber into the little skiff to start this phase of the journey. Now, having halved the distance, they paddled forward as silently as was possible under the circumstances. The Moon was starting to set and when that happened they would be left with only with starlight to see by. That suited Carter and the other two commandos. They could move as well by night as most soldiers could in daylight and the bright band of the Milky Way provided a more generous amount of light than they would have had under cloudy skies.

Before leaving the Motor Launch the four men had applied streaks of camouflage cream to their faces, necks and hands. Not even the naval rating was excused. His face could reflect light as much as anyone's and been seen from the shore if it caught the moonlight. Only the commandos were dressed in their crude ghillie suits. The packs on their backs were filled with only two commodities, water and ammunition. Food could wait until they were back on board the launch, but the Sun would dehydrate them quickly once it rose. Carter hoped they wouldn't need the ammunition but wasn't going to risk being without it. The Motor Launch wouldn't return until midnight the next night and that was a long time to have to sustain a firefight if they were discovered.

The skiff grounded itself on the bottom when they were still about fifty yards from the shore. "Sandbank." The rating whispered. Carter didn't doubt him. He placed his paddle on the bottom boards of the boat and stepped over the side into about two feet of water. Lighter, the skiff bobbed loose. Grabbing the painter attached to the bow, Carter pulled the boat a few yards further forward, until it grounded again. Green and Wishaw stepped out of the skiff on the far side and between them they turned it until it was pointing back out to sea. Giving it a final shove, the rating started to paddle back the way they had come.

Wordlessly, the three commandos turned back towards the shore and waded on, the cool water dragging at their boots and puttees. The sea was so calm there was hardly a ripple disturbing the surface, except for those made by the three men.

The water became shallower, the ground sloping gradually upward towards the beach, where a thin line of white bubbles marked the edge. Ahead, a darker line showed the ground rising into undulating dunes. Beyond that they couldn't see, but the Admiralty chart had shown contour lines, indicating higher ground. The last line had been drawn about two hundred yards from the shore. No estimate of the topography was made beyond that point as the Royal Navy wasn't interested in what lay inland.

Carter turned them to face along the beach and they made their way slowly forward, taking care to make no noise. The stayed within the line of foam to ensure that their footprints were eradicated as soon as they were made. It would take only one native to find one print made by a moulded sole British Army issue boot for their presence to be discovered and a search for them started.

Unlike the rest of the armed forces, the commandos didn't wear the traditional "ammo boots", with their thick leather soles and hobnails. They made too much noise as they struck the ground. For them, rubber soles were moulded directly to the uppers. The boots were more expensive than the product manufactured in Northamptonshire, but made far less noise. They also left a distinctive footprint that told the enemy exactly who they were dealing with. Not that the pirates would be familiar with the imprint. Not yet, anyway. Carter was anxious to delay that discovery until he had a lot more men at his back.

The bay curved gently out towards a small headland, all that marked the end of this stretch of beach and the start of the next. Carter kept his route straight, rising into the dunes as the bay arced away from him. The dunes gave way to a harder, rockier surface. Reaching a summit Carter lowered himself to the ground and took in what he could see.

As the Motor Launch had passed Alsourah, a mile out to sea, they had seen a twinkling of firelight and that was what Carter was now seeking out. There wasn't much left of it to be seen. Just a red smudge of embers. But it marked where the habitation lay. With sandbanks lying to the north of Alsourah, they had opted to land on the southern side where there was less risk of the launch running aground.

Carter led them back down the slope, away from the inhabited area. There was little chance of them being silhouetted against the skyline, but Carter wasn't taking even that slim chance. Turning inland the ground rose gently upwards. Carter wanted them to be as high as possible when they stopped. Not only would it allow them to see further, it would also be harder for them to be observed by someone on the lower ground.

There must have been buildings below them, because when Carter turned back towards the firelight again there were more spots visible. Half a dozen now rather than the single spot he had seen earlier. They were still dim red smudges, but at night they shone like beacons.

Wishaw scouted the area, looking for concealment that met his exacting standards. He returned to collect Carter and Green and guided them another fifty yards inland to an outcropping of rocks that broke through the thin soil. "This will do." He whispered into Carter's ear. Taking off their heavy packs, they settled themselves behind the low cover. There was nothing they could do to allow them to take up a position to watch the village until they saw what the ground was like. They didn't want to be sticking their heads above the rocks. It would be far better if they could peer between them.

Carter remembered what Phillips had said about the stonefish. If they were in the sea, what dangerous fauna might there be on land? Carpet vipers and horned vipers were common across the region. They had been told that in Algeria. At night they would bury themselves or take refuge in holes in the ground, to insulate themselves against the cool of the night and retain their body heat. But where might they appear once the sun came up? If one of them was bitten it would be the end. They had no-one they could call on for assistance. Would the pirates help them? Hardly likely. Even if they were willing to, it was extremely unlikely that they would possess any anti-venom.

Then there were the scorpions. Almost every soldier had seen at least one by now. The big black ones were the most deadly, but even the small ones could inflict a disabling sting. There would be bound to be some of those around once the sun rose. They would have to be careful where they put their hands.

Wishaw had been quite clear; once dawn had broken and they had taken up their positions, there could be no movement. The slightest shift in position could give them away. Even to move down the slope, crawling backwards until they were out of all possible sight, would take ten or fifteen minutes. And that would just allow them to take a drink of water.

No, Carter had to be able to rotate the three of them. No more than two watching the pirates while the third stayed back, away from possible observation. They would change places every hour, giving a maximum of two hours without taking a drink. It would be a long time to be without water, as they had discovered during training in Algeria and El Ataka. They were much further south now. The heat would be more severe. He had a thought.

"More cam cream." He instructed in a whisper. "Really smear it on. It will help keep the Sun off your skin. Make sure you have plenty on the back of your neck."

He reached into his pack and took out the small round tin. Dipping his fingers in he dug his nails into the soft surface and scooped some out. Placing the tin on the ground he smeared it across his other hand and then used both of them to coat his neck beneath the hairline. He needed a haircut, he realised, as he felt the longer wisps just above his shirt collar.

As soon as there was enough light, they adjusted their positions so that they could see without being seen. The rocks weren't high, but they didn't need to be. They lay across the top of the ridge like a set of broken teeth, offering a number of places where they could lie and keep watch. Carter sent Green back down the reverse slope of the low hill while he and Wishaw took the first watch.

Wishaw rested the barrel of his Lee Enfield No 4 rifle[1] onto a V in the rocks and lay behind it, his eye pressed against the telescopic sight. The shape of the weapon was lumpy, deliberately made that way by wrapping canvass around it to disguise its shape and stifle any rattling from the sling swivels. Carter shuffled into position, pulling his poncho over his head to disguise his own shape. It would also help to protect him from the Sun, even though it would trap heat in close to his body. Every choice was a compromise.

Wishaw didn't need a poncho; he had his homemade ghillie suit. Carter rested his binoculars on the rocks in front of him, then lay his notebook and pencil within easy reach.

Below them shapes started to form as the weak dawn light reached the beach.

The largest structure down there was a walled compound, almost glowing white in the dim light, the bulk of which was made up of a dwelling of some sort. It stood about a hundred yards inland from the beach. A second building, this time without a compound, stood about fifty feet further away, marking the far side of what might be called a village. The rest of the area between the compound and the beach was filled with tents. Carter had seen the like of them before, used by the nomadic tribes that travelled the old trade routes through Algeria, south of the Atlas Mountains. Those tribes had been Berbers.

These would be Bedouin, Carter supposed. Like the Berbers, they plied the ancient trade routes with their families and herds of animals, living a life that was unchanged for centuries, perhaps millennia. Caravans of nomads had plied the trade routes during the time of Jesus, Carter seemed to remember being taught.

He counted the tents, twenty of them, each capable of housing a complete family. Picking up his notebook he started to sketch the layout of the camp.

Along the edge of the sea, lying on the brilliant white sand, were the boats. There were a dozen skiffs of the type they had used the previous evening and a few other types of small boat. The long arms of oars projected over the sides of these. The skiffs each had an outboard motor attached to the transom, tilted to keep the propeller clear of the water and prevent it being damaged by any hidden rocks beneath.

A man emerged from one of the tents, weighed down by a large bundle. He staggered to the nearest skiff and dropped the bundle into the boat, before turning and returning once more to his tent. He appeared again seconds later, carrying another bundle which he also dropped into the boat. Movement from the compound attracted Carter's attention. Carefully he shifted his position so he could identify it.

It wasn't difficult to identify. A large, bearded man strode purposefully though the village. Even at this distance Carter could see his air of authority. His mouth opened and closed as he called something to the smaller man, who was now standing motionless at the edge of the water.

The large man strode on, the waving of his arms making his agitation clear. Reaching the skiff, he pushed the smaller man to one side, reached into the boat and picked up one of the bundles. He thrust it towards the man, who refused to take it. An argument developed. At their distance none of the words carried to Wishaw and Carter, but it didn't take words for Carter to know they were arguing. He suspected that the smaller man wanted to leave and the larger, probably the village's headman, wasn't about to allow that. Was this a reaction to the capture of the pirates the evening before? It was a possibility, with the less brave deciding that the risk of capture was too high.

The large man threw the bundle to the ground and the smaller man bent to pick it up, before dropping it back into the skiff. As he turned back to face the larger man, he found himself facing a gun that the large man had drawn from the sash around his middle.

The jerking of the gun's short barrel told Carter that threats were being made, but the smaller man wasn't cowed. A bright flash of light appeared in the gap between the two men before the faint sound of the gun's report reached their ears. The smaller man sagged at the knees, then crumpled to the ground, his body half in and half out of the water.

Wishaw let out a low growl and settled himself more comfortably behind his rifle. Turning his head towards him, Carter saw Wishaw's knuckle whitening as he took up the first pressure on the sniper rifle's trigger.

"Don't fire!" Carter hissed.

"But …"

"But nothing. Don't fire." The air of finality came through Carter's whisper and Wishaw relaxed the tension in his trigger finger. Exhaling audibly, the sniper seemed to deflate.

The camp seemed to come alive at the sound of the shot. Faces appeared at the entrances of the tents, but only one emerged fully. A female, dressed from head to toe in a black burka. She ran towards the stricken man, her arms waving. Falling to her knees she tried to rouse the fallen man, but Carter thought it unlikely that he was still alive.

The large man picked the bundle out of the skiff again and threw it at the woman, knocking her sideways, off balance. A child, no more than four or five years of age, appeared from the same tent as the woman and ran towards her, his little legs a blur of motion. He threw himself around his mother's neck as though trying to protect her.

A ring of figures gathered to form around the little tableau; the men forming a semi-circle from the edge of the sea on one side to the edge on the other. Females hovered behind them, straining to see between the men. Children snuck through gaps between legs, trying to get a glimpse of the dead body.

The large man turned and pushed his way through the throng and marched back to the compound. Nobody remonstrated with him. His authority and power had been more than adequately demonstrated.

Men picked up the body and led the way to the far side of the village. Others collected tools and soon the sound of shovels striking stone could be heard.

Carter had counted the men. There were twenty five, plus the headman but discounting the corpse.

Women and children; that complicated matters. Carter had assumed they would only have to deal with male pirates. Whatever plan he came up with would have to cater for the women. He couldn't risk them or the children being injured. While women and children were killed in warfare, this wasn't war. At best it was police work, which was something that the commandos weren't used to doing. They were a blunt instrument, used to strike fear into the enemy, not nursemaid children.

It would be a problem he would have to solve before they returned to El Ataka.

With the dead man buried, the men returned to their dwellings. A lot of them went to the house that didn't have a wall around it, presumably the barracks for the single men. Carter didn't know much about Arab culture, but he did know that men were very protective of their wives and daughters. No man could be alone with a woman she wasn't either related to by blood or married to. That probably meant that there was just one man in each of the tents. Simple arithmetic told him there must be five men living in the barracks, plus the headman in his house. He probably had a family in there with him.

But that maths didn't add up. He had seen a lot more than five men head for the smaller building. Of course, nine men had been captured on the dhow the previous evening. Some of those would have lived in the tents with the women, while others would have lived in the barracks. So it was unlikely they could establish which tents held men and which didn't, unless they saw the men enter the tents.

The men returned into the open carrying rolled mats, accompanied by the older boys. They arranged the mats into a line, facing roughly south. Morning prayers. Carter knew the routine from the calling of Muezzins from the towers of the mosques in Algiers and Suez. Five times a day the call to prayer sounded out, the first time before dawn broke. The morning's events had delayed the morning prayers but not led to them being cancelled completely.

Each man seemed to pray on his own, but all performing the same ritual of standing, kneeling and bowing. It lasted just a few minutes before the men started to roll up their mats again and go about whatever work they were to do that day. They had just beaten the sunrise, the latest designated time for prayer.

With the sun now fully up, the final details of the camp revealed themselves. At the far end of the beach was a stack of oil drums, next to which were some smaller containers which the binoculars revealed to be British army issue flimsies, just as Appleby had described. That must be the fuel dump. Inland from that was a railed compound containing a dozen or so sheep, or maybe they were goats. Carter was never sure which was which. In this part of the world they both looked the same to him. As he watched, a couple of children headed towards them. Removing some rails they allowed the animals out and they at once headed inland, followed by their small goatherds. Carter turned his head to see where they were heading. There was a broad valley stretching inland, with a clump of palm trees about half a mile away. That must be their water source. The presence of the trees meant there must be water, which was why the thirsty animals were so anxious to get there.

Almost at the same time a number of women emerged from the tents, each carrying a large jug. They gathered together, holding some sort of discussion, before they turned to follow the goats inland. Carter suspected it was a journey they made several times a day.

Although the sun was up, the low line of rocks still offered some shade. But Carter could feel the heat on the backs of his legs that told him they were in direct sunlight. The light khaki drill cloth would protect his legs from sunburn, but they also prevented air from circulating. The heat would become uncomfortable before long.

Carter completed his sketch map and pushed his notepad into his pocket. He would get Green to make his own version and they would compare notes later. Green was a good draughtsman, with a keen eye for detail. If Carter had missed anything, Green would pick it up.

"I could have killed that murdering Ayrab." Wishaw whispered, just loud enough for his voice to carry to Carter. There was a suggestion of bitterness in his voice.

Was he bragging about his skills with a rifle? Or just pointing out that he could have administered swift justice, Carter wondered. He decided to give Wishaw the benefit of the doubt.

"That isn't what we're here for." He replied, equally softly. "No point in trying to stay hidden, then firing off guns. They're armed and would have come looking for us."

"But that was murder. Plain and simple." Wishaw continued to protest.

"So, we add it to the charges when we come back to get them." Assuming they were allowed to come back. It reminded Carter that they were on the territory of a foreign power and were liable to be arrested themselves, if their presence was discovered.

Green crawled quietly up to join them.

"Make more noise, why don't you!" Wishaw grumped, still not happy about not being able to fire on the headman. In fact, Green had approached almost silently.

"Time for your break, Lucky." Green whispered. Carter handed him the binoculars, picked up his Tommy gun and slid carefully backwards until he was sure he couldn't be seen from the village. Only then did he remove the poncho and rise into a crouch to scuttle a few yards further down the slope towards the beach, where his pack lay with those of Green and Wishaw.

He pulled a water canteen from within and gulped greedily at the already warm water. He had to force himself not to drink too much in one go. It would be a long day and they would need every drop of water that they had brought with them.

[1] The Short Magazine Lee Enfield No 4 Mk1 (SMLE No 4) was the standard infantry rifle used by the British and Australian armies from 1941 onwards. At its basic level it was only an upgraded version of the original Lee Enfield that had been introduced in 1904 and had served throughout World War I. The SMLE No 4 was highly accurate at a range of up to half a mile with ordinary sights. Most soldiers could hit a man-sized target at 300 yards without

difficulty. The only variation for the sniper version was the 3.5 x magnification telescopic sight fitted above the barrel.

4 – Night Raid

The motor launch came smoothly to a stop on the outside of a trot of two other launches. It had hardly come to a standstill when the figure of Lt Cdr Culshaw could be seen making his way across the gangways connecting the boats.

The naval harbour was crowded with more shipping than it could really handle. Carter could make out the ensigns[1] of a dozen Empire and allied nations. Out in the approaches to the canal the Motor Launch had passed through a mass of other shipping, both naval and commercial. There could be no doubt that something big was being prepared. To Carter's untrained eye it looked as though the amount of shipping had trebled in the short time he had been absent from the city.

Phillips greeted Curshaw at the rail and exchanged salutes, before Carter went forward to have his hand shaken.

"All went well, I trust?" Curshaw asked.

"So long as the dhow made it back, yes." Carter replied.

"It's on its way. I got a telephone call from your camp telling me that your commandos were disembarking there. But we have some good news. At least I think it's good. London has agreed the plan to raid the pirates' base if it's on Saudi Arabian soil."

"Well, that is certainly where the camp is." Carter confirmed. "I spent the whole of yesterday getting a suntan while I did a recce of it."

"Do you have a plan?"

"Pretty much. I'd have to run it by my CO but, yes, I think it's feasible for us to take it without loss of life."

"A fine swansong for our squadron, then." Curshaw smiled.

"Oh, what's happening to you?"

"The Red Sea Inshore Squadron is disbanding early in July. The exact date hasn't been announced yet. Then, when all this shipping has sailed through the canal, we follow behind and become the

Eastern Mediterranean Inshore Squadron. What our orders will be I have no idea as yet, but I suspect we'll be acting as guard boats for the ports along the Egyptian and Libyan coast, while the frigates and corvettes go and grab all the medals and the glory along with you Army types."

"Will you miss the Red Sea?"

"Hardly, old chap. All we've had here up to now has been gyppie tummy and frustration. At least north of Port Said we'll have a chance to do our proper job, which is sub hunting. We'll be refitting our depth-charge racks before we leave. We haven't needed them down here."

"Well, one bridge at a time. I'd better get back to camp and have a chat with my CO."

"Which is why I'm here. I have a truck waiting for you and your men."

[1] Aboard ships, national flags that are flown at the front of a vessel are called "jacks", as in Union Jack and are flown on jack staffs. On land the correct name for the British national flag is "The Union Flag". Flags flown at the rear of ships are called ensigns. Ensigns are the flags usually flown during daylight hours while at sea. The Royal Navy has its own Ensign, known as the White Ensign and that of the British merchant navy is called the Red Ensign. There is also a Blue Ensign that may be flown by the members of certain yacht clubs, all of which contain the prefix "Royal" in their name. The author wishes to thank a former member of the Merchant Navy for this information, having got it wrong in an earlier book in the series.

* * *

With the pleasantries over, Carter gave Lt Col Vernon a verbal report of the operation and his subsequent reconnaissance of Alsourah.

"You shouldn't really have gone ashore, Steven. "Vernon chided. "It could have caused a heck of a diplomatic storm. But I suppose that all's well that ends well, as Shakespeare would have it. And, as you point out, it has saved us a couple of days preparation time now that we have the go ahead for phase two of the operation. When would you want to mount it?" Culshaw directed the question to Culshaw.

"That would be down to you, Sir. This time we're just the transport. It will be a commando operation, at least in name."

Carter stifled a smile. The Royal Navy was shifting the blame in advance, just in case things went wrong and the Saudi Arabian government got wind of the raid.

"Well, Steven?"

"The sooner the better, while we still have an almost full Moon, but that would be your decision, Sir. I assume you'll be taking command."

"I'd love to, but we've got far too much on here right now. I have to go up to Cairo tomorrow for another briefing and I have no idea when I'll be back. That also rules out the 2IC, as he'll be taking command here. I take it you won't be using the whole commando."

"No, Sir. I was thinking two troops would be enough."

"Precisely. So the other four troops would stay behind and continue with their training here. How long do you think you need?"

"What transport do we have?" Carter asked Culshaw.

"We've been given command of the Prince Leopold, because it was assumed you'd be using landing craft to go ashore. Other than that we can use all, or none, of the three Motor Launches in my flotilla."

"So how long would the Prince Leopold take to get to a position to launch the landing craft?

"If we left at dawn, she'd be there by dawn the next day."

"In that case we leave at midnight, so we can go ashore under cover of darkness when we arrive. We'd be in position to launch our attack at dawn. All being well we'd be back in our landing craft an hour after that and back on the Leopold not much later. We could leave at midnight tonight, if we can get all the stores we need loaded in time. I can brief the men while we're at sea. There's nothing complicated about the plan. What day is it today?"

"Friday." Vernon supplied.

"In that case we'd be back here by Monday afternoon. Call it Tuesday morning at the latest."

"OK, Steven. But before I give you the go-ahead, you had better explain your plan." Vernon settled himself back in his chair, looking at Carter expectantly.

There was a chalk board standing in the corner of the tent, with a list of outstanding actions listed on it. Carter lifted it down and checked the reverse, finding it blank, just as he had hoped. He turned it over and started to sketch the layout of the camp from memory. He then drew symbols[1] on, indicating the formations that he would deploy and where they would be positioned, before adding the final arrows that showed them striking the village.

"What about the extraction?" Vernon asked.

"We'll need six landing craft for that." Carter replied. "Four of them for our own men, one for the male prisoners and one for women and children. We have to keep them separate if we don't want to start a riot. We'll send up a Very flare to call them in when we're ready and they'll come direct into the beach in front of the village. We put the prisoners on board, get aboard ourselves and withdraw to the Prince Leopold, waiting for us in international waters. The two landing craft for the prisoners will need Egyptian police on board, but we can board them at the same time as the commandos and brief them at the same time. That Constable Masry seemed like a sound chap and his English is good, so I'd like to take him along as police liaison if possible."

"I'm sure we can arrange that." Curshaw responded. "Will the police go ashore with your men?"

"No. I don't want a bunch of flat-footed coppers blundering about in the dark and giving the game away. So long as they're on board the landing craft, that's all we need."

"It's a simple plan, Steven." Vernon nodded. "Which is why I like it. Not much that can go wrong, apart from the usual premature risk of discovery. And the added complication of the Saudi Arabian authorities making an unplanned appearance. But you'll have to deal with either event as best you can. Just make sure you don't kill any officials. That really would set the cat among the pigeons."

"We saw no sign of any Saudi Arabians authorities during our recce, Sir. No patrol boats, no vehicles. We didn't even see any telephone lines that could connect the village to civilisation."

"Let's hope things stay that way. As with all things, if you don't get caught there's not much chance of the Saudi Arabians being able to prove anything." Vernon stood and clapped Carter on the back. "You can take your own troop and 3 Troop, plus any of the men that went with you on the dhow. I'm sure they'd like to be in at the death so to speak. I'm giving you tactical command on the ground. Anything you say will count as an order from me."

"Thank you, Sir."

"Save your thanks until you get back. If it all goes tits up, it will be you that will be court martialled."

With those ominous words, Vernon dismissed them.

[1] Armies use standard sets of symbols to indicate the size and position of formations from the smallest, an 8 man section, to whole divisions and corps. Additional symbols are used to indicate specialist units such as armour, artillery, engineers etc. Colours are used to differentiate own forces, allies and enemy forces. Readers wishing to find out more about the symbols currently used by the British Army should search "NATO Joint Military Symbology" on the internet.

* * *

The engine noise dropped as the landing craft's Cox'n reduced the power. They were close inshore now and if the craft grounded too heavily it might not be able to pull itself off the mixture of sandbanks and coral that lay just beneath the sea's surface.

The tension inside the craft was palpable, as it always was just before the bow ramp dropped. Nobody knew what would happen. Normally there was a mad dash for the shore to escape the 'murder hole'[1], as it was known, the narrow gap in the landing craft's bow which offered enemy machine gunners a packed target as the commandos tumbled out.

But that wasn't the way they would attack tonight. The ramp would be lowered gently, so as not to create a splash. The men would then step out into the water one by one, making as little noise as possible and wade ashore rather than rush. Carter had been quite explicit about that in his briefing.

Reaching out over the bow ramp a sailor lowered a pole into the water, feeling the depth of the sea. Word was passed back to the Cox'n at the rear. Still no bottom, safe to continue. To either side the other three landing craft were keeping station, each boat feelings its way slowly towards the shore. While the water beneath one craft may be clear of obstructions, there could be rocks or sand bars just a few feet away beneath the next craft.

Carter heard a faint grinding sound as the craft to their right found the bottom. He gave the order for his men to brace themselves. It couldn't be long before they, too, were brought to a halt. Sure enough, Carter heard the message being passed that the man hanging over the bow had found the bottom. A few seconds later, barely ten yards further towards the beach, a vibration caused the landing craft to shudder as it ground to a halt.

The naval rating slid back down from his perch. At the back of the boat the Cox'n operated a switch and the drum holding the chains that controlled the ramp started to turn and the bow ramp started to drop.

Carter felt the men behind him pushing, anxious to be ashore as always. "Wait!" he snapped, struggling to keep his voice low. "There's no rush. Not this time."

As the ramp reached a manageable angle, Carter stepped along it towards the edge. It reached the horizontal, then water started to lap over as it dipped into the sea. Only when the chains started to go slack did Carter step off the end. The water reached above his knees, lapping only a little higher as the small waves rushed past on their way to the shore.

Gripping his Tommy gun in both hands he started to wade. The moon lit up his path, showing that he had about thirty or forty yards to go to reach the beach, glistening whitely just beyond the thin line of foam that marked the limit of the sea.

He heard the sloshing of water behind him as his men followed, their thighs pushing the sea aside as they forced their way towards land. The noise sounded loud in the silence but was probably inaudible more than a few yards away. "Keep behind me!" he hissed. If this was a false beach and there as a sudden change in depth, he wanted himself to be the only one who sank. They hadn't brought their large packs, so he was unlikely to be dragged down, but he would have to sacrifice his weapon if he had to swim to save his life.

The beach began to rise beneath his feet and he was out of the water. No challenge had rung out, nor any cry of alarm. The men behind him spread out to their left and right, providing the most effective formation from which to open fire if it became necessary.

Tpr Wishaw led 3 Troop ashore, their troop commander Andrew Fraser close behind. He led them up the slope from the beach while Carter's 4 Troop waited. They would form two lines along the low ridge overlooking the village, keeping their heads down until an hour before dawn. Then they would move down the slope on the other side and into position. Wishaw had a good eye for terrain and he and Carter had plotted the route to take while they had lain baking under the sun during their reconnaissance.

Commandos are good at waiting. They could lie for hours in wet grass or half in and out of the sea if necessary, without making a sound or moving a muscle. It was a discipline hard learnt at Achnacarry and one which had saved many lives. It would save many more before the war was over.

The Moon set, leaving them in total darkness except for the thin light of the stars that coated the heavens. The sight never ceased to amaze Carter. There seemed to be so many more stars than they could see at home, in England. Someone had told him it was because the streetlights made it harder for the pin pricks of the stars to make themselves seen. The nearest streetlight to where they currently were, was probably Sharm El-Sheikh, if there.

Carter felt a movement beside him and warm breath next to his ear. "No sign of any movement in the village." Wishaw breathed. Carter slid back the sleeve of his shirt and checked the luminous hands of his watch. Two hours until dawn.

"OK." He breathed back. "Get back to 3 Troop. Don't move until it's time."

If they went down to the village early it was unlikely that anyone would discover them, but there was always the risk of someone with a weak bladder leaving one of the tents. The biggest risk was the goats (or were they sheep?) getting spooked and starting to bleat. The goatherds would respond to that sound in the same way as a mother would wake when her child whimpered.

Carter shivered. He was always amazed by how cold it got at night in this part of the world. Something to do with the clear skies and the ground giving up the heat it stored during the day. He didn't pretend to understand it,

The line of figures ahead of them rose, black against black, and moved to the top of the hill. The route they had chosen was narrow, so they would turn to the right into single file to make the descent. Carter allowed the second hand of his watch to circle the face twice, before nudging the men to his right and left, signalling that they were leaving. The message was passed silently along the line as they rose and followed 3 Troop.

Their pace was so slow and cautious that they took most of the available hour to reach their objectives. They passed through 3 Troop, who formed the perimeter and took up their positions beside the tents. Each man laid his bayonet tipped rifle on the ground and drew his commando dagger.

The eastern horizon grew lighter as dawn approached. Just as it grew dark quickly, so did it become light just as fast in the morning. Carter allowed them five minutes more to give them enough light by which to see.

He placed his whistle between his lips, drew a breath of air into his lungs and blew one long blast. The daggers slashed down, cutting the guy ropes on the tents and allowing them to collapse slowly onto the occupants sleeping inside, imprisoning them within the heavy cloth.

Meanwhile, at the mud built barracks and the headman's house, soldiers from 3 Troop pulled the pins on small cannisters and lobbed them through the open rectangles of the windows, before running back to a safe distance to prepare for the buildings to be evacuated.

Tear gas, they called it. It had first been used in the trenches of World War I. Now it was used as a riot control agent. Curshaw had been able to lay hands on half a dozen small bombs, courtesy of the Egyptian police.

Men started tumbling from the front of the building, rubbing at their streaming eyes. It was the worst possible thing to do, but it was an instinctive reaction. Commandos rushed forwards, grabbing the helpless and unresisting men and throwing them to the ground before securing their hands.

Struggling figures emerged from the collapsed tents to find needle sharp bayonet points hovering inches from their noses. They didn't try to resist, just raised their hands and clambered to their feet.

There was only one point of resistance. At the compound surrounding the headman's house the commandos backed away as the headman himself emerged. In front of him he pushed a cowering woman, dressed in black from head to foot. At her head he pointed his revolver; a British army issue Webley. He shouted something in Arabic. It needed no translation.

"I've got a clear shot." Wishaw shouted.

"No. Too risky." Carter shouted back. He didn't doubt Wishaw's aim, but it was possible that the man would pull the trigger even as he died, killing the woman.

A child clung to the woman's leg. Carter recognised the little boy as being the one with the woman whose husband had been killed. So that was what that was about. The headman had taken a fancy to the woman and the dead man had been trying to remove her from his reach. Or maybe he really had been afraid that their hideout had been discovered and had just been trying to escape; then the headman had taken his widow anyway.

The man started walking backwards, dragging the woman along with him. They were headed towards the distant palm trees, now just visible in the growing light. Was there a means of escape in that direction? They had no maps of the area, so there could be an entire city there that they didn't know about. Well, not a city, but certainly another village.

The man stumbled, turning his ankle. The woman took her chance and went to attack him, raking at his eyes with claw like hands. As he fell the man dropped the gun, then scuttled backwards, crablike, out of her reach. He managed to get back to his feet, pausing to decide if he could reach the gun. A shot over his head from Wishaw made him decide he couldn't. He ran.

But the woman could reach the gun and she did. Picking it up in both hands she raised it and pulled the trigger. It was a lucky shot, the recoil of the weapon in her small hands forcing her to drop it once again. But the bullet hit the man in the leg. He fell face down, grasping at the growing blossom of blood that appeared at thigh level on his gallabiyah.

The woman let out a shriek and ran to where he lay. Realising the danger, he turned onto his back. The woman's hands were extended again, her fingers arcing into talons. Instinctively he put his hands up to protect his eyes, which he knew would be the woman's main target. It is what killed him.

With his arms raised, the woman could see the elaborately jewelled hilt of his knife in its sheath held at the man's waist. She grabbed at it, drawing and stabbing in one smooth motion, the knife sinking deep into the man's chest.

She withdrew it and stabbed again, repeating until the front of his gallabiyah was covered in blood and the man had long left this world.

It was only the child, grabbing at her mother's clothes, that returned her to the real world. She stood, ruffled the child's hair and walked back towards the village. The commandos stood aside to let her past, even though she had left the knife sticking out of the man's ribs. Slowly, almost in a dream, she made her way down to the water's edge and sat down. Letting the sea wash the blood from her hands. The child joined her, wrapping its small arms around her neck.

"What're you lot gawkin' at?" Troop Sgt Maj Chalk's voice bellowed across the village to break the spell. "Get them prisoners secured and down to the water's edge."

Even Carter was surprised at the sudden and unexpected violence of the woman's actions.

"There's a biddy[1] I wouldn't want to upset." O'Driscoll remarked as he escorted three prisoners shoreward.

"The female of the species is deadlier than the male, Paddy." Carter replied.

"Very profound, Sorr. Did you just make that up?"

"No, but Kipling did, in one of his poems[3]."

"Ah, there was a wise man, Sorr." His voice faded as he continued to make his way to the goat pen where half a dozen men from 3 Troop were corralling the prisoners. The goats themselves had been let free to wander. It wasn't a secure prison, but the threat from the bayonets and the grim, camouflaged faces of the commandos were sufficient deterrent to prevent any ideas of escape. The women were being herded into a separate area on the other side of the village.

With the prisoners secure, the commandos started the destruction of the rest of the camp. The skiffs and other boats were dragged out of the water and piled up with the tents, petrol from the fuel dump poured over them in readiness for a massive bonfire. A smaller party searched the building for any weapons or valuables. They found a chest containing money and Carter put it under the guard of two men. The Egyptian government would decide what to do with that.

The pirates' weapons were all gathered up and stripped, the components scattered across the sea to prevent them being used again.

The first of the landing craft arrived in response to the flares sent up by Carter's Very pistol. The women were nudged into one, reluctant to lose sight of their menfolk, perhaps fearing that they were to be killed; or worse. Egyptian police officers stood ready to formally arrest them. The men were then pushed and prodded into a second landing craft.

3 Troop and half of 4 Troop boarded three of the remaining four craft, leaving Carter with thirty men to finish the job. The site needed to be cleared of any trace that the British Army had been there. Not so much as a spent Very pistol cartridge could be left behind.

A trail of petrol was laid to the water's edge, his men boarded the landing craft and Carter struck a match, letting it fall to the ground. Flame streaked across the sand, splitting into three streams. Two went to the barracks building and the dead headman's house, while the final one set light to the tents and the boats.

As Carter's landing craft backed away from the beach, he pulled himself up onto the closed ramp and took careful aim with the Very pistol. Pulling the trigger he fired a flare at what was left of the fuel dump. There was satisfying explosion followed by a blast of heated air. Carter slid down inside the safety of the craft as it reached deeper water and turned to head out to sea, towards the waiting Prince Leopold.

[1] Taken from the murder holes built into the ceilings of gatehouses of castles which allowed defenders to fire arrows down into the packed rank of attackers trying to breach the gate, or to pour boiling liquids onto their heads. In the film 'Saving Private Ryan', Tom Hanks, in his role as Capt Miller, can be heard telling his men to get away from the murder hole as they storm ashore from their landing craft on D-Day.

[2] Biddy – Irish slang for a woman, usually implying a gossip or nag.

[3] A poem entitled "The Female of the Species" written in 1911. The exact words are "For the female of the species is more deadly than the male" and forms the last line of each of the first four of the thirteen verses. It is reprised with a slight variation in the final verse. The phrase also appeared in a 1928 Bulldog Drummond novel, but is probably best known nowadays from the 1996 recording released by the band Space.

* * *

Back on board the landing ship, Carter went to join his men in their accommodation, going from man to man, slapping them on the back in congratulation for a job well done. The Purser had opened his alcohol stocks and the ship's captain had given permission for each man to be given one bottle of cold Stella beer[1].

Spying a huddle of Egyptian police officers nursing glasses of fruit cordial, Carter went across and drew Constable Masry to one side.

"Can you thank your colleagues for their work." Carter asked.

"Of course. They will be pleased."

"The woman, the one who committed murder …"

"I know of no murder, Sir." Masry said. Carter wasn't sure, but he thought he saw a twitch at the corner of Masry's lips. Carter had the sense not to pursue the matter.

"I must explain." Masry leant in to take Carter into his confidence. "Many women we arrested are slaves, kept by the men. Their lives are ruined. No man will marry them. Best hope is if family take pity, otherwise …" He shrugged. "So, everyone have trouble enough and I do not have body or murder weapon, so no murder." Again, Carter thought he saw a twitch.

"I saw the dead man kill another man, who the woman seemed to be living with. I assume he was the father of her child. They seemed quite fond of their men." Carter observed.

"I have seen before. They are … what is word? Everything they need they get from men."

"Dependent?"

"Yes, that is it. They dependent on men for everything. So they get very attached. Now life get difficult for them. Some may starve. Some may have to get work in Suez, you know, where soldiers go at night."

Carter did know. He reminded himself that the culture in the Middle East was considerably different to that which he knew. "Well, everything passed off well, and thank you once again for your efforts."

"Sir, Captain's compliments." A breathless naval rating called to Carter. "Can you join him on the bridge, urgent like, Sir."

Carter passed his beer to the nearest commando, who took it with a broad smile, then followed the sailor through the narrow corridors that the travelling public never saw in the pre-war days when the ship had plied its trade across the English Channel.

"Ah, Steven, thought you should be here for this. We've got company approaching." Lt Cdr Norton pointed across the bridge wing towards the north east where a boat could be seen bouncing across the small waves towards them. The flag of Saudi Arabia streamed from a flag staff at the taffrail.

Norton offered Carter the use of a pair of powerful naval binoculars. Through them Carter could see the boat a lot more clearly. It wasn't large, hardly bigger than a cabin cruiser that might be seen on the Norfolk Broads. A wheelhouse was sited in the middle, with a well deck behind. In front a Vickers machine gun stood behind a low sandbag wall but there was no crew manning it. Glistening from the wheelhouse roof was a whip aerial, suggesting that help could be summoned if needed.

"How do you think the alarm was raised?" Norton asked. It couldn't be a coincidence that a fast patrol boat had just turned up out of the blue.

"Perhaps there's a village in that oasis behind the beach." Carter suggested. "We didn't carry out a recce inland. Maybe they have a telephone there. And of course, we did leave a column of smoke behind us. Moses used one of those to guide the children of Israel across the Sinai, if my memories of Sunday School are correct[1]."

"Well, we're in international waters and he's too small to try to stop us. What do you suggest?"

"He has a radio. He could whistle up something with a bit more firepower. Perhaps if we have a chat with him, we can convince him we're just an innocent troopship in transit for Suez. Let's face it, there have been plenty of those in recent weeks."

"OK. We'll see what he wants. But I suggest you have a wash and brush up first. All those stripes of yours are likely to give the game away."

Carter checked the back of his hands and realised he was still smeared with cam cream. His face and neck would be as well. Norton was right. He might as well have a sign above his head saying "commando raid".

"You can use my day cabin, just behind the bridge." Norton smiled. "Feel free to use anything you need."

Looking in the mirror above the small sink, Carter could see that he looked bedraggled. Not only was his face streaked with black and brown cream, but his hair was awry as well. A clean shirt wouldn't have gone amiss either, but he had no time for that. He cleaned himself up and returned to the bridge. His green beret was in his cabin on the accommodation deck and the patrol boat was now too close for him to go and get it.

A figure appeared in the well deck of the patrol boat, a metal cone in his hand; a loud hailer. He was dressed in a conventional tropical style uniform of khaki shirt and trousers, with gold at his shoulders to denote his rank. On his head was a typical Bedouin red and white chequered keffiyeh, held in place by a black agal, a rope like ring.

"Heave-to and prepare to be boarded." The man's voice sounded tinny as he hailed the Prince Leopold." But the man's accent spoke of attendance at one of Britain's more expensive schools.

Norton strolled out onto the bridge wing, taking his time. He picked up a hand held microphone so that he could use the ship's own public address system. "We are a ship of his Britannic Majesty's Royal Navy sailing in international waters." Norton's voice boomed out across the water. "On what authority do you order us to heave to?" It was a game, both officers knew that.

"On the authority of His Majesty King Saud of Saudi Arabia. I believe you have violated Saudi Arabian territory and demand that you heave-to for inspection."

"And if I refuse?" Norton tried hard to keep the smile off his face.

"A protest will be made to your government." Was the best that the officer could reply. He was engaged in a fruitless task and he knew it, but he, like Norton, had to go through the motions.

"In order to avoid a diplomatic incident," Norton replied, "I will allow you and one member of your crew to board, but I'm not heaving-to. You will have to board while we continue sailing."

Norton returned inside and called a rating over to him. "My compliments to the Bosun and ask him to put a ladder over the side to receive our visitor. Usual courtesies for a visiting captain."

Even the captain of a tiny patrol boat had to be shown the respect due to his station, no matter how modest his craft. Again, it was all part of the diplomatic game.

A few minutes later the officer and a naval rating were shown onto the bridge. He saluted Norton, who replied in kind.

"*As-Salaam Alaikum*" he said, touching his right hand to his heart, his lips and his forehead in the traditional Arabic greeting.

"*Wa-Alaikum Salaam*" Norton replied.

"I am Lt Al-Ebeid of His Majesty King Saud's Navy." The man introduced himself.

"Lt Cdr Norton. This is Captain Carter."

"A soldier, I see." Al-Ebeid replied. "Perhaps he is the one I should be talking to."

"I command this ship." Norton replied, somewhat stiffly. "Now, what nonsense is this about us violating Saudi Arabian territory?"

"This morning there was an attack on a peaceful fishing village not far from here. Your ship was observed standing off-shore. It is assumed that the attackers came from here."

"And why would the British attack a peaceful fishing village?" Norton responded. "The last time I heard, the nations of Saudi Arabia and the United Kingdom were on peaceful and friendly terms."

This seemed to flummox the officer, but it was a reasonable question. If there had been an attack, it must have been motivated by something.

"I er … I have no idea. But there are witnesses to the attack."

"Have you spoken to them? Have they identified the attackers as British? There are known to be pirates operating along this coast. Perhaps it was they who attacked the village."

It was a master stroke. If the officer identified the villagers as pirates, providing a motive for a British incursion, he would have to justify the Saudi Arabian authorities not taking any action against them. On the other hand, if the attackers weren't positively identified as British, then the possibility existed that they might have been pirates. Carter felt sure that the officer knew who was operating boats along the stretch of coast he patrolled, so he would know where the pirates were. Perhaps he was protecting them; or maybe just following orders from above.

The officer decided that bluster would serve him best. "I am here to identify the attackers. I demand to be allowed to search this vessel."

Deciding that things had gone far enough, Carter decided to intervene. "I am in charge of one hundred and twenty soldiers aboard this ship, Lieutenant. They are hot, which is making them bad tempered. If you think that you and your man here are going to be able to subject this ship to a search, then you are welcome to try."

"You are threatening me, Captain?" The Saudi seemed genuinely shocked.

"No. I'm just telling you what you will have to deal with. If you want to search the ship, I'm sure Lt Cdr Norton would allow it." Carter knew full well that Norton would do no such thing, but Al-Ebeid didn't know that.

"Look, Lieutenant." Norton decided to diffuse the situation. "I'm sure our presence in the area is just a coincidence; a case of mistaken identity. You have done your duty and checked us out."

"I must submit a report."

"And your report can say whatever you wish. Now, let there be no hard feelings. I'm sure that the war is leaving you short of some supplies." Carter could see where this was leading. Had Norton had this in mind all along? "Is there anything you can't get hold of that we might be able to assist with?"

The visitor tried to keep a smile from his face, but didn't quite manage it. "Well, actually there is. My wife's father has rather a taste for Scotch whisky. Not for me, you understand. Allah, may His name be praised, forbids it. But my father-in-law, he doesn't always observe the rules."

"I understand." Norton suppressed his own smile. There was no doubt in his mind who the whisky was really for. "I'll arrange for a case to be at the side rail when you get there."

There were some pleasantries and the Saudi naval officer departed.

"You had that planned all along, didn't you?" Carter grinned.

"While you were cleaning up I sent a message for the wardroom steward to have a case of whisky ready." Norton acknowledged. "Just a little oil for the wheels. He'll now exonerate us for any involvement in the raid and probably take our hint and blame it on pirates."

A sailor came onto the bridge and offered a clipboard to the captain. Norton read the top sheet of paper. "Ah, it looks like things are under way back in Suez." He said, looking at Carter. "After we've dropped off the prisoners and their police escort, we're to anchor off El-Ataka and be ready to receive stores and passengers. I'm to report to the Port Commodore for a full briefing."

"It must be the big operation we've been training for."

"You and every soldier, sailor and airman from the Red Sea to the Atlantic." Norton replied. He flipped the top signal flimsy over and read the next one in the sheaf. "One for you." He said. "There's a General due at your camp to carry out a review of your training. Your CO says to make sure your men are turned out properly when you march back through the gates." He unclipped the bit of paper and handed it over to Carter.

"I better go and let the men know."

[1] A popular brand of beer brewed in Egypt at the time of World War II and drunk by most of the British troops based there. Not connected to Stella Artois.

[2] Book of Exodus 40:38

5 – Operation Husky

The camp was s hive of activity when Carter marched his two troops up from the beach and through the camp gates. On one side there were lorries disgorging cargo into the arms of waiting commandos, while on the other, cargo was being heaped up in neat stacks ready for transfer to the beach. A short line of staff cars stood in front of the HQ tent, with MPs standing outside keeping eavesdroppers at bay.

Calling his men to a halt, Carter dismissed them, sending them back to their tents to await orders. They were well rested after their cruise back up the Gulf of Suez to the port. The prisoners had been hustled from the ship by the Egyptian police, at least fifty more of them waiting on the quayside. Carter had no doubt they were there to be seen as much as they were to contain the prisoners. There was a lesson to be learned about the risks of piracy and the best way to do that was to make a public spectacle of the arrival of the pirates.

The prisoners were herded onto lorries, the backs of them closed in with only tiny barred windows at the top to allow any ventilation. Carter tried to feel pity for them, then remembered the floating bodies of the crew of a missing dhow and all the pity he might have had evaporated. Seeing the females dragged away, none too gently, was a different matter. Most of them were blameless, but they would be treated no differently to the men. The best they could hope for was to escape prison and then have a very uncertain future.

Carter caught sight of the Sergeant Major. If anyone knew what was going on, he would.

"Mr Finch[1]." He called.

The Sgt Major stopped berating the men he was supervising and turned to put up a crisp salute. "Capt Carter. Welcome back Sir. What can I do for you?"

"You can start by telling me what's going on."

"I don't have that much of an idea, as yet. General Dempsey[2] arrived this morning and we put on a bit of a show for him, putting the commando through its paces so to speak, then these lorries started arriving. I'm guessing we're off sometime soon, but the CO hasn't briefed us yet."

Carter suspected that the Sgt Major knew more; he always did. But he was being discreet and Carter couldn't blame him for that. He was the CO's right-hand man, which was a privileged position.

"Well, 3 and 4 troops are available if you need them."

"I probably will, in due course. We'll need men aboard the Leopold to receive these stores and stow them wherever the fish'eds … beggin' your pardon, the Navy want to stow them."

"There seems to be a lot of stuff. More than we would normally take on an operation."

"Yes, there is. But we've got to get from here to wherever we're going and that's going to take a while. Then I suspect we'll be using the Leopold as a floating barracks, so we've got to have everything on board that we need to keep us alive for several weeks."

"When you put it that way, I guess it's not that much, really."

"Don't you believe it, Sir. There's another twenty trucks due today. I suggest you tell your men to start packing, because once I put them aboard the Leopold, I doubt they'll be coming ashore again."

The Sgt Major glanced over Carter's shoulder and sprang to attention. "General's coming, Sir." He whispered, before bellowing a command for everyone within earshot to come to attention.

Carter turned around in time to see a tall, thin officer leave the tent, followed by a retinue of aids and, finally, the CO. Carter saluted. "As you were, carry on, carry on." The General called, waving his swagger stick. Carter dropped his salute but remained at attention.

In a flurry of hot dust, the convoy of staff cars pulled away, leaving the camp to its own devices.

"Sgt Maj Finch" The CO signalled to the Warrant Officer.

"Scuse me Sir. I think I'm about to get my orders." Finch hurried across and disappeared inside the HQ tent behind the CO.

[1] Warrant Officers are often addressed as "Mister" by officers in all three branches of the armed forces. It stems back to the Royal Navy during the days of sail, when the senior non-commissioned professionals on board ship were given the title "Master": Sailing Master, Master Gunner, Master Carpenter etc. Over time this changed to "Mister". Junior ranks address Warrant Officers as "Sir".

[2] Lt Gen (later General) Miles Dempsey DSO MC was the commanding officer of XIII Corps of the 8th Army from December 1942 until he returned to the UK in October 1943 with General Montgomery, to assist in the planning of D Day. He was later knighted and garnered a chest full of awards from both Britain and allied nations. When Sgt Maj Finch referred to him as "General" rather than Lt General, he wasn't being disrespectful. It is the normal short form used in the army, in the same way as a Lt Col will often be referred to as Colonel.

* * *

After two days of hectic activity, evening fell aboard the Prince Leopold. Half the commando's officers waited in the First Class lounge for the arrival of the CO. They chatted amongst themselves, mainly about the luck of 1, 2 and 6 troops being billeted aboard the Dunera[1], a modern passenger liner pressed into naval service as a troopship.

"We got the landing craft." Carter observed. "That means we're going ashore first." He said confidently. Heads nodded in agreement. Whatever their mission, they were the priority. But it only partially made up for the fact that half the commando would be travelling in relative luxury.

"Not that much luxury." The QM said. "As well as our lads there's a battalion of Jock infantry and an artillery Field Regiment on board. That's nearly her capacity. In peacetime she was only licensed for four hundred passengers of all classes. Even now she's only supposed to carry fifteen hundred troops.

With only one hundred and eighty commandos on board, the Prince Leopold no longer seemed so crowded.

The officers stiffened to attention as the CO entered.

"At ease, gentlemen." He said, taking up a position in front of a series of covered easels and a table that was also concealed by a blanket. "As you will have gathered, this is it. This is what we have been training for. Once I start this briefing, no one will be allowed ashore, so if you have any urgent business, I suggest you say so now."

There was a dutiful chorus of laughter before the CO held up his hand for silence. He pulled the blanket off the first easel, to reveal a map of the Mediterranean Sea. Arrows were stretched across it, starting from various points in North Africa, but all ending at one place. An island off the coast of Italy that looked a bit like a rugby ball about to be kicked by a booted foot.

"We're heading for Sicily, gentlemen, the invasion of which is designated Operation Husky. From here we will sail up the Suez Canal to Port Said, where we will form into a convoy. From Port Said we will sail along the coast so as to remain under RAF air cover, as far as the Gulf of Sidra[2] in Libya, roughly due north of Benghazi. From there we'll turn north west to pass close by Malta, again to take advantage of air cover, before heading due north to arrive off Sicily on the morning of 10th July." As Vernon spoke, he traced the route along the arrows until his finger tapped on the island that was their destination.

"Not Italy, then?" Someone said. For weeks they had assumed that Italy was their destination. Some had said Greece, but no one had really taken that seriously.

"No. It was considered, I believe, but that would leave our west flank exposed. There are naval and air forces in Sicily. So that's where we're going first." He lifted the blackboard from its easel and turned it over to reveal a larger scale map of their destination.

Clustered around the south eastern corner were a series of arrows, denoting the formations that would go ashore and where they were destined to land.

"The Americans will be travelling from Tunisia and Algeria and landing on the southern coast in the Gulf of Gela. From there they'll strike inland to link up with us. The Americans will continue their attack through the centre of the island, while we take the coastal route. The British landing beaches" he continued, "Are along the coast of what is called the Gulf of Noto, between the southern-most tip of the island and the town of Syracuse. Ultimately, we're looking to reach Messina, cutting off the German and Italian supplies to the island, forcing them to surrender. I understand that there is an element rivalry between Monty and General Patton about who will get there first."

This brought a further round of laughter. Patton's reputation as a glory hunter was well established after his campaign in Tunisia and many considered Montgomery to be in the same mould.

"Now, you are no doubt wondering what our role in this little shindig is going to be and also why we've been split up into two parties."

There were murmurings of agreement.

"The fact is, we've been given two separate objectives. 1, 2 and 6 troops, under the 2IC, have been given the shore defences at the northern end of the landing beaches to capture, to the west of a place called Punto Murro di Porco, which is just south of Syracuse. It's official designation for the operation is Beach 44. That's why they've been practicing on those sorts of installations at El Ataka. They go in about thirty minutes before the main landings start, to neutralise whatever forces the Italians and Germans have lurking there.

But we, 3, 4 and 5 troops, are going in earlier." You could have heard a pin drop. "We will be landing here," he tapped the map on a headland projecting into the bay, a mile to the south of Punto Murro do Porco. "There's a prominent rock there called the *Scoglio*

Imbiancanto, which is where we land. From there we march due west, inland, to capture an artillery battery sited close to the village of Cassibile, that is threatening the beaches." He tapped a black dot on the map some distance inland. "It is an important objective, gentlemen, and once we hit the beach we have just ninety minutes to take it."

There was some muttering about that. The way the commando had rehearsed was for three troops to capture the shore defences then for the other three to pass through them to advance on what was supposed to be an artillery battery inland. To find that their three troops had to capture both the beach and the battery came as a surprise.

"Don't worry, gentlemen." Vernon understood what his men were thinking. "The Scoglio has been chosen because it isn't a well defended stretch of land. It's rocky and hard to get at, just like El Ataka."

This brought a knowing chuckle. "And because it is hard to get at, it's poorly defended, as no one would be foolish enough to try to land there. But the Italians have never had to fight the commandos before, so they can be forgiven their ignorance."

This brought a louder laugh, breaking some of the tension that had built up. But poorly defended wasn't the same as undefended, Carter knew. They could lose valuable time dealing with just one stubborn machine gun position.

"You will all get plenty of time to study the maps, the aerial photographs and this." Vernon uncovered a table containing a model, showing a stretch of rocky coastline and a patchwork of fields that had miniature guns positioned on the inland side. The village of Cassibile, represented by small box like shapes, stood a short distance from the guns. "That's a model of the ground we have to cover."

The officers pushed forward, anxious to see a three-dimensional representation of their objective. It told them so much more than maps and photographs.

Vernon laid out the rest of the plan for them, but it wasn't much more than hit the beach, march inland and attack the battery. The tactical details of the final attack were described, but everyone knew that those would probably change. Who knew how the enemy would react when a hundred and eighty commandos arrived on their doorstep? No plan survived first contact with the enemy. They all knew that.

The commandos would be heavily burdened as they marched inland. Since arriving in Egypt they had been equipped with three inch[3] mortars to supplement their much smaller two inch versions. Without transport to carry the mortar bombs, each man had to carry one with them and they weighed ten pounds each. They also had to carry their own weapons, spare ammunition, spare magazines for the Bren guns and all their other kit. Even if they achieved their objective there was no guarantee the landings would be successful and they had to plan to remain defending the battery against counter-attack until relieved. Worst case scenario might mean them having to remain there for days.

But that was negative thinking, Carter told himself. A hundred and eighty commandos were more than a match for a bunch of Italian gunners who had probably never heard a shot fired in anger.

"After we've captured the battery and blown up the guns, we move to Cassibile village and rendezvous with the 2IC's party to await our next orders. Let's hope Monty doesn't forget about us in all the kerfuffle that will be happening on the beaches."

But Monty wouldn't forget about 15 Commando, although they would come to wish he had.

---

[1] Like the Prince Leopold, the Dunera was a real ship and her passenger capacity was as described. Cargo holds were converted to provide capacity for so many troops. She was originally owned by the British-India Steam Navigation Company. In 1960 she was disposed of by the Admiralty and refitted as an educational cruise ship, complete with classrooms, swimming pool and games room,

carrying one hundred adult cabin passengers and eight hundred and thirty four school children. She was scrapped in 1967.

[2] Also referred to as the Gulf of Sirte. Sidra is the recognised name; Sirte is a city at the western end of the gulf, south of Tripoli. As a city Sirte it was only established in the early 1900s by the invading Italians, built on the ruins of an older Ottoman fortification.

[3] Although referred to as the three inch mortar, it's calibre was slightly over 3.2 inches, or 81 mm. This is still the standard calibre for the more modern mortars used by the British Army. The complete mortar assembly of baseplate, barrel and bipod weighed 115 lbs and had to be carried by its three man crew, so they couldn't carry ammunition as well. By 1943 the range of the mortar had increased to approximately 2,800 metres, or 3,000 yards.

* * *

Peering through the tiny porthole, almost blinded by the sunrise, Carter could look out across the flat northern plain of the Sinai. Visible in the distance was a train, also heading north, a long series of flatcars loaded down with Sherman tanks, a new addition to Britain's armoury since America had joined the war. At the rear of the train was a series of dilapidated looking carriages, no doubt carrying the tanks' crews.

Rumour said they were a good tank; about the only weapon capable of dealing with the German Tiger tanks and even then they had to be at close range. Artillery could kill a Tiger, of course, but artillery had no protection against counter-fire. But the Sherman had performed well in the open spaces of Tunisia, so there were high hopes for it in Italy, which was more mountainous and therefore provided less room for manoeuvre.

The ship had still been at anchor when Carter had gone to bed the night before, but the sound of sailors hurrying around, readying the ship for departure had been evident. Now they were well along the

Suez Canal. He wondered if they had passed through the Great Bitter Lake, where north and southbound shipping was able to pass. Probably. Although the ships didn't travel quickly through the canal, they could make the journey in little more than half a day. He would know soon enough.

Angus Fraser snorted and turned over in his sleep. As captains they shared the cabin. The more junior officers had to sleep four to a room. It was still better than the men, who swung in hammocks in what was once the passenger lounges of the old cross channel ferry. Taking his opportunity before Fraser awoke, Carter washed and shaved before dressing and going up on deck to get some fresh air.

It was still quite cool in the early morning, made more-so by the breeze created by the ship's forward motion. Cool enough to raise goose-bumps on his arm. That wouldn't last, of course. It was high summer and they could expect daytime temperatures of up to eighty five degrees. The metal surfaces of the ship would become hot enough to fry eggs. They knew that because they'd tried it while they'd been in the Red Sea.

He crossed to the port side and looked out. The land there was green, the vegetation spreading out from the Nile delta, invisible in the distance. Carter could see a farmer leading a donkey cart laden with crops.

If they stopped long enough, Carter wondered if he'd get time to visit Alexandria. He'd always had a romantic notion of the city, ever since reading about it as a child; about how Alexander the Great had founded a city in his own name in Egypt, about its great library and the huge lighthouse that had been one of the seven wonders of the ancient world. He knew that both the library and the lighthouse were long gone, but he would still love to see the city.

Probably not, he thought. If he was allowed ashore the rest of the men would have to be allowed as well and in a city like Port Said that was far from advisable. If Suez had a bad reputation, the city at the northern end of the canal was worse.

He glanced ahead to see another ship ahead of them. He couldn't identify it; some sort of merchantman by the look of it. He leaned out over the rail so that he could see back past the central superstructure. Sure enough, there was another ship behind. That was more easily recognisable as a warship, a destroyer judging by its size, but he couldn't see its ensign. The Australians and New Zealanders were heavily involved with this operation, so it might be one of theirs.

Carter's nose twitched as the smell of bacon wafted towards him. A sailor had just emerged through a gangway and was leaning on the side rail, tucking into a sandwich. Breakfast, thought Carter. Then they would start the round of briefings for the men. Between now and their arrival off the shores of Sicily, they would go over the plan time after time until everyone had the whole thing off pat; word perfect. The men would become bored with the repetition, but experience had shown that one of them would miss something if they didn't have it rammed home.

As well as the briefings there would be some training, first-aid mainly as there wasn't anywhere they could practice anything else. Once in the Mediterranean they might be allowed some target practice, firing at disused oil drums. But that depended on their position in the convoy. They couldn't risk hitting some poor bloke on another ship with a ricochet. But they would exercise the mortar crews, going through dry runs on deck, assembling the mortars and then taking them apart again. Lining up on imaginary targets and dropping imaginary bombs down the tubes. They had two Vickers machine guns as well now. The same sort of training would be done with them.

There was talk of setting up a specialist heavy weapons troop to look after the new weapons. Carter hoped he wasn't picked to lead that. Being tied down to heavy equipment wasn't very exciting. Some of the officers and NCOs had already been sent on fire control training courses while they had been in Egypt. They were the most likely candidates for the job. But Carter had been in the army long enough to know that wasn't always the way things worked. Besides, they were going into combat; the trained officers and NCOs might not make it. Other men had undertaken training in signals skills; laying telephone wires and operating field radios so that fire control could be exercised from forward positions.

On that gloomy thought he gave the sailor a farewell nod and left him to his sandwich, while he made his way back below decks to the wardroom in search of his own breakfast.

* * *

It was too much to hope that they weren't expected. Fighters had chased off enemy reconnaissance aircraft, but not until they must have seen the armada heading westwards. Then there were the Italian submarines. Two laggards from the various convoys had been sunk, picked off by torpedoes as they struggled to maintain the pace that was being set.

And then there was the enemy on their own side. It was only a few weeks earlier that Winston Churchill himself had told the BBC that "something big was about to happen". The enemy would have been particularly dense not to have guessed that it involved the Mediterranean Sea. The men had roundly cursed Churchill's stupidity, but there was nothing that could be done now.

The landing craft carrying the CO, The QM, Carter and half of his troop was lowered until it was bumping along the surface of the sea as the Prince Leopold maintained a steady course and speed, but the water was dragging it backwards. The Cox'n applied power, driving the craft forward until it was keeping pace with the bigger craft and the lifeboat falls[1], to which the craft was still attached, were more or less vertical. This was a manoeuvre that had been practiced many times. The crew of the landing craft knew what they were doing.

On a word of command from the landing craft's skipper, the falls were released and the Cox'n turned the boat away from the Prince Leopold's side, heading due west towards the distant shore. The object they were looking for was so small that it was still invisible; a canoe manned by a naval rating and launched from a submarine, marking the beach they were due to land on.

The other five landing craft joined the first in two lines astern. They would move into line abreast as they drew closer. Like this they presented a smaller target to waiting gunners.

"Damned canoe's in the wrong place." Carter heard Vernon say from the front of the Landing craft. "Must have drifted with the wind." Carter strained his neck to try to pick out the flashing signal that the canoeist was supposed to send, but he couldn't see over the high slab of the ramp.

"Are you sure, Sir." It was the QM's voice. He was acting as 2IC in the absence of Teddy Couples.

"Those mountains behind the signal light; they should be further north. I'd say he's drifted at least half a mile."

A destroyer loomed out of the darkness, making to pass behind the flotilla on some errand of its own. Vernon fought his way backwards through the packed ranks of soldiers until he could use the electric loudhailer system in the Coxon's small bridge housing."

"Ahoy there." The metallic voice boomed out. "Can you give us a bearing for the *Scoglio*?"

There was a short pause, then "Bearing two-six-eight." Came the reply.

"There, I told you." Vernon said with some satisfaction as he passed Carter on his way back to the bow of the craft. "At least ten degrees off course." Carter felt the landing craft change direction and the five others followed suit, like ducklings following their mother.

They continued on their way until the pinnacle of rock appeared in front of them. It was two hundred feet high and fifty feet across at its base. Hard to miss in daylight, but in the darkness they could have passed it by at a hundred yards distance and not known it was there. With a ten degree error they might have landed half a mile away and without any visual cues they would have had no idea where they were until the sun rose. If it hadn't been for Vernon's sharp eyes, picking out the silhouette of the mountains against the stars, that is what would have happened. Being on the wrong beach would have been bad enough, but if it was also well defended they could have been cut to ribbons.

Two hundred yards from the beach a machine gun started firing from the shore. What had spooked the crew was impossible to say. Perhaps they'd heard the exchange between Vernon and the destroyer; perhaps they'd just picked out the dark shapes of the landing craft against the sea. Or maybe they'd heard a wandering goat and just panicked. The Lewis guns mounted on either side of the ramps of the two leading craft returned fire and, after a few more random bursts, the gun on shore fell silent.

Intelligence reports said the Italians were demoralised. Was that the first indication that the reports were true?

The ramp dropped and the men stormed ashore, scrambling over the heaped rocks, only to be stopped by barbed wire. Cutters were unstrapped from packs and paths cut through. Behind the wire the commandos found half a dozen pillboxes, the first line of the enemy's defences. All but one was empty. The one that was manned was quickly dealt with by grenades and Tommy guns, and the commando rushed on. The noise they had made meant their presence would be known about, but their advantage was that the commandos knew where they were going; the enemy had to guess.

Behind them the landing craft raised their ramps and backed off from the beach. They were needed elsewhere.

Carter was aware of the sound of aircraft engines above their heads, which reminded him that the enemy had other things to think about than a beach landing. Paratroops flown in from North Africa were landing inland, seizing strategic crossroads and river crossings. An enemy behind was a more pressing matter than an enemy in front. Those landings had been hours earlier, of course, but the aircraft arriving now would be dropping heavier equipment and supplies.

A hundred yards inland Carter called his men to a halt. NCOs checked their men were present and reported to the Lieutenants. Ernie Barraclough and Arthur Murray reported to Carter. All present and correct. He went forward to find the CO, who was huddled over his map with the QM, examining it by the wan light of a shaded torch.

"4 Troop all present, Sir." Carter whispered.

"Good. We'll be moving off in a couple of minutes. Keep close up. We don't want any gaps forming that might cause people to wander off and get lost."

The instruction was unnecessary. They had rehearsed this so many times they could do it in their sleep. Carter made his way back to his troop, sandwiched between 3 and 5 troops. The NCOs had formed the men up into two files. For the moment they were sat on the ground, resting their heavy burdens. Never stand when you can sit; never sit when you can lie down. Every commando adhered to the mantra. It went on to say never to miss the chance to eat, drink or sleep, but for the moment those options weren't available.

Movement rippled along the line as the men rose and stepped forward, only to stop again, like traffic on a busy road. They had to move at the pace of the scouts, who decided if the route was clear or if there was danger.

Slowly the troop inched forward until it reached the first barrier, a high drystone wall. This was the terrain they had to cross to get to the battery. A series of stony fields, each surrounded by its own wall. A dozen walls to cross without accidently discharging a weapon or dropping anything that might make a noise. It was slow going. Very slow.

By the time they were crossing the third wall Carter was growing impatient. He checked his watch, alarmed to see how much of their ninety minutes had already been consumed. At that rate of progress they would be late capturing the battery and that was bound to cost lives as the first wave of troops started their landings on the wide open beaches.

Telling Ernie Barraclough to take charge and keep the men moving, Carter moved quickly ahead, passing 3 Troop. He found the CO and the QM crouched in the deep shadow of the next wall, deep in conversation.

"What do you want, Steven?" Vernon sounded a bit tetchy, something Carter wasn't used to hearing from him.

"Sorry, Sir. Just wondering what the hold-up is."

"The scouts keep seeing ghosts." Vernon said, his frustration evident. "Look, could you go forward and gee them up a bit."

"Of course, Sir. Where are they right now?"

"Halfway across this next field, last time I saw them. They think they've spotted a sentry, though what a sentry would be doing out here in the middle of nowhere, I have no idea."

"OK, Sir." He handed his Tommy gun to the QM, stood up and reached for the top of the wall. Swinging his legs, he got a boot on top and hauled himself up until he was lying flat along the top, then dropped down the other side, bracing his legs to act as shock absorbers. Even then he felt his knees protesting at the combined weight of himself and his kit. He reached back and collected his Tommy gun from the QM before moving forward at a crouching run.

The scouts had moved forward as far as the next wall, but were now crouched in its shadow, spaced along it at twenty yard intervals.

"What's the problem?" Carter hissed, almost tripping over the nearest man in the dark.

"I think there's a sentry ahead, Sir." The man whispered.

"Where?"

"About twenty yards along on the right."

Removing his steel helmet, Carter raised his head above the top of the wall and peered into the darkness. He could make out the line of the right hand wall, heading into the distance Towards the far end of the field. There was something there, about twenty yards along, just as the scout had reported, but was it a man? To Carter's eyes it looked more like a heap of rubble, perhaps where a portion of the wall had collapsed.

Carter reached around his back and pulled an object from his belt. It was a tip that a pal from 16 Cdo had told him, after encountering a similar problem during a raid in France.

"Take a catapult, old bean." He had advised. "If you get a lucky shot in, a sentry is bound to cry out and give himself away. Even if you miss, the sound of the stone hitting something is sure to make the sentry move. Maybe he'll even issue a challenge. That way you won't waste time creeping up on fence posts and the like."

So Carter had taken to carrying a catapult. He found a pebble beneath his feet and fitted it to the leather patch in the middle of the thick rubber chord. Pulling backwards as far as he could, he stood up, took aim at the presumed sentry and released. He heard the sound of the pebble smack against a stone, he even saw the small spark that it made, but there was no movement from the mound.

"No one there." He told the sentry, more abruptly than he meant to. He couldn't blame the soldier for being cautious. After all, who would want to be responsible for leading the whole commando into an ambush? He handed his Tommy gun over for safe keeping while he crossed the wall, then took it back along with the soldier's rifle as he followed. "Give me the map." He instructed. Using his shaded torch, he checked their position against the pencil marks on the map that the soldier had made, before starting off into the night. "Keep up with me." He hissed back. The sentry paused to flash the "come on" signal with his torch, to the troops behind, then followed Carter.

To his right and left the other two scouts kept in line abreast. He didn't force the pace too much. There was a difference between careful scouting and a headlong rush, but they did move more quickly, but checking carefully before crossing each wall. Only when they were about two hundred yards from the battery did Carter bring them to a complete halt. In front of them was a dry riverbed, running right to left across their line of advance, taking it across the front of the Italian guns. Carter imagined the layout in his head, his image of the model so clear, he thought he might be able to touch it.

They were at the south east corner of the battery, exactly where they had intended to arrive.

Carter's eyes were seared by a brilliant flash, his ears assaulted by the sound of a heavy gun being fired. It meant the fleet had been spotted offshore and fire orders relayed to the battery commander. Just a single shot, probably to establish the range. As the echoes of the discharge died away, Carter could hear voices shouting orders as the gun was reloaded. Carter sent the scout back to find the CO and report their arrival at their appointed jumping off point for the attack.

The guns of the battery crashed out, firing a volley of shells out to sea. It focused everyone's minds, if that were still necessary. Carter could hardly forget that they were deep into enemy territory with a full Italian force of anything up to four hundred men in front of them.

Vernon arrived and began to issue hushed orders to deploy ready for the assault. A dozen men from 3 Troop were sent along the river bed with 2 inch mortars to provide harassing fire. A three inch mortar was sent out onto the left hand flank to fire along the line of the guns, along with another dozen men and four Bren guns to protect it and provide enfilading fire. Angus Fraser was given command of that party.

The rest of the force were sent by a circuitous route to take up positions at the rear of the battery. They were the assault party and would be led by the CO himself, two troops attacking with the remainder of 3 Troop in reserve. So far, they seemed to be undetected.

The firing of the guns would help their cause. Both the gunners and the sentries would be deafened by the sound and the muzzle flashes would degrade their night vision.

The attack force marched steadily forward. Even if they were now discovered it would make no difference. They were committed. Fifty yards from the rear of the battery, according to the map, Vernon brought them to a halt once more. The line wavered as some men didn't get the whispered order, but then came to a standstill, the men shuffling backwards and forwards as they straightened the line.

Vernon nudged his batman and he raised his bugle to his lips. Faltering on the first note, he quickly recovered to sound the advance, the signal to start the attack. In the riverbed and to the flank, the mortars and Bren guns opened up with harassing fire. Interspersed, Carter heard the whip crack of Lee-Enfields and the panicked shouting of the artillery men in the battery. The attacking line stepped forward, their rifles and Tommy guns held in front of them, cocked and ready to fire. Parachute flares soared into the sky to illuminate the battery, but they were focused on the eastern edge, keeping the main attacking force in semi-darkness, as they were supposed to. They were a distraction for the enemy to keep them looking in that direction.

The Italians weren't going to give up without a fight. Automatic weapons opened up from defensive positions, sending tracer rounds criss-crossing the battery and sending some of the commandos diving for cover. But the firing was wild and inaccurate, so the soldiers scrambled to their feet once again, continuing the attack.

Bangalore torpedoes[2] were slid under the barbed wire of the defences and discharged, blowing holes through which the commandos could pass. Vernon called the advance to a halt again and the men dropped to one knee to steady their aim, one elbow resting on their knee before opening fire. Another volley of parachute flares soared into the sky and Vernon called for the advance to continue once again. Carter was wondering if any of his men had been hit, but had no time to turn and check. He had to keep moving, so that his men would follow.

The soldiers now fired from the hip as they dashed forward in short spurts. Fire, re-cock the weapon, run, halt, fire, re-cock the weapon, run, halt. They concentrated on the sources of the counter-fire, helped by the glow of the tracer rounds. They themselves didn't use tracer[3], as it gave away their positions too easily. The rhythm had to be maintained. Make sure you have men on either side; it wouldn't do to become isolated. Only go to ground if you come under direct fire.

But as they closed on the rear of the battery they pressed home the attack with bayonets. After the firing of a Very flare, the Bren guns and the mortars fell silent, so as to avoid hitting their own men. From the riverbed the commandos in front of the battery rose and charged forwards, anxious to be in at the kill. Although the Italians fought back, they had been taken by surprise and the fight soon went out of them. As soon as one threw down his weapon and raised his hands, it started a flood of surrenders.

The NCOs started to regain control of their men, preventing any abuses of the prisoners. Men high on adrenalin didn't stop to think, they just acted. They herded the dispirited Italian gunners to one side and started to prepare the guns for demolition. Sgt Major Chalk found Carter and made his report. "Only one casualty. Young Merchant cut his hand on some barbed wire. Nothing serious.

The story was repeated across the commando. No casualties except for minor scrapes and bruises.

As dawn broke over the sea, the prisoners were marched out of their battery, the three troops following behind in high spirits. About a hundred yards out the CO brought them to a halt and turned them back to face the way they had come. Waving his hand he gave the signal for the guns to be blown up. One by the one the blast echoed across the countryside. Bits of artillery flew skywards to come crashing down to the ground. Carter checked his watch. Since arriving on the shore, just eighty five minutes had elapsed. Vernon's promise to General Dempsey had been kept with just five minutes to spare.

One final huge blast went off, knocking everyone off their feet. The men staggered, clutching at their ears, which had been stunned into deafness. Some idiot had set charges on the ammunition dump and about a thousand artillery shells had exploded. Fortunately, no one was injured, but that was more by luck than judgement.

Getting back to their feet and continuing along the road, the commando made its way to the village of Cassibile, the explosion still keeping their ears ringing. After sentries had been set and some crude defensive positions constructed, the men were given permission to have some breakfast. They needed no second bidding. Soon mess tins of water were bubbling away for tea and bully beef was being hacked into slices and smeared onto hardtack biscuits. Where the villagers were, it wasn't possible to say. There were signs of them having been present until just before the commandos' arrival. Carter suspected they would have headed inland, away from the invading forces.

The first new arrivals weren't the 2IC's half of the commando, as expected, but a Scottish infantry battalion, marching in lines along either side of the road with pipers leading the way, playing Scotland The Brave. They were quite put out to find they weren't the first to arrive in the village.

The Scotsmen didn't stay long, just a long enough for a brief exchange of banter before they marched on towards their next objective. In a few brief moments, the commandos' position behind enemy lines had become a resting place behind the Allied lines.

[1] "Falls" are the maritime name given to the ropes that are used to raise and lower the lifeboats on board a ship. The have a quick release mechanism to allow the lifeboat to "fall" the final inches to land in the sea. On the ships used by the commandos, the lifeboats were replaced by landing craft. This required some modification of the ship, as landing craft are much longer and heavier than lifeboats.

[2] Bangalore torpedoes were invented in India during the First World War. They are made up of 5 ft lengths of 2 inch diameter pipe which screw together into longer lengths to allow them to be pushed ahead of an attacking force and under skeins of barbed wire. They can be assembled into lengths of up to 50 ft (approximately). The pipes at the front end are filled with explosives and the one at the

very front usually has a conical nose to prevent it digging into the ground as it is pushed forward. The weapon was fired electrically along wires connected to a standard blasting cap. The Bangalore torpedo is still in use today in updated versions using modern technology and materials.

[3] A special coating on the outside of tracer bullets ignites after the bullet is fired, making the bullets visible in the dark. They are useful for indicating the location of a target to other soldiers. Most armies use tracer rounds sparingly, however, because they also reveal the position of the weapon that is firing them.

* * *

It was midday before the three troops of commandos under the command of the 2IC arrived. Maj Couples looked very unhappy. Carter called over Ronnie Pickering, 2 Troop's commander.

"What's got the 2IC into such a tizzy?" Carter asked.
"Our landing was a complete shambles." Came the reply.
"Fancy a cuppa while you tell the story?" Carter asked, signalling to Paddy O'Driscoll. He was a man who could always be counted on to have some tea brewing.
"Where do I start?" Pickering asked. "We hadn't even boarded the landing craft when things started going wrong." Pickering took a tin mug from O'Driscoll. Thanking him, he blew on it to start it cooling.
"The landing craft were coming to us after they dropped you off, but only five out of the six turned up. What happened to the other one we never found out. so we all crammed into the other five. Believe me, we were far from comfortable. We had a motor launch in front of us, acting as guide but we lost that in the dark. The 2IC got the flotilla turned towards the Duchess of Bedford[1] and checked our course with her. Turned out that we were on the right bearing."
"We had to do that as well. Our canoe had drifted off station and we needed to get a course from a destroyer."

"Seems to have been a lot of that going on." Pickering observed, taking a sip of his tea. "Anyway, we carried on and then found ourselves on the wrong side of a flotilla of Royal Scots Fusiliers. We slowed down to pass behind them and regain our station, but missed the marker buoy that had been dropped; or maybe it hadn't been dropped. We must have passed right across the front of Beach 44, where we were supposed to land and ended up off Murro de Porco Bay. The flotilla commander wanted to turn back to the Dunera on the grounds we were lost, but the 2IC had a go at him, telling him that it didn't matter, so long as we got to shore somewhere, even if it was the wrong beach. I think the bloke was a bit windy myself, first time he'd been on a real landing, but I suppose that applied to a lot of the Navy crews.

By that time we could hear gunfire, so we knew the landings had started and we weren't part of them. Then we came across a downed glider[2] with a whole load of men clinging to it for dear life, just wearing their underwear. How they had survived is a miracle because they must have been weighed down by their equipment when they went into the water. We squeezed them into the landing craft somehow.

We were just about to run into Beach 44, which was where we were supposed to land, when a shell from a battery inland hit a headland to our right. We think it may have been the first shots from the battery you were attacking."

"Yes, it opened fire before we were able to start our attack."

"Anyway, even though we weren't sure it was aimed at us, that caused the flotilla commander to try to turn around again and the 2IC had a right go at him before he would turn back. Threatened to have him court martialled for cowardice if he didn't take us into the beach. By then we were hopelessly late, of course. We found that we were behind Brigadier Tarleton of 17th Infantry Brigade[3], who was a bit put out to find we were behind him when we should have been in front, dealing with the defences that his men were now attacking.

Anyway, the Brigadier said we could go ashore with him, so we formed a sort of escort either side of his HQ craft.

Well, we made it ashore and took up defensive positions along the railway line until 17th Brigade headed north towards Syracuse, which is when we were released to make our way here."

"So no action for you so far."

"No. Bit of a damp squib, all told. I'm pretty sure none of our lot even fired their weapons. Did you hear that massive explosion though?"

"You heard that?"

"They probably heard it back in Cairo."

"Well, that was us." Carter told him the story of the exploding ammunition dump, which brought a smile to Pickering's face for the first time.

"Ronnie!" A call came from behind them. Carter turned to see the 2IC heading towards them, a determined look on his face.

"Get your men together, Ronnie. The CO has found another job for us."

Carter made to rise as Pickering stood, but the 2IC waved him back down. "You're not involved this time, Steven."

"Anything interesting?" Carter asked as Pickering went off to find his troop.

"There's an Italian strong point about half a mile in front of us and it's mortaring 17th Brigade and stopping their advance. They've tried a couple of frontal assaults, but the Ities are pretty well dug in, so we've been asked to try to find a back door to see if we can winkle them out that way."

"Are you sure you don't need an extra pair of hands?"

The 2IC laughed. "Always up for a scrap, eh Steven? But not this time. I think I've got enough men for the job." He headed off to where Pickering's troop were gathering, preventing Carter from entering another plea.

The day wore on with no more action for Carter's half of the commando. They rotated the men in the defensive positions and the

CO sent out patrols to make sure that the lines weren't being infiltrated. Although the beachhead seemed to be well established, there were gaps between the advancing formations that an enemy could exploit if he identified them.

Carter was back from just such a patrol when the CO called across to summon him to an O Group.

Carter found that the 2IC was there, looking far happier than he had earlier in the day. His mission must have gone well, Carter thought.

"We're to move out to the high ground on the left of the beachhead and defend it. The Americans have been slowed up and haven't managed to make enough progress to link up with us on that side yet, so we're going to be holding the flank until they arrive." He pointed to the map, where the contours showed a ridge separating the coast from the interior of the island. "Be ready to move out in fifteen minutes. Make sure you settle your mess bills before you go." There was a chuckle. During the afternoon some of the villagers had returned to their homes and the commandos had purchased some items of fresh food from them, eggs being in particularly high demand.

[1] The Duchess of Bedford was another merchant ship pressed into wartime service to carry troops. Launched in Glasgow in 1928 she was requisitioned for wartime service in 1939. She was refitted in 1947 and renamed the Empress of France. She remained in service until she was scrapped in December 1960.

[2] As well as paratroops, the airborne brigade also sent infantry to Sicily in gliders, the first time such a method of transport had been used by the British other than in trials. A number of the gliders came down too soon, crashing into the sea. At least two hundred and fifty soldiers died as a result. The incident described above was genuine.

[3] 17th Infantry Brigade had been part of 10th Army serving in Iraq, Trans Jordan and Palestine, before being detached to take part in Operation Ironclad (5th May – 6th November 1942), the invasion of Madagascar to prevent the Germans from using the Vichy French controlled island as a U Boat base. After that they were attached to XIII Corps, 8th Army for the invasion of Sicily. They were made up of the 2nd Btn Royal Scots Fusiliers, 2nd Btn Northamptonshire Regiment, 6th Btn Seaforth Highlanders and 156th (Lancashire Yeomanry) Field Regiment, Royal Artillery.

* * *

It was just past midnight when Carter was woken and summoned to join the 2IC. He felt as though he had hardly slept; indeed, he had checked the sentries only an hour earlier. Already present in the barn they were using as an HQ was Molly Brown of 6 Troop, Carter's old pal from 4 Troop when he first joined the Commando. The 2IC wasted no time on early morning pleasantries; he wasn't that sort.

"The CO's been ordered to send out a fighting patrol into an area between Cassibile and a place called Torre Ognina. Torre means tower, but I have no idea if that's a building or a topographical feature. There's some sort of fortification in the area giving a few problems, so we've got to try and find it and silence it."

The 2IC laid his map flat in the ground and shone a torch on it. "This is the route we'll take." Carter and Brown quickly marked the route on their own maps. They would need to know it if they became separated. "We'll be on the road north from here until we reach the railway junction. After that, we're operating blind. Unless we can locate friendly troops who can give us more information, we'll have to spread out and move forward in a line until we locate the strong point. I have no idea if we're looking for a building, trenches or just holes in the ground. But we've no time to do a recce because 17th Brigade want to move forward at first light and we've got to sort this place out before they can do that. Once we've found it, we'll regroup and work out a plan of attack. I doubt it will be any more fancy than 'head down and charge'. Makes sure you've got plenty of bombs for your two inch mortars, because we'll use them to soften the target up before we go in."

"Any chance of using the three inchers as well?" Molly Brown asked. "They're far more powerful."

"If the two inchers can't do the job, I'll radio back to the CO for fire support. We should still be in range. But we'll have to wait and see. Now, be ready to move out in one hour. Make sure your men get a cup of tea and some food inside them before we go, because we won't be stopping to have a picnic."

"I wonder how we got picked for this?" Molly Brown mused as they made their way back through the village to find their men.

"Well, I got it because my troop's the best in the commando. Obviously, you're coming along so we can show you how we do things." Carter grinned into the darkness.

Brown said a very rude word and Carter laughed in response. "Just time for a shave before breakfast." Carter observed. It wouldn't do to be seen by the enemy in an unshaven state.

"Then we smother ourselves with cam cream so they won't know if we've shaved or not." Brown observed dryly.

"But we'll know, Molly. And that makes all the difference."

* * *

The two troops, with the 2IC in the lead, made good time along the road to the junction. Here they came across a group of RASC[1] drivers, standing around their trucks.

"We've been ordered not to move forward until that Itie strong point's been dealt with, Sir." The senior man, a Corporal, explained.

"Do you know where it is?" The 2IC asked.

"We heard firing coming from in front, Sir. I can probably show you on a map."

The 2IC spread his map over the wheel arch of the nearest truck and used his shaded torch to illuminate it. The Corporal surveyed the terrain in front of them, trying to pick out landmarks in the dark, before stabbing a grease stained finger onto the map. "That would be it, Sir."

"You're sure/"

"As sure as I can be in the dark, Sir. We haven't heard much recently though. I sort of assumed they'd either been dealt with or they've withdrawn."

"OK. Thanks. We'll be coming back this way, so we'll let you know if the way ahead is clear."

Considering himself to be dismissed, the Corporal withdrew back to the company of his mates, while Brown and Carter moved closer to try to get a look at the 2IC's map, where the soldier had indicated.

"It looks a farm of some sort." The 2IC reported. "One large building and a few smaller ones. The map says it's called Torre Cuba. Presumably it refers to the same tower as Torre Ognina. I'm going to take a couple of men forward to scout and see if I can get a look at the place; see what we're up against."

Carter and Brown organised their men into a defensive ring around the trucks, something that the RASC drivers hadn't thought to do. Then they settled down to wait. They had long ago learnt the lesson that warfare was ninety five percent sitting around waiting for something to happen, interspersed with five percent of frantic and dangerous activity.

It was about thirty minutes later that the 2IC returned. "Looks like it might be a tough nut to crack." He reported. He started sketching a plan on the ground using the point of his Commando dagger. "It's a large square compound surrounding a house, with a couple of outbuildings on the outside. There's a gate on the east side, with a road that probably connects to the one we're on. The outbuildings look much newer, like they've been added on. They've cut loopholes into the wall through which they can observe and lay down defensive fire. I'm guessing they've got their mortars set up inside the compound, firing over the wall. The upper rooms of the house have a clear view out, so I reckon that the observers will be up there directing fire. They'll probably have snipers up there as well."

"What's the plan?"

"6 Troop will crawl up on the southern and western sides and start firing to distract them. You can use Bren guns and drop mortar bombs on them as well. Meanwhile, Steven, you and I will lead your troop around to the front. I'm going to try to crawl up to the gate and plant an explosive charge on it. If that works, your troop will charge through and take on the occupants."

"If it doesn't work?"

"We fire the mortars at it until the gate falls off, then you charge."

Carter nodded his understanding. He had fired a two inch mortar almost horizontally once before. It kicked like a mule, but it fired a bomb on a flat trajectory, just what was needed to break down a gate without having to use a battering ram. "Molly, when you see a red flare, stop sending mortar bombs over, but you can keep firing on the upper floor of the house to try to keep the snipers at bay. Cease fire when you see a green flare."

"Understood." Molly replied.

The 2 IC consulted his watch. "I want both troops in position by oh four hundred hours. Molly, you commence firing at that time. That gives us about an hour before dawn to finish the job and get 17th Brigade on the move again."

"They'll owe us a drink for doing it." Molly said.

"Given that they had to clear the coastal defences that we were supposed to have cleared for them," The 2IC reminded him, "I think that honours will just about be even. Now, let's get moving."

The ground ahead of them was reasonably flat, divided up into fields by stone walls. It was the wrong time of year for crops in Sicily's hot, dry climate, so the fields were bare. The walls weren't as high as those they'd had to cross on their way to the Cassibile battery, but they still had to be crossed with caution in order to prevent any sound from waking up the farm's defenders. Every chink of equipment on stone, every rattle of detached masonry, caused them to freeze, waiting for any reaction from the big square of deeper shadow in front of them.

At last Carter's troop were in position on either side of the approach road to the farm, crouched in the shadows of the walls that edged it. The 2IC and the Sergeant who had accompanied him, huddled together over a satchel of explosives. This was Sergeant Connors of 6 Troop, the recognised expert within the commando on all matters related to causing explosions.

If they were using conventional materials, the satchel would be filled with Explosives 808, as it was known. A plasticine like substance that smelt of almonds. They would probably use a pencil timer to set the charge off. As its name implied, it was shaped like a pencil. It was initiated by crushing it with a pair of pliers, which would release acid to start to eat its way through the wire that held the trigger back, which would set off the detonator, which in turn would set off the main charge. A two minute fuse should be enough for the 2IC to get far enough away to avoid being killed by his own bomb.

Carter held his breath as the 2IC edged his way forward along the line of the wall until he was within yards of the gate. There he paused to wait. Carter was surprised to see that the Italians hadn't broken the wall down to give themselves a clear field of fire. But they were garrison troops, probably not the best trained and they had probably imagined their country would never be invaded.

The second hand on Carter's watch crawled around and as it passed the twelve position the sound of gunfire broke out from Carter's left, the south side, followed closely by the crump of mortar bombs exploding inside the compound. Firing broke out from the defenders, spitting rounds in all directions, including the north, where there were no commandos. Panic, thought Carter.

Which is what the 2IC had counted on. He made a dash forward, keeping his head down below the parapet of the wall. The Italians sent up parachute flares, trying to identify the source of danger. By their light Carter saw the 2IC hang the satchel bomb on one of the large metal rings that were positioned close to where the two sides of the solid wooden gates met.

The 2IC didn't hang around. The satchel was still swinging gently from side to side as he withdrew in a scuttling run. He must have been seen, because a stream of tracer stitched its way towards him, striking sparks where the bullets hit the top of the wall. But the 2IC kept going, putting the maximum distance between himself and his deadly cargo. He slid to a halt beside Carter.

"All set?" He puffed.

"Yes." Carter grunted. His men didn't need to be told to be ready to attack.

Two minutes can seem like an eternity at times and so it seemed to Carter on this occasion, as the pencil fuse did its work. But when the blast came it was unexpected in its ferocity.

There was a brilliant flash followed by the thunderous blast which dragged at Carter's face and clothing. Carter's hearing seemed to shut down for the second time in twenty fours hours, in order to protect itself. Almost at once debris started to rain around them.

The 2IC seemed to be shouting something, but Carter couldn't hear what it was. Perhaps he was telling him to charge. It didn't matter, because that was what Carter was going to do anyway.

He stood up, feeling the men closest to him doing the same. Gripping his Tommy gun tightly, he shouted the single word "Charge!" at the top of his voice, then ran forward. Even his own voice had sounded muffled, as though he was disconnected from his own ears. A group of men tumbled over the wall to the right, heading for the outbuildings, just as Carter had briefed them. The remainder followed Carter or tried to get past him in the narrow lane. Carter could never understand the eagerness to be first into the enemy lines. Perfectly ordinary, quietly spoken blokes seemed to get taken over by a desire to be first. Or maybe it was others slowing down, not wanting to be the ones exposed to danger.

Such were Carter's thoughts as he closed the hundred yard gap between him and the farm's perimeter wall. Any thought was better than contemplating the pain of a bullet piercing his flesh.

The defenders nearest to the gate seemed to have stopped firing, probably stunned by the explosion. That gave them some breathing space. Once they were close to the walls of the compound the loopholes the Italians were firing through wouldn't allow them to train their weapons around far enough to be able to fire on them. Neither would the snipers be able to depress their barrels to shoot at the onrushing commandos, thanks to the height of the wall. What was designed to keep out the local burglars would prevent a sniper from picking out a target.

As they reached the shattered gate, its' supporting pillars tumbled into heaps of rubble, there was a sudden hiatus as the commandos jammed into the opening, before exploding inwards like a champagne cork popping. Carter went down onto one knee, trained his Tommy gun along the wall to his left and opened fire. He saw a figure drop back from the wall, rolling on the floor in agony. Another tried to fire back before he also fell.

The hammer of Carter's weapon clicked on the Tommy gun's chamber as the magazine emptied. He pulled a fresh stick from his ammunition pouch, released the empty mag to drop to the floor, then pushed the new one into place. Hauling back on the cocking handle, he scanned the farmyard in an arc. But in the seconds he had taken to reload, the commandos had rushed past him and were blocking his field of fire. He saw a trooper, it might have been Glass, raise his bayoneted rifle and stab down into the body of a defender.

A mortar bomb crashed onto the roof of the farmhouse and Carter realised he had forgotten to fire the signal for Molly brown's troop to stop the bombardment. He pulled the Very pistol from his belt, cocked it and pointed it skywards, pulling the trigger. The flare shot up, but not before another mortar bomb fell. Fortunately it was in a portion of the yard that seemed to be empty.

He saw why. The defenders had retreated into a corner and were huddled together, their hands above their heads. Two commandos marched towards them, their rifles extended in front of them, ready to stab. He was just about to shout a warning to them to honour the surrender when they came to stop a few yards away from the frightened Italians. They lowered their weapons and one of them took out a packet of cigarettes and started to light one. Carter was about to shout at him to put his cigarette out when he realised there was no reason why the trooper shouldn't smoke. He would hardly be giving away their position. The only reason to stop him smoking was that he hadn't been given permission to smoke and that didn't seem an adequate reason, given the tension they were all under.

Ahead of them figures erupted from the house and Carter raised his weapon to fire, before realising two things. The first was that they were wearing British uniform and the second was that they were unarmed. Behind them came a group of Italians, hands held high above their heads.

From a window in the upper floor a white bedsheet was unfurling as a flag of surrender.

"Cease fire." The 2IC's voice cut across the small battlefield. "Cease firing."

Carter reloaded the Very pistol with its second cartridge and fired off the green flare. Silence fell as the message reached the eyes of Molly Brown's troop.

Commandos hurried past Carter and started to round up the Italians and herd them into the centre of the courtyard, where they could be searched. The count would come to one officer and fifty one men of the Italian 206th Coastal Division. Another five Italians would be found to have died in the attack. Plus one British prisoner who had been too eager to leave the comparative safety of the farmhouse and who had rushed out to greet his rescuers and run into a stray bullet.

The British turned out to be airborne infantry who had landed by glider a couple of hundred yards from the farmhouse and who had been taken prisoner. A few of their comrades had managed to escape into the night.

"How did the Italians treat you?" Carter asked the officer from the group of British prisoners.

"Not bad. Though I wasn't too keen on their food. Some long thin stuff like string, covered in some sort of gravy.

"That was spaghetti." Ernie Barraclough chuckled. Having holidayed in Italy before the war, he was the closest thing the commando had to an expert on the country and its people "It's a type of pasta, which is made from flour and water. Best get used to it if you're staying in Italy. They eat a lot of pasta."

"I think I'll stick to my meat and two veg." The officer chuckled.

"We'll take you back as far as our positions, then you can go on down to the beach with the prisoners." Carter continued. "Someone there will be able to point you in the direction of Division HQ. They'll know what to do with you."

"If it's all the same to you, we'd rather just collect our kit from the Italians and go and look for our unit."

"There's no guarantee they'll still be where they were supposed to be. You could end up trekking a long way, just to be sent back to the beach anyway." Carter said. But he could see why the infantrymen would want to be on their way. Being seen arriving on the beach with a party of Italian prisoners under the guard of commandos, wouldn't look good.

"We'll be OK. Our unit was supposed to hold for up to two days, so they're probably still out there somewhere. Can I take a look at your map?"

Carter handed the folded sheet over, pointing to their current location.

"We're about five miles from where we're supposed to be." The infantry officer informed him. "We should be much further west, in those hills there." He pointed to beyond 15 Cdo's current location. "There's a bridge there that we were supposed to take."

"We haven't heard what's happening out that way. It's well outside our operating area."

"What about enemy troops between here and there?"

"No idea, I'm afraid. That's why it would be better ..."

"We'll take our chances." The officer said forcefully. A man arrived, another of the former prisoners, laden with kit, some of which he placed on the ground beside the officer.

"OK. Good luck then." Carter said, really meaning it. He wouldn't have relished the idea of crossing five miles of unknown territory with no idea of what may lie in front of him. The British front line had spread west, the troops from the more southerly landing beaches punching forward to try to link up with the Americans, but Carter had no idea how far they had got.

The officer led his men out of the farmyard and out of Carter's life. Well, he thought he was out of his life, but they would meet again, though neither of them knew it at that time.

"Steven. Send a message back to those RASC chappies and let them know the road's clear now." The 2IC's voice broke into Carter's reverie.

[1] Royal Army Service Corps. The providers of transport and other logistics services for the Army at that time. Nicknamed "Run Away, Someone's Coming".

6 – Agony

Dawn on 13th July found 15 Commando lined up on the beach, ready to board landing craft. The message had come through during the night that they were to withdraw to their landing ship, their part in Operation Husky now over.

Along the beach from them an LS(T)[1] was disgorging its cargo of Sherman tanks onto the beach. It was the start of a new phase of the operation, that would see tanks driving an armoured battering ram through the enemy's lines towards the Straights of Messina; or so it was hoped by Montgomery.

They heard the sound of aero engines and the commandos scattered and threw themselves flat onto the sand. The Luftwaffe hadn't been much in evidence for the first two days of the operation, but now they were back with a vengeance. Fighters from the Royal Navy's aircraft carriers, positioned beyond the horizon, did their best to keep the bombers at bay, but it was usually a matter of luck whether or not they could intercept, despite their ships' radar.

But the Ju 88 roared over their heads without dropping its bombs, heading out into the bay to attack one of the merchant ships. As the men regained their feet and started to form lines again, great gouts of water rose from around a merchant vessel[2]. At least one bomb actually struck the ship, sending smoke and debris skywards. The men looked on horrified as the bow section broke off and started to sink, a great fire engulfing the rest of the ship. Warships close by speeded to her aid, but it was obvious to the onlookers on shore that very few on board would have survived.

Belatedly, a pair of Seafires[3] appeared and the JU 88 turned for home, harried from above and behind.

"Anyone seen the CO?" Andrew Fraser approached, seemingly not in any hurry.

"He was picked up in a Jeep just after we got here." Ernie Barraclough supplied.

"Oh. I wonder if he's off getting a slap on the wrist for us not taking the beach defences on Day 1." Fraser said.

Carter gave him a sideways look. "That's a gloomy sort of view to take, Andrew. It may be that he's getting a pat on the back for us capturing the Cassibile battery and clearing out Torre Cuba."

"Monty's not one for handing out plaudits." Fraser observed. "He's good with the men, but hard on the officers."

It was true that Montgomery had a lot of charisma when it came to addressing the front-line troops.

"Maybe it's another mission." Barraclough suggested.

"No, can't be that." Arthur Murray, Carter's other Lieutenant chipped in. "They wouldn't send us back to the ship if it was another mission."

"Unless it's another landing." Carter reminded him of the main role of the commandos: mounting sudden attacks from the sea.

They were interrupted by the arrival of the landing craft and Fraser had to return to his troop. They were surprised to find twelve landing craft had been sent for them, as the Prince Leopold only carried six.

The men filed aboard and stood in their rows. Landing craft didn't allow space to sit down, at least, not when fully laden. The ramps were raised and the craft backed off the beach and turned to face out to sea.

The Prince Leopold hadn't been visible from the shore, so it was assumed that she was lying beyond the Punto Murro di Porco, in Syracuse Bay. The landing craft were certainly heading in that direction.

The sea was calm, so even the worst sailors amongst them managed to hang onto their breakfasts. The high sides of the landing craft didn't afford much of a view. High above them a formation of Liberator bombers, as the RAF referred to the B-24, was heading westwards towards the island they had left behind.

"You might want to take a look at this." The Cox'n's voice came over the loudspeaker system.

Carter craned his neck to see forward, but he was jammed into the middle of the landing craft. He pushed his way to the front and pulled himself up onto the ramp.

Ahead of them the Prince Leopold stood, dressed from bow to stern; "dressed overall" as the Navy would say. The full ship's crew, or so it seemed, lined the rail.

The sound of Bosun's pipes chirped across the water to them and the sailors lifted their caps to sound three loud cheers.[4]

"It seems that the Navy is pleased to see us." Carter observed. "Three men, step forward." He ordered.

With three men standing just behind the ramp, Carter ordered them to fire a volley into the air from their rifles, making sure it was aimed well away from the ship in front of them. Salutes were usually fired with blank ammunition, but they had none of that.

[1] LS(T) – Landing ship tank.

[2] This ship is likely to have been the SS Timothy Pickering, an American "Liberty" ship. She was sunk with the loss of 3 officers and 19 crew, plus 16 guards and 127 British soldiers who were on board. The remnants of her hull were later sunk by a British torpedo fired from a destroyer. Only 29 of the 194 American and British personnel on board survived.

[3] The Seafire was a version of the Spitfire, modified to enable it to operate from aircraft carriers.

[4] This is the actual welcome received by 3 Cdo when they returned to their ship on 13th July 1943.

* * *

Not only had the Navy prepared them a welcome, but they had also prepared breakfast. Although the men had eaten before starting the march back to the beach, they never missed an opportunity to eat. The very best rations had been released from the storerooms and someone must have been ashore, because there were freshly fried eggs on the menu, which were always a luxury item.

After their meal, the commandos were dismissed to go below decks and start to clean their kit. Weapons took the highest priority, followed by the laundering of clothes and then their repair. Barbed wire and rocks took a heavy roll on the lightweight uniforms issued for the warmer climate. Reunited with the kitbags, the soldiers were able to change into clean uniforms.

Around midday word went through the ship that the CO had been sighted arriving on a motor launch. It was only minutes later that the officers were summoned to the First Class lounge, which served as both officer's mess and briefing room. The CO was already present, along with the 2IC.

"First of all, gentlemen, I bring you thanks for your efforts directly from General Montgomery. He was extremely pleased with what we did both on Day 1, when we captured the Cassibile battery, but also afterwards. The need to protect the left flank hadn't really been considered because it was expected that we would link up with the Americans within hours, but as they say in Ayrshire, 'The best-laid plans of mice and men often go awry'[1]. No matter how carefully an operation is planned, something may still go wrong with it."

This brought the expected chuckle, easing the tension somewhat.

"So impressed was Monty, that he's found another job for us."

This brought an outbreak of whispered conversation. Two operations in such a short space of time was unexpected in the commandos. They could go for weeks, even months, between ops.

"Calm down, gentlemen." Vernon interrupted them. "It is a measure of the esteem in which we are held by Monty that he has given us this job. I think that we can say that the rules have changed since we left Egypt."

He stepped to one side and Sgt Maj Finch carried a blackboard into the centre of the room, accompanied by a naval rating carrying the easel. Turning the blackboard over, a map of coastline was revealed.

"This is the only map we have, so you are all going to have to make your own copies. The Navy have kindly provided a stock of foolscap[2] paper for the purpose." There was a sudden movement forward. "But please, gentlemen, let me finish the briefing first."

The room relaxed a little and some laughter was exchanged.

"Now," Continued the CO. "The next major objective for 8th Army is the port city of Catania, here to the north." Vernon tapped the map at its top edge. "There is only one road that will take them there directly, which is this one." He traced the route, leaving Syracuse and heading north inland from the coast. "Catania is a deep-water port, making it far better for our ships to dock than the fishing port at Syracuse. There is also an airfield, which we want to capture, both for our own use and to prevent the Luftwaffe from using it.

There is one fly in the ointment or, more accurately, two. The road crosses two bridges. One crosses the Gornalunga Canal at a place called Primasole." Vernon tapped the map again, "and one near the small village of Agnone. Primasole Bridge is to be assaulted from the air by a parachute brigade who will be flown in from their base in North Africa. The bridge called Ponte, over the river Gabriel, is ours. It lies about ten miles north of the small town of Lentini and about seven miles inland; at least, seven miles by the route we'll be taking. We are to take the bridge before dawn tomorrow …" There was an outbreak of murmuring at the short timescale. The CO waited for it to die down " … yes, tomorrow morning. At dawn 50th Division will attack Lentini before advancing north along the road to come to our relief. They should be with us by lunchtime and at Primasole Bridge by sunset. If those bridges are blown, then it could mean several days of delay, giving the Germans time to reinforce the island."

"Surely the river won't be a problem at this time of year, Sir." A voice came from the back, one of the junior officers who had only recently joined the commando. "They can just roll right through the river bed."

"If that were the case, Kevin, then General Montgomery wouldn't be sending us." Everyone felt for Kevin's embarrassment. "The fact is that the river runs through a ravine at the point where the road crosses it. Infantry could climb down and get back out again, so long as they weren't under fire, but there's no way across for tanks or wheeled vehicles. So, the bridge must be captured intact if the impetus of the attack is to be maintained." He glared at the assembled officers. "Now, does anyone else wish to question the Commander-in-Chief's orders?"

It seemed that no one did.

"This is a textbook commando operation, gentlemen. It will be a night landing on an enemy occupied shore, followed by a forced march inland to our bridge. I feel honoured that Monty has chosen us to carry out the attack." He didn't mention that there were very few other units present in Sicily that could do the job, which rather limited Montgomery's options.

With that, the CO continued with the tactical brief. They were to land close to the village of Agnone before heading directly inland to reach the Catania to Syracuse railway line. They would then follow the railway through Agnone station and then onwards until they reached a tunnel. At that point they would climb up and over the hill which the tunnel ran through, until they reached the valley of the River Gabriel. They would cross that and make their way along the northern bank to take the bridge from the rear, the side from which the Italian guards wouldn't be expecting them.

"Why don't we just walk through the tunnel, Sir?" Kevin asked again. A groan went up from the more experienced officers. Kevin ignored it. "It must be easier going than clambering over the hill."

"Would anyone care to enlighten Kevin?" The CO asked with a wry smile. They say that there's no such thing as a stupid question, but for the commandos, or any experienced soldier for that matter, that one was pretty stupid.

Andrew Fraser accepted the CO's invitation. "Because, laddie, a machine gunner positioned at the far end of the tunnel could keep the whole 8th Army at bay until eternity if he had enough ammunition. There's no cover inside a tunnel. It becomes a long, dark killing ground."

The CO took pity on the young officer. "Don't worry, Kevin. These are lessons to be learnt. Just be thankful you won't have to learn that one the hard way."

There was a sympathetic chuckle around the room. Most of the officers had made such a blunder at some time, but not all so publicly.

They heard the ship's whistle blast out a signal, meaning they were getting under way. The journey wouldn't be a long one, but it would lead to a far longer night.

[1] Robert Burns, "To A Mouse".

[2] It is sometimes easy to forget in these days of standardised paper sizes, that at one time paper suppliers all manufactured paper of different sizes. Foolscap folio, to give it its full name, was the one commonly used by government departments before the arrival of the office printer forced a move to a standard size. The dimensions of foolscap were 13 in x 8½ in (343 x 216 mm), compared to 11.69 in x 8.27 in (297 x 210 mm) for A4. Manufacturers used to identify their brands with a watermark, in this case it was a man wearing a "fool's cap and bells", giving the paper its name. First seen in Germany in 1479, the foolscap watermark was introduced to England in 1510 by John Spilman, a German who founded a paper mill in Kent.

* * *

Carter left the sketching of the maps to Arthur Murray, who had some promising artistic talent. "My favourite artist is Picasso." He had once confided. Carter suggested he restricted himself to a more conventional style on this occasion, especially when it came to the positioning of key features.

Taking himself down to the lower decks he rounded up his troop, before splitting them into two groups, one which he would brief and the other which would be briefed by Ernie Barraclough. He would repeat the briefing again before they boarded the landing craft, so that the essentials wouldn't be forgotten, but the main thrust would be "follow me, because I've got the only map." The lack of detail supplied to the CO translated into a greater lack of detail for his own men.

"If we're heading twenty miles north," Prof Green interrupted, "why is the Sun on the right when it should be on the left?"

"Well spotted, Green." Carter always addressed him more formally when they were with the rest of the troop. The late afternoon Sun was streaming through the Starboard side port holes for everyone to see. "It's part of the deception plan. We sail south until we're over the horizon and out of sight of any observers on land. That way they'll think we're going somewhere else. Then we circle back, staying out of sight of land. We won't head back in towards the Sicilian coast again until after dark, when we can't be seen."

The rest of the briefing was taken up with passwords, radio call-signs, and the order of march. Carter was able to sketch the map onto the bulkhead from memory, using the butt end of a stick of chalk. It couldn't be detailed, but it gave a general idea of where they were going and what they were doing.

"1 Troop are tasked with going inland by the most direct route to clear Agnone station and village. We keep to their south until they've finished, then we pass them by using the railway line. From then on, we'll be the lead troop, with 3 Troop behind us to defuse the demolition charges once we get there. 5 Troop will be behind them.

It's our job to take the bridge, then defend the south side. 5 Troop will defend the north side. We've only got enough landing craft for 4 troops, so 2 and 6 troops will follow behind, once we've landed and sent the LCs back. 2 Troop because they've got the heavy weapons and will only slow us down and 6 troop because they're the reserve. Those two troops will be under the command of the 2IC."

The 2IC had grimaced when he had been told that, but otherwise had kept his own counsel. It was his place to always be the bridesmaid and never the bride.

As always, Carter finished the briefing by answering questions. There weren't many. It was a night operation and they were unpredictable and the men knew that. He asked a few questions of his own, just to make sure that the men understood their roles and then told the men to get as much sleep as they could. They would be fed before boarding the landing craft, which would probably be the last hot meal they'd get until they were back on board the Prince Leopold the next afternoon.

* * *

As always, it was the run into the beach that was the hardest part mentally. Each man stood alone with his thoughts, but they were all thinking pretty much the same thing. Were the defences manned: how well were they manned; what sort of weaponry would they be using; would they stand and fight or would the enemy run? So many questions, none of which could be answered until the ramp at the front of the landing craft dropped open.

The Italian weaponry was pretty poor. That had already been discovered. Their machine guns fired very slowly compared to both the British and the German guns. The officers carried pistols that were designed to fit in a woman's handbag and had little stopping power. It was rare for an Italian officer to carry a rifle or submachine gun. Even their grenades were small; red devils they were called, no larger than an egg and made of some sort of plastic. The shrapnel didn't seem to cut through anything much. They also had a one man operated tank, but it could be stopped by a machine gun, which made it more of a liability than an asset.

But Carter's main thoughts were about getting off the beach. It was long and relatively flat, which meant that it would be festooned with barbed wire. They had brought Bangalore Torpedoes to deal with it, but it would mean all two hundred men being stuck on an exposed beach until they could be assembled and fired.

At about two hundred yards out the Italians started firing their machine guns. They were sited in pillboxes, that much the attacker knew from the limited aerial photographs that had been available. The landing craft answered back with Lewis guns, mounted either side of the small wheel houses. With sea an almost flat clam, the Lewis gunners were able to get some accurate fire and one by one the Italian guns fell silent; all but one, which seemed to be more persistent. Whether the gunners had been hit, had fled or had just ceased firing in order to avoid attracting the attention of the Lewis guns, no one knew.

"Stand by." The command came over the loudspeaker system. It meant they were fifty yards out from the beach. Carter braced himself, ready to be flung forward as the landing craft ground itself against the beach. He felt the engine's vibrations die as the power was reduced and the landing craft was allowed to continue under its own momentum.

There was a lurch as it struck, then the bow ramp dropped open with a rattling of chains and an outward surge of water. Opening his mouth to shout the order to advance, Carter was almost flattened as his men surged past him, eager to get onto the beach and find some cover before the enemy could zero in on the craft.

The single machine gun continued firing, but the bullets were undirected and did no more harm than to kick up gouts of sand and water.

A Bren gun opened fire on the machine gun that was still firing. Using the distraction it caused, Carter dashed forward about fifty feet until he encountered the barbed wire. It seemed to form a jungle of looping coils, glittering in the moonlight. Even a Bangalore torpedo would struggle to create a viable gap. He edged sideways, looking for a place where the wire might be less deep. A dark regular shape became discernible as he approached one of the pillboxes. It wasn't the one that had the machine gun firing, but Carter wasn't about to take any chances. He unhooked a grenade from his webbing. Letting his Tommy gun hang from its strap, he used his free hand to feel for the pin.

Keeping his head low, well below the deeper darkness of the firing apertures, Carter rushed towards the pillbox and crouched beneath the opening. He pulled the pin, let the safety catch fly off and counted to five. On the last word he tossed the grenade through the firing port and heard it bounce off a wall and rattle around the floor. Then there was the sharp crack of the explosion and brief bloom of light above his head. He was just about to return along the wire, still looking for a way through, when he saw that the coils didn't quite reach the solid sides of the pillbox. There was a gap at least wide enough to take a man. Perhaps it had been created by the defenders to allow them access to the beach, but for Carter it was the answer to his prayers.

"Over here 4 Troop!" he called. Men started to rise from the sand and run towards him.

"Through here!" He pointed the way for the first arrivals. They needed no second bidding. They filed through and spread out on the far side of the pillbox.

If everything was going to plan, 1 Troop would be making their way to the far end of the beach, which would give them a more direct line to Agnone village. Carter and Fraser's 3 Troop were to avoid that by striking inland. By the time they arrived at the village 1 Troop should have subdued any defenders.

"All through." Fred Chalk informed him, bringing up the rear of 4 Troop.

"Good man. Through you go." As soon as his Sgt Major was through Carter followed behind. They were off the beach.

There was a burst of submachinegun fire. Carter realised that it was being aimed back at the pillbox; being aimed at him! As he threw himself to the ground, he saw that two figures were falling alongside him. One of his men hurried back and helped him to his feet.

"Sorry, Lucky. I was shooting at them." Sgt Carney apologised profusely as he indicated two bodies on the ground beside the pillbox's entrance. One was unmistakable German, Carter saw from his steel helmet. The other was Italian, wearing a more rounded, pudding bowl style of helmet. "I reckon they were waiting for us to get past and then shoot us in the back."

More likely waiting for us to get past and then sneak down onto the beach and get away, Carter thought, but he didn't say it. The two men must have evacuated the pillbox before Carter had thrown his grenade, or they would both have been killed by the small bomb. But it meant there were probably other enemy still in the area. They had better take care.

Another machinegun rained fire at them, coming from an angle above their heads. For the first time Carter realised that behind the pillboxes at beach level there was another series, mounted on a low cliff, the second line of defence. They were arranged in a staggered line, so that the rear ones could fire between the ones in front, but at the same time cover the rear doors of the front line. In daylight it would have been an effective defensive position, but at night they hadn't realised the commando had found a way through the wire until the first line of defence had been breached.

But now it meant that the troop was going to have to cross the pillbox's killing ground and eliminate it. Another machine gun opened up from their right and created a crossfire. "Arthur!" Carter called into the darkness.

"Over here." Came the reply. He was on the right, as he should have been. Ernie Barraclough had been detailed to take his men to the left.

"Look after that pillbox on your side."

"OK, Lucky." The reply came back from Murray.

Ahead of him Carter could hear Barraclough issuing orders, his voice rising above the clatter of gunfire. Men started running to the left, away from the stream of bullets. Once again the enemy was unwittingly helping them by using tracer. It made it easier for the commandos to see where they were aiming. Barraclough kept a Bren gun firing on the pillbox, attracting the attention of the gunners while his other force moved out on its flank in relative safety. Was there another pillbox out that way? Carter couldn't tell. The cliffs weren't steep. Barraclough's men wouldn't have any problem scaling them. So long as the gunners kept looking this way, Carter thought.

A mortar coughed and a bomb fell close to the pillbox. That would help to keep their eyes focused forward as well. Good on Ernie, Carter thought.

To the right more gunfire erupted as Arthur Murray's section engaged the more distant target. They were taking a more direct approach, advancing in small groups, one running while another provided covering fire, then swapping over, leapfrogging past each other. It was a dangerous tactic against an enemy in a hardened position like a pillbox. All the gunner had to do was keep up a steady rate of fire and the section was it his mercy. Carter made a mental note to have a chat with Murray about that when the action was over. Inexperience such as that could cost men their lives. Had he ever been that inexperienced? He supposed he must have been.

The muffled sound of a grenade exploding brought Carter's mind back to the nearer pillbox. Barraclough's assault force had reached its objective and lobbed a grenade through the firing port. A second grenade went off, a flash lighting up the pillbox's interior before the light died again. A Tommy gun started firing as someone went in through the rear door and hosed down the walls, as they called it. If the occupants had any idea about surrendering, it was already too late.

On the right Murray's attack had stalled short of the base of the cliff as the machine gun pinned down the attackers. Carter rushed forward and tapped the nearest four men on their shoulders.

"With me!" he commanded, setting off at a run, moving at right angles to the beach. He heard boots striking the ground as the men followed him. They had started off about fifty yards from the pillbox, but quickly closed the gap down to ten. Thanks to Barraclough they were able to get behind the pillbox. He called a halt and crouched down.

"Grenades." Carter instructed. "I want two of you to creep up on the front, get below the firing ports and lob your grenades inside." Other than artillery fire or flame throwers, it was the only way pillboxes were vulnerable. Once an enemy was that close the occupants were as good as dead.

"You other two, come with me. We're going in the back door."

He led the two men forward as the dim figures of the other pair scuttled along to his right. "Fix bayonets!" he whispered to the two men. He didn't know why he was whispering. A bull roaring wouldn't have been heard above the clatter of the machine gun.

"I go in first with this," Carter hefted his Tommy gun, "then you come past me and finish off anyone who's still moving."

Carter got into position. There was no back door, as such. A blast from a bomb or an artillery shell could warp a metal door and trap the occupants inside. It would be a waste of time to fit a wooden door. Carter took a position to one side, screened from the blast of the grenades by the thick, reinforced concrete. His two men went to the far side. There was a flash followed instantly by the crack of two grenades exploding. Carter ran through the door while the occupants, had they survived, would still be gathering their shattered wits. He started firing almost before he had crossed the threshold, dragging his gun from left to right to cover the entire interior. The hammer clicked as it fell on an empty chamber. Carter dodged to the left, knowing that if he didn't, he'd be bowled over by two hefty commandos. Sure enough, they were past him and looking for something, anything, to stab with their bayonets.

"Both dead" One of the men reported, sounding a little bit disappointed. "Looks like the grenades got them." Carter stepped forward to take a closer look. On the floor, beneath their weapon, lay two heaps. If it hadn't been for the gleam of blood he might have thought they were just piles of abandoned clothing.

"OK. Let's go." There was no point in them staying where they were. Leaning towards the firing port he shouted out into the night.

"OK, Arthur. You can bring your men up now." There would be some ribbing from Barraclough later, with his men having to go to Murray's rescue. Then Carter would remind Barraclough that it was he who had led the attack. Just to reinforce to Barraclough that it had been a team effort.

But that was for later. Right now, the clock was ticking and they had a lot of ground to cover if they wanted to capture the bridge while it was still dark.

He checked his watch. They had hit the beach at midnight, if they'd been on time, which he hadn't checked. It was now zero zero twenty. Not bad to have cleared the beach defences so quickly.

Barraclough was forming his men up into two files, while Murray's men were hurrying across to join them. "Any casualties?" Carter asked. If there were, they would have to be taken back to the beach to wait for the return of the landing craft with the second wave.

"Not in my section, Lucky." Barraclough reported.

"One minor injury in my section." Murray puffed as he arrived. "He's fit to continue though."

"OK. Let's go then. Ernie. Tell your scouts, bearing oh nine oh until they cut the railway line. Then stop and wait for us to catch up."

They set off at quite a fast pace. The fighting that had already taken place would have woken any sleeping defenders, so stealth was an unnecessary luxury at that moment. Carter provided the scouts with a compass bearing, not too worried if they stuck to it or not. So long as they weren't too far off they were bound to cut the railway line at some point. They have to be out by ninety degrees to miss it completely and he doubted they would collectively make that sort of error.

To the right there was still the rattle and clatter of gunfire, interspersed with the crack of grenades. Some stretches of the beach were better defended than others, it seemed. But Carter noted that some of the firing was coming from inland now, suggesting that the rest of the commando was making progress.

Above him he was aware of the drone of aircraft engines, travelling south to north. That would be the Paras, he concluded, on their way to Primasole Bridge. He looked up, seeing stars wink in and out of view as aircraft passed across them. In the distance a searchlight beam stood upright in the night, but it didn't seem to be lighting anything up. There were occasional flashes of anti-aircraft shells exploding, but whether they hit anything or not was a mystery, invisible at that distance.

Carter also heard the sound of aircraft travelling north to south, coming from in front of him. Must be the empty aircraft returning to North Africa, he assumed. But then his mind told him he was wrong. There was something about the sound of the engines that didn't make sense. He halted in his tracks, apologising reflexively as one of the commandos barged into him, not expecting him to stop so suddenly.

Those aircraft weren't continuing south, he realised. They were turning somewhere in front of him and flying away, towards the west. Why should that be? There was nothing out there except enemy occupied territory, followed by open sea until they reached Spain.

He walked on, hurrying to catch up with his men. That was the trouble with night landings. Nothing made sense if you couldn't see what was happening. The mind played tricks, making people imagine things, filling in the gaps in information to try to make it comprehensible.

Things began to make a little more sense shortly afterwards. A commando came up to him, a corporal from one of his sections. "Found this guy wandering around lookin' a bit lost, Lucky."

The man was wearing a parachute smock and wore a domed parachutist's helmet. He snapped to attention, allowing his Sten gun to hang at his side. "Sgt Marsh, 2nd Parachute battalion, Sir." The man reported. "I think we've been dropped in the wrong place."

"You have. You're 15 miles south of Primasole. How many of there are you?"

"A full stick, Sir. Twenty men including me. I've managed to gather us all together. We're about a hundred yards over that way." He pointed north west. "I heard some fighting so I came this way to try to find out what was going on."

"That would have been us coming off the beach. Well, Sgt, you've got a long walk ahead of you. Head due north and you'll get where you're going. Oh, there's a couple of hundred commandos out there, so make sure you don't get caught up in a fight with your own side. The password is Waverley and the reply is Wallaby." Once again the words had been chosen because of the supposed inability of the Germans to pronounce the letter W. One day, Carter had thought at the briefing, we're going to meet a German with a speech impediment who pronounces his W's in the English way and it will cost someone his life.

"Thank you, Sir. Hope all goes well for you."

"And for you, Sergeant." Then the paratrooper was gone into the darkness.

But that still didn't explain the aircraft turning west, Carter thought. The short interruption had allowed his men to get ahead of him, so Carter ran to catch up. He found them crouching in the darkness, waiting for him. In front of them was the railway line, sitting above the surrounding countryside on a raised track bed.

One of the scouts reported to him; it was Danny Glass. "There's paratroops on the other side, Lucky."

"I know, I just met one of them. They're British."

"Since when have British paratroops spoken German? One of them nearly landed on top of me. I heard him call out, looking for his mate I think. Sounded like he "Woe Bisto hands", but that don't make sense, 'cos he wouldn't be making gravy at this time o' night."

"Are you sure he didn't say '*Wo Bist Du, Hans*?'" Carter asked.

"Yes, come to think of it, that did sound like what he said."

"Well, you're right. He was German. It means 'Where are you, Hans?' How far on the other side of the railway were they?"

"He was no more than twenty feet away from me. He was still dragging his parachute together. He went off towards the west.

That helped to make sense of what Carter had heard. If the Germans were dropping paratroops into Sicily to strengthen their front line, they would come from the north. The aircraft would have to turn to go back to where they came from, so they were turning west, then they would probably turn again to head for home.

But what should he, Carter, do about them? He had his full troop; sixty men. But how many Germans were there? At least a full battalion. It seemed unlikely they would drop less than that. It might well be as much as a full airborne division, maybe three thousand men. He couldn't take them on, it would be suicide. And they were moving away from the commandos, heading inland. That conclusion made up Carter's mind for him. He called his officers and NCOs close, so he could brief them.

"It looks like there's Jerry paratroops on the other side of the railway. If they know we're here, they haven't let on, so I propose we ignore them. We carry on up the railway line as planned. Keep scouts on the left-hand side, on the lookout for the Jerries, but don't engage unless your life depends on it."

"Is that wise, Lucky?" Ernie Barraclough asked in a whisper. "I mean, leaving an enemy behind us."

"I know it's unorthodox and I'd rather not, but our mission is to get to the bridge and capture it, so that is what we will do unless the Jerries stop us. The mission comes first; always!" He paused, letting his instruction sink in. "Besides, we're already behind enemy lines, so any way we go we're going to have them behind us. The Jerries paratroops don't know we're here, so they won't come looking for us. No doubt they've got a mission of their own. Hopefully it doesn't involve securing the Ponte bridge."

That ended the argument. Fred Chalk detailed new scouts, fresh eyes to prevent them running into anything unexpected. As well as sending them ahead, there were additional men placed on the flank to provide advance warning if the paratroops were still in the area. They were back on the march again.

The railway sleepers were just the right distance apart from the commandos to stride out along them without crunching on the stony track bed. It allowed them to make quick progress. A halt was called when a firefight erupted some way in front of them. That had to be 1 Troop clearing the village of Agnone, Carter thought. The fighting lasted for about five minutes then silence returned. Carter ordered his men forward once again.

Not knowing where precisely they had joined the railway, Carter was unable to estimate how far they had to go to reach Agnone station. It could be anywhere between a mile and two miles. They would just have to trudge on into the darkness until the scout reported their arrival.

There was also the distinct possibility that they might encounter a train. The Axis commanders would know that the British breakout from their bridgehead was underway and would surely want to reinforce and resupply their front line. The railway offered them a useful way of doing that. They would hear a train coming, of course, and would be able to get clear of the line, but if it was carrying troops the train commander might decide to stop and make a fight of it if the commandos' presence was detected. It was another thing to keep Carter's mind occupied as he tramped along the railway sleepers.

The scouts brought them to a halt as soon as they saw the railway station. Moving forward in short rushes, they went to do a reconnaissance. Carter moved up to the front of the troop to wait for their report. They weren't gone for long.

"No sign of the Ities." The scout reported. "There's man there, though, a commando. Badly wounded by the look of him."

"OK, carry on until you can see the tunnel, then stop again." Carter sent him on his way, before signalling to the troop to continue the advance.

It wasn't much of a station. There was a long, low platform, rising barely a foot above the tracks and running for about fifty yards. The local trains obviously didn't have many carriages. In terms of buildings there was just the one; it was hardly bigger than a garden shed. It probably provided just enough space for a ticket seller.

Leaning against one corner, Carter found the man the scout had referred to. He had a bandage around his eyes and blood smeared his face and shirt. Across his knees was a Tommy gun, but his hands were loose around it. Beside him sat two grenades. He wouldn't have been able to use his weapons, but for a commando to be without them would be emasculating. If it wasn't for his shock of blond hair, Carter wouldn't have recognised him.

"You look the worse for wear." Carter said, crouching down beside 1 Troop's sergeant.

"You should see the other guy!" Sgt Brody attempted some humour, but Carter could tell he was in great pain.

"They made a fight of it, then."

"Not really. Got this when a grenade went off right in front of my face. Then they scarpered before the rest of the boys could get amongst them."

"Where's the rest of your troop?"

"Gone to do a house-to-house through the village. We think there's still some Ities hiding under beds and we don't want them behind us. They'll be back shortly, then they'll take me back to the beach to be evacuated."

"They should have taken you straight back to the beach."

"They wanted to. I refused. Get the job done first. I'll keep for a while. I knew you lads were on your way."

"Is there anything I can do?"

"Nah, thanks. Not unless you've got any chocolate. I just fancy a nice bit of chocolate."

"Sorry. I never eat the stuff. I might have some boiled sweets in my pack."

"Got plenty of those myself. But thanks for the offer."

"OK, well, 3 Troop's right behind us. Maybe they've got some chocolate you can have."

"Those stingy bastards won't share." He laughed, then coughed. Perhaps Brody's eyes weren't the only injury he had suffered, Carter thought.

"Well, I've got to get going before my troop starts wandering around like a lot of lost sheep. You take care."

Carter rose to go, taking a long look at the injured man. Would this be the last time he would ever speak to him? He hoped not. Brody was a good soldier and also a good man. He'd be a great loss to the commando.

But these sorts of things happen in war, Carter told himself. He turned and headed after his men, who were disappearing into the darkness.

They made fast progress along the railway line to the tunnel and the scouts brought them to a halt well short of it. A tunnel would be a natural place to defend.

"No sign of any sentries." The scout soon reported. "There's gun pits either side of the entrance, but if there was anyone posted there they've done a runner already."

"Did you find the track over the top?" Carter asked. It would be much harder if they had to march on a compass bearing.

"Yes. About fifty yards down. There must have been a wall there at some time. All that's left is some rubble and a pair of old gate posts. The track goes up the hill from there. Cedric's gone up to take a look-see."

Cedric was Tpr Ramsbottom, a taciturn Yorkshireman who had transferred in from 7 Cdo while they had been in North Africa. He may have been short on conversation, but he was a good commando, from everything Carter had seen so far.

"OK, get back in front and guide the troop to the gate. I'll be right behind you."

They found Ramsbottom waiting at the pair of old gateposts. "I went up the hill for about a hundred yards." He made his report. "Nothing along there."

"OK, lead the way. Keep going until you reach the top, then wait for me."

Ahead along the railway line Carter could make out the dark maw of the tunnel entrance. The path had probably been made by the passing of the feet of the workers who had dug it out. They would have had to go back and forth over the top of the hill as they dug from both ends towards the middle. Others must have kept using it, because it was clear of any vegetation. Perhaps local farmers or shepherds still made use of the route. So long as no enemy soldiers had chosen to camp out on it, Carter thought. Attacking uphill in the dark would be no picnic.

The climb wasn't severe, certainly not challenging for commandos. When they reached the top they continued down the far side until they found their way blocked by the River Gabriel. "I'll see if we can get across." Arthur Murray volunteered. He stepped gingerly into the water, feeling for the bottom with his booted foot. Suddenly he was gone, the water claiming him as the weight of his kit dragged him under. He appeared again just as swiftly, bobbing to the surface about halfway towards the other side. He struck out for the far bank until he found firm footing again.

That had been unexpected. In the height of an Italian summer Carter had assumed the river would be down to a trickle, but it seemed to be still in full flood. He signalled to Murray to keep going to their left, while he led the troop along the other side, looking for a safer crossing place.

The water shallowed rapidly, suggesting that the place where Murray had fallen in was some sort of sink hole, where water had gathered, possibly behind an obstruction. A scout found a place where it was only ankle deep, splashing and gurgling over boulders swept down from further upstream. Apart from the impetuous Arthur Murray, the rest of the troop crossed almost dry-shod. Carter sent a trooper back to the end of the path to guide the following troops in the right direction and detailed another man to mark the crossing point, before he climbed the slope on the far side. At the top he found he was on the crest of a ridge running left to right across his path. He turned left and led the troop along the rocky top.

He found the hapless Arthur Murray waiting for them, wringing water out of his socks.

"I had to drop my pack and webbing. My Tommy gun went as well." He apologised.

"You're lucky to be alive at all." Carter undid his belt and slipped his holstered Webley off it, slid the lanyard over his head and handed the whole lot to his subordinate. "You can use this for the moment. Not much use for anything other than close quarters, but I'm sure the Ities will yield some rifles to us when we take the bridge and you can have one of those." Fishing in his ammunition pouches he found a box of ammunition for the handgun and handed that over as well.

Murray grunted his thanks as Carter turned and followed his men along the top of the ravine.

The scouts called them to a halt after about half an hour.

"The road is just up ahead. About a hundred yards." Ramsbottom whispered in his ear.

"Show me." Carter whispered back.

The soldier crept forward again, keeping low so as not to show up as a silhouette against the moonlit sky. It took them about ten minutes to cover the hundred yards. Silence was now their friend if they didn't want to alert the sentries on the bridge. After all the fighting, they were bound to be wide awake, imagining what might be approaching them out in the darkness. Little did they know.

Ramsbottom pointed and Carter saw their objective for the first time. Under the bright moonlight, Carter could see that the road ran downhill from his right until it reached the bridge, crossed it and then continued on a straight line into the distance. The bridge itself was no more than thirty yards long, spanning the river which ran through a shallow ravine below. A pillbox was set into the parapet towards the far side, protecting an approach from the south. The plan to approach from the north had worked in their favour. Just the two sentries protected the north side, pacing slowly back and forth close to sandbagged machinegun emplacements built on the verges beside the road.

On the far side of the bridge were more sandbags, with another sentry perched on top taking his ease, while another stood looking over the parapet, staring at the river flowing by underneath. There were more pillboxes arranged to defend the southern bank, four of them. The two furthest to the left and right were almost on the edge of the ravine, protecting against a flank approach. The other two were further forward, set up to provide crossfire to the front and along the line of the road. If they had approached from the south they would have been faced with a one hundred and eighty degree arc of fire. But on this side there seemed to be nothing other than the two sentries. Behind the ridge was an orchard of some sort; probably an orange or lemon grove, protected by a hedge.

"What's in there?" Carter asked, pointing.

"Not sure. I didn't look." Ramsbottom replied, slightly embarrassed to have overlooked such obvious cover.

"Well, take a look now. I'll wait here."

The scout scuttled off towards the hedge and was back a few minutes later.

"There's pillbox. It seems to be covering the road, but it could probably turn its guns on our rear when we advance down the hill."

"OK. Thanks, I'll bear that in mind. Stay here. I'm going back to brief the troop on the plan of attack now that I can see what we're up against. When your section gets here, you join them. Your section will be attacking that pillbox, so you'll need to guide them."

"OK ... and sorry I missed it."

"Not the end of the world, Ramsbottom." Carter was in a forgiving mood, his mind better occupied with how best to take the bridge. The textbook way was to attack both ends at once, but that was rarely achievable. With that option discarded, the best method was to be fast and take the bridge before the enemy had time to react. With most of the defences facing southwards, they at least had the advantage of attacking from the rear.

Carter half stood and made his way back to the waiting troop.

Arthur Murray had caught up with them, still dripping water in a pool around his feet. Carter called up Ernie Barraclough, the Sgt Major and the sergeants that each officer had to act as their second in command.

"I'm going to keep this as simple as possible." Carter informed them, whispering as loudly as he dared. They were at least a hundred yards from the nearest pair of enemy ears, but they all knew how far sound travelled at night. "Arthur, your section will stay on the high ground and cover our backs. There's an orchard of some sort with a hedge around it with a pillbox hidden there. Ramsbottom will show you. There's probably another on the far side of the road, so once you've dealt with the first one, cross over and make sure of the other side. Then set up defensive positions. But don't do anything until you hear my team going in for the attack.

That will be your men, Ernie. We'll go down the hill as quietly as possible until we're either thirty yards out or until the sentries spot us, whichever comes first. Then we rush the bridge. I'll take Easy section hell for leather to the other side. Make sure they've got grenades ready to drop into the pillbox on the bridge. Once we're on the far side, Easy and Fox section will go left with me and we take the two pill boxes on the left flank. George and How sections go right and take the other two.

Now, Ernie, I want your Bren gunners up here along the ridge with Arthur's. Arthur, you lend Ernie eight men with rifles to fill the gaps. Arthur, when we go in, you start laying down covering fire on the far bank.

Fred," Carter addressed his Sgt Major, "Make sure you have a Very pistol loaded with a red flare. Once we're on the far side of the bridge, fire the flare. That will be your signal to cease fire up here, Arthur. Everyone know what they have to do?"

They all nodded their heads to indicate they understood the plan. "OK. Ten minutes to brief your men, then we move."

The five men split up, going back to join their sections in the darkness, leaving Carter on his own with his thoughts once again.

7 – The Bridge

Who kicked the stone, Carter would never know, but it clattered across the hard ground. The sentries stopped their chattering and turned towards the harsh sound, unslinging their rifles at the same time. Carter was farther away from the bridge than he would have liked to have been, but it was close enough.

Raising his Tommy gun, Carter fired a short burst towards the sentries before yelling "Charge!" at the top of his voice. He fired again and saw one of the men fall to the floor, writhing in agony. The second sentry dived for cover behind the sandbags. Carter lowered his head and started running. It was a matter of personal pride that he should be the first across the bridge.

Carter had closed the gap quickly and was on the bridge. Someone else would take care of the second sentry. The pillbox built into the bridge's parapet stayed silent. It didn't mean it was empty, just that whoever was inside had been looking in the wrong direction. Bren gun fire started to rain down from the ridge as Arthur Murray's men laid down covering fire above their heads. A two inch mortar bomb exploded on the road. Carter hadn't mentioned mortars, but Murray was entitled to use his initiative. Sparks bounced off the sides and roofs of the pillboxes, showing where point three-oh-three ammunition was striking. The sound of ricocheting bullets whined away into the night. The fusillade wouldn't do any damage, but it would prevent the occupants of the pillboxes from trying to exit through the rear doors.

As Carter reached the far side of the bridge the crack of a grenade told him that someone had dealt with the pillbox that was now behind him. He crouched in the shelter of the sandbagged emplacements to allow time for his men to catch up with him. The two sentries on that side of the river had disappeared.

Feeling bodies behind him, Carter stood once again, levelling his Tommy gun. "Easy Section, with me!" he shouted over his shoulder, just as the bright red glare of a Very flare lit up the sky. He sprinted for the furthest pillbox, nearly fifty yards away. He was no more than half way when two figures stumbled out, their hands held high over their heads.

"No shoot!" one shouted. "No shoot! *Ci arrendiamo!*"

Carter slowed to a walk, allowing his men to run past him. They would know what to do with the prisoners. He looked over to where Fox Section were approaching the nearer pillbox. The occupants of that were surrendering as well.

"Sir!" a voice hailed him from behind. Carter turned to see the stocky frame of Fred Chalk approaching, prodding an Italian ahead of him with the muzzle of his Tommy gun. "I think this is the Itie CO." He announced.

The sound of fresh gunfire from the top of the hill attracted Carter's attention briefly. That was Arthur Murray's boys going into the orchard. He had more than enough fire power to deal with a couple of pillboxes. They would probably surrender anyway, just like the ones in front of him.

The Italian came to a halt, drew himself up to his full height, which wasn't very tall to start with and saluted. "Capitano Bianchi." He announced, before dropping the salute and offering his hand. Carter took it and gave it a brief shake, magnanimous in victory. A trickle of blood ran down the side of the Italian's face, probably caused by grenade shrapnel. Carter noticed a row of medal ribbons on the Italian's chest.

"Steven Carter, Captain."

"We are from number 904 Fortress Battalion." The Italian informed him, without waiting to be asked. "I beg you be good with my men. They are no more than boys really. I left my best men in Libya. These … you understand, they are not the best."

So the Italian was a veteran of North Africa. That explained the medal ribbons, anyway. And the men he commanded were probably barely trained lads.

"Your men are safe with me, Capitano. We will move them up the hill out of harm's way. What can you tell me about what lies between us and the town of Lentini?"

"I am sorry, Capitano Carter. You know I can't answer that."

It was worth a try, Carter smiled inwardly. But the Italian was right. Apart from number, rank, name and unit the officer wasn't obliged to tell him anything and Carter didn't have time right then to conduct an interrogation. The CO would probably try again when he arrived.

"You may keep your sidearm, Capitano …" Then Carter remembered the last enemy officer he had allowed to remain armed after he had surrendered. "… on second thoughts, no. I would request you hand your weapon over."

The Italian shrugged his shoulders but didn't object. He just removed his pistol from its shiny leather holster and offered it to Carter. Fred Chalk took the small weapon and pushed it into his belt.

Soldiers were now gathering all around Carter, which meant they presented a juicy target to any enemy with a machine gun. "Sgt Carney, Sgt Franklyn; what are all these men doing hanging around my bridge? Get them into defensive positions."

He turned back to his prisoner. "If you would like to go with my Sgt Major, you can gather up your men."

He dismissed the defeated officer by the simple expedient of turning his back on him and walking back across the bridge. More soldiers were streaming down the hill; that was 3 Troop arriving. He waited at the northern end of the bridge to greet Andrew Fraser.

It was the CO who arrived first, striding ahead of 3 Troop as though he was inspecting his estate. "Well done, Steven. What's the state of play?"

"The bridge is secure, about a dozen Italians taken prisoner; three dead. No casualties in my troop. I've got half of my troop up on the top of the hill watching our back and the other half across the river."

"Good. I'll replace your men on the hill with 5 Troop when they get here and yours can go across and strengthen the southern defences. Once 2 Troop turn up we should be quite a formidable force."

"Did you hear about the paratroops, Sir?" Carter asked.

"Yes. Trust the RAF to drop them in the wrong place."

"Not the British ones, Sir. The German ones."

There was a moment of silence. "German paratroops, Steven? I know nothing of them."

"They were dropping to the west of us. I didn't want to engage them in case we got bogged down in a fight, so I came straight here. I did send a runner to try to find you."

"Well, he didn't find me. Probably still wandering around in the dark. OK, well, there's not much we can do about them. Any idea of their strength?"

"Not really, Sir. But I wouldn't expect any less than a battalion, unless they were strays, like our boys."

"Yes, I agree. That rather complicates matters. The *Fallschirmjäger* are elite troops; probably the best the Jerries have. If they're here in any numbers, we'll have a fight on our hands if they suspect we've taken the bridge."

"We only used small arms to take the bridge, Sir. Depending how far away they are they may not have heard us. Or maybe they'll think we're jumpy Ities, shooting at shadows."

"Let's hope so. Is there anywhere I can set up a command post?"

"I was going to set my Troop HQ up in the pillbox on the bridge. You could use that."

"It's a bit low down. I'd prefer something a bit higher up, where I can see across country when it gets light."

"There's a pillbox in the orange grove at the top of the slope."

"That sounds the sort of place. If any more troop commanders arrive here, send them up to see me. I'll decide where to put them. In the meantime, 3 Troop can get on with removing the demolition charges. I'm putting you in charge down here until the 2IC arrives. When he gets here, he'll take over as forward commander."

"Understood, Sir."

They parted company and Carter went back across the bridge to inspect the pillbox. Inside the circular interior he found a central pillar that dominated the room. On the southern side a dead Italian lay beneath a machine gun, with his loader beside him, badly wounded. Carter tutted. The wounded man should have been dealt with by now. On the far side of the pillar was a tiny desk, on which lay a field telephone, a folded map, a pad and a pencil. The Italian officer must have been using the pillbox as his HQ as well. Carter went outside and summoned a party to deal with the body and the wounded Italian, then went inside to inspect the map by the light of his torch.

It didn't tell him much. Most of the symbols indicated troop dispositions that were days out of date, There was no front line drawn, which suggested that the Italian hadn't been told where the line was. Carter lifted the handset of the field telephone. There was no sound from it. That was bad. A strategic asset such as a bridge should have had communications with the next higher level of command. Carter wondered how long the phone had been out of order. If the map was any guide, it was at least three days. Not his problem, he decided. But if the phone was out of order, it meant that the next level of enemy command had no idea that their troops no longer held the bridge. Which was good in one way. It meant that they were unlikely to try to retake it. On the other hand, it meant that traffic would still be using the road, thinking it was safe to do so. With the coming of the dawn, the British advance on Lentini would mean that ammunition would need to be supplied and casualties would need to be evacuated. That would mean the bridge's defenders would soon be discovered.

"Cosy in here." Ernie Barraclough said as he ducked his tall frame through the pillbox's low entrance.

"It's the best we've got. How are the defences looking?"

"Arthur has sent my Bren gunners down, so I've put one in each pillbox. We could use the Italian machine guns but they're shit, so we'll only use them if we run out of Bren ammunition. I've got four men in each pillbox. In between I've got the rest of the men digging slit trenches."

"I'll come out in a minute and take a look. When Arthur comes down to join us, we can rest the men in shifts, but no naked lights until after sunrise. Oh, and you better send a runner up to tell Arthur not to molest any traffic coming down the road. It will give away the fact that the bridge is now in our hands. So long as it doesn't stop to check, they won't know the difference in the dark."

No sooner were the words out of Carter's mouth when a Bren gun opened fire. Carter ran out onto the bridge, searching for the source of the firing. It was coming from the top of the hill. At least two Bren guns were firing long burst along the road towards the north. Carter was about to order them to cease firing when he realised it was too late. Whatever the gunners were firing at would already know that they were there and it would take too long to get a runner up the hill anyway.

Above the sound of the Brens, Carter could hear the roar of an engine. It sounded like a lorry. Sure enough, the slits of headlamps appeared at the top of the hill as the driver tried to run the gauntlet of the crossfire. A grenade exploded on the road in front of the vehicle, doing no harm. But a second was better aimed and the glass in the cab of the lorry exploded into shards. At once the lorry slewed to one side, running off the road. Carter could see soldiers standing up, firing their rifles into the rear of the vehicle as it careered down the hill, bumping and bouncing over stones and other obstructions. It must have hit something larger, because it started to topple over. Gravity took hold of it and helped it on its way, until it slid to a stop on its side. A commando ran down the hill, raised his arm and threw something at the back of the lorry. It had to be a grenade.

There was the crack of an explosion, then the sound of a small war starting. Bullets cracked and whined from the back of the vehicle.

"Bloody hell." Ernie swore. "It's an ammunition carrier."

That certainly seemed to be the case. The grenade must have started a fire in the back of the vehicle, causing small arms ammunition to start exploding in the heat. Flames started to flicker along the canvass awning that enclosed the rear of the vehicle and more ammunition started to cook off. Then came louder rumbles of explosions, with bright flames shooting into the night. Artillery ammunition, Carter assumed. Or maybe demolition explosives. It didn't matter. The lorry was turning the night sky into a reasonable facsimile of Guy Fawkes night back home, before the war put a stop to such things.

At times the noise was deafening and Carter had to withdraw into the pillbox in order to avoid the shrapnel that was whizzing through the air. The lorry continued to explode for a further ten minutes, with shrapnel and small arms rounds pinging off the hardened concrete of the pillbox.

"I think we can say the enemy now know we're here." Barraclough shouted above the racket.

"True." Carter shouted back. "If I were anywhere in the area, I'd be preparing a recce patrol to come and take a look at what was happening up here."

"Which way will they come?"

"Could be either. Those paratroops can't be far away and the Italians must have troops billeted in the next village to the north." Carter consulted the Italian map. "That would be a place called San Leonardo, on the coast a few miles north of Agnone. By road they could be here in minutes."

"It would take a brave Italian to chance it. That must have sounded like the whole of 50th Division was engaged. It would be a bit rich for a small village garrison."

"You're probably right. So that leaves the paratroops. They're far more experienced."

"But I doubt we'll see them before dawn. They don't know the terrain any better than us."

Carter checked his watch. "Dawn isn't that far away." The noises had quietened, limited to the odd stray bullet exploding. Carter risked looking out of the pillbox towards the east. "Yes, the sky is lightening over the coast. Time for 'stand-to' anyway[1]."

It was at that point that an artillery barrage started up to their south. Flashes of light lit up the horizon, followed by the explosion of heavy calibre shells. The ground vibrated under their feet.

"Looks like 50th Division are on their way." Barraclough observed. "We'll soon be relieved now."

"Let's hope so." Carter replied. Knowing that there was anything up to a thousand elite enemy troops between him and the relief force didn't make for pleasant thoughts. Even if they only retreated, they would be coming straight towards Carter's defensive positions.

As the sun rose, Carter clambered up onto the top of the pillbox so that he could see further along the road to the south. There was nothing visible to the naked eye and even his binoculars revealed no more than the smoke of the artillery barrage. No sign of troops crossing the fields or walking down the sides of the road. But if the enemy knew what he was doing, he wouldn't be coming by a direct route. Just as Carter had crossed the river to approach the bridge from the rear, so might the commander of an enemy patrol take a more circuitous route. The river offered only an illusory barrier; an enemy that didn't mind getting their feet wet wouldn't balk at crossing it.

Andrew Fraser, 3 Troops commander, appeared clambering up the side of the ravine to the southern end of the bridge. "You make a fine target for a sniper." He called up to Carter, still standing on top of the pillbox. Carter took the hint and jumped down to the ground.

"How's it going under the bridge?" he asked.

"All done. It would have made quite a bang if all those explosives had gone off. I couldn't find the firing wire though."

"It's inside the pillbox, still wrapped around a drum. The firing handle is there as well. I think the bridge commander was a bit nervous about the bridge going up underneath him, so he was waiting to see the army advancing down the road before he connected it all up to the charges. It meant he didn't have time to do anything when we came out of the night from behind him."

"Lucky for us, otherwise that march across country would have been for nothing. Anyway, what do you want me to do with my men now."

"I'd get them onto the north bank for now. The CO's set up shop at the top of the hill. You'd better go and see where he wants you."

1 and 6 troops would have arrived by now, Carter thought. That made them a pretty daunting defence force should the enemy turn up. With the bridge to slow the enemy down and with three inch mortars and Vickers machine guns at the top of the hill, it would be a pretty brave commander that risked a frontal assault. Or a very stupid one.

But Carter didn't intend waiting for the enemy to come and find him. With Arthur Murray's men now down from the top of the hill he had more men than he needed for the immediate future. He went and found Murray, sitting behind a pillbox brewing up a cup of tea.

Carter squatted beside him. "I'd like you to send out a couple of patrols. One to the east side of the road and another to the west. Send them out to patrol an arc about half a mile in front of us. If they see anything, they're to count heads, then get back here as quickly as possible.

"Do you want me to go with them?"

"No. Just send out two sections with a corporal in charge of each. That should be enough. I don't want them taking the enemy on if they find them. No stupid heroics and they should try not to be seen. Just get back here as quickly as possible."

"OK."

"What have you got for breakfast?" Carter asked.

"The usual. My men chipped in some bully and biscuits. It'll do until the army gets here."

"The plan says they'll be here by lunchtime."

"Since when did plans work like that? At least we know the fight has started."

The rumble of artillery was continuing, though it hadn't got any louder. Was that significant? There was no way of knowing.

"Have you got yourself a better weapon?"

"Yes. I've got an Italian rifle now and enough ammunition to keep me going for a while."

"Good. Let me know as soon as those patrols get back." Carter instructed, turning around to return to the bridge.

The tension suppressed Carter's appetite, but he knew he had to eat or he would suffer for it later. He couldn't keep his body going on adrenaline alone. He returned to the pillbox and munched his way through some hardtack biscuits topped with sardines, the only alternative they had to bully beef. Paddy O'Driscoll appeared bearing a mug of tea. "That'll do yez good, Sorr." He said.

"Thanks. What are you doing here?" Carter asked.

"Me and Danny boy have been sent by Lt Barraclough to man a Bren gun in here." He explained, just as Danny Glass appeared through the entrance to the pillbox, the Bren gun balanced across his shoulder and a haversack of magazines in his free hand.

"Oh, here you are." Glass grumped at his companion. "I thought I was going to have to carry all that Bren ammo myself."

"I'm just going back to get it now." The Irishman protested, ducking back through the door.

"I hope you two aren't going to sit here bickering all morning." The two troopers, close friends, were well known for arguing like an old married couple, disagreeing on almost everything as a matter of principle. Glass was an ardent Chelsea football supporter, but had been heard disagreeing with O'Driscoll on the merits of his team because O'Driscoll had suggested they'd had a good time before the war.

"We'll go somewhere else if you want us to." Glass said, flatly. He was one of only three men that Carter would allow to speak to him like that. When you've faced death together the way they had, a certain degree of licence is granted, despite King's Regulations.

"Just keep it down, that's all I ask." Carter said.

Glass rested the barrel of his Bren gun on the thick ledge of the firing aperture, pushing the weapon far enough through that it balanced without him having to hold the butt of the weapon. He crouched down behind it and peered out. "There's someone running towards us." He said. "Looks like Sidewell from Able section."

Crouching down, Carter looked over Glass's shoulder. "He must be from the patrol that went out." He turned and left the pillbox, intent on hearing what the soldier had to say.

Sidewell ran first to his own officer's position behind the eastern pillbox, but Murray stood and directed the trooper to the approaching Carter, getting up to follow him.

"Cpl Henry's compliments, Sir." The commando came to a halt in front of Carter. "Enemy sighted to the south east. Platoon strength, heading this way."

"How far away?" Carter asked.

"About five hundred yards in front of us when we spotted them and we wuz about half a mile out."

So, less than a mile. It wouldn't take them long to reach the bridge, even moving covertly. There was plenty of cover for them to use, in the form of drystone walls and scrubby hedges.

"Germans or Italians?"

"Definitely German, from their helmets. They looked like they know what they're doing, as well. I only got a glimpse of them before the corporal sent me back with the message."

"But the corporal is sure they were in platoon strength." Carter knew that fear often inflated the numbers of the enemy. Earlier in the war Carter knew that the crew of a single Heinkel bomber, shot down over Wiltshire, had been reported as a full-scale airborne invasion.

"He was pretty sure."

Carter knew Henry quite well. He was an experienced NCO. If he said it was a platoon, then it probably was.

"What is Cpl Henry doing now?"

"He said he was going to keep the enemy in sight and withdraw in front of them. If they change direction or get reinforced, he's going to send another runner."

"Right, Arthur." Carter turned to Murray. "Get the men stood-to and tell Ernie to do the same. I'll go and report to the CO."

Making his way back across the bridge Carter's stomach gave a twist of anxiety. They would see action again soon. He made his way through the positions that 3 Troop were digging, part way up the hill on the north side of the river, providing a second line of defence should it be needed. Carter felt sure it would be. His troop could defend against a German platoon, but if the enemy brought up reinforcements, a withdrawal from the south bank of the river was almost inevitable. The climb to the top of the hill took only a couple of minutes and Carter found the CO in the pillbox that had been captured that morning.

"I've had a report of a platoon sized formation of Germans approaching from the south east, Sir." Carter reported. "That would be the right sort of direction to make them part of the paratroop landing from last night."

"Let's take a look." Vernon said, reaching for his binoculars. "How far away?"

"Less than a mile from the bridge. I sent patrols out as soon as it got light."

"I know, I saw them go. A sound precaution, Steven." They arrived at the hedge that surrounded the orange grove and raised their binoculars, looking for any sign of the enemy.

"Got them, Sir." Carter reported. "About two finger widths to the left of the bridge and about six hundred yards from it."

"You have sharp eyes, Steven. I can't see anything … wait, yes, there was one, just crossing a gateway." The CO lowered his binoculars as he considered what to do. "They have a pretty good idea that we're here, otherwise they wouldn't be creeping around like that, trying not to be seen. They'll know exactly where we are as soon as they see your front line. I think we may as well try to persuade them to stay back a bit." Pausing, he wrote something on a page of his notebook.

"Ecclestone!" he summoned his HQ clerk. The man appeared as though he had been waiting for the summons, which he might well have been.

"Take this to the mortar teams." He handed the note over. "They are to fire one bomb for effect, then wait my order to adjust aim."

"Very good, Sir." The trooper vanished as speedily as he had arrived.

They heard the cough of the mortar firing only a minute later then, after a delay, saw the gout of stones and debris that the exploding bomb sent up. The bomb had fallen short, but that wasn't unusual. It was difficult to judge distance with any degree of accuracy. The miracle was that the bomb had landed within fifty feet of the last place they had seen the German soldier.

But it provoked a reaction. Figures broke cover and scurried to put distance between themselves and the explosion. They did know what they were doing. Troops clustered together made for an easier target to hit. By putting distance between themselves they made much smaller individual targets.

"Down twenty." The CO instructed the mortar operators to adjust the angle of the mortar tubes to send the bombs a little further. Ecclestone hurried to relay the order. The response was another bomb, this time landing in the area where the enemy had last been seen.

"Both tubes, three bomb salvo." The CO instructed. Skilled operators could fire quickly enough to keep three bombs in the air at any time, so the enemy would find it hard to guess how many tubes the Commando had. Had six bombs been fired quickly from two tubes? Or had six bombs been fired from six tubes? Anything that kept the enemy off balance was a good tactic.

As each bomb fired, the aim of the tubes changed fractionally as the vibration of the discharge shifted the baseplates. So the six bombs peppered the target area. It wasn't the explosions of the bombs that was dangerous, but the shrapnel that was thrown around; razor sharp splinters of metal accompanied by clods of earth and stones. A direct hit was rare, but the bombs were still deadly even if they missed by several yards.

"That won't stop them, of course." The CO acknowledged his satisfaction with the mortar strikes, "But it will make them stop and think."

"I'd better get back down to my men." Carter said. There was nothing he could do up there and his men would need to know that he wasn't avoiding the fight that they all knew was coming.

"Yes, you had." The CO's face took on a serious expression. "Look, Steven, no heroics, do you hear? Withdraw if you need to. We can hold the bridge well enough from this side if we have to. The enemy will have to cross the river and we have enough firepower to prevent that. We've got the flanks well anchored, so anything less than a brigade strength assault can be fought off. 50th Division will be here soon enough. You can hear their artillery already."

"I have no plans to be a hero today, Sir." Carter grinned.

"Good man."

But the sound of the artillery wasn't the good news that the CO tried to make out. The British artillery would have fallen silent as soon as the infantry moved into Lentini; to keep firing only risked killing their own men. The enemy, Germans or Italians, would also have ceased fire as they withdrew their guns to prevent them being overrun and captured. Only light artillery would have remained to try to pick off advancing tanks. The continuation of the barrage suggested that the enemy were putting up a fight for the town and if that were the case, it was impossible to say when relief might arrive.

In addition, a retreating army would probably need to cross the bridge to escape, which would bring even more enemy to them. It was going to be a long day, Carter felt sure.

As he reached the bridge again, Carter was met by Arthur Murray, in the company of Cpl Dawkins. "Baker section are back from their patrol." He reported. "They didn't see any troops, but they reported seeing a lot of dust and haze off to the west.

"You think that was significant?" Carter asked the corporal.

"Yes, Sir. The last time I saw anything like that was in Tunisia, when those tanks and halftracks were chasing us."

Carter stayed silent. Their intelligence for the raid had said there was no armour in this part of Sicily, so theoretically Dawkins was wrong about whatever was raising the dust. But he was another reliable man. It was unlikely that he was wrong about seeing it, only about his interpretation of its cause.

But if it wasn't tracked vehicles raising the dust, what was it?

"OK, thank you Dawkins. Go and take up your position."

As they watched the corporal's retreating back, Arthur Murray asked the obvious question. "You think it's tanks, don't you?"

"I think we have to consider the possibility. Where they've come from is another matter. But if they're heading south they aren't our problem."

"They'll slow down 50th Division, though."

"They might. But we'll have to wait and see. The CO says we're to hold for as long as we can, then get back across the bridge. I only intend retreating if it becomes obvious we're going to be overrun. Our big advantage is holding the pillboxes. We can keep the Bren guns firing until the cows come home from there. Make sure they've got enough ammunition. Detail men to go and get more from the troops behind us, if necessary."

"No problem."

Carter went off to find Ernie Barraclough to repeat his orders.

[1] All armies "stand-to", ie man their defences, at dawn and dusk as those are the most likely times for a surprise attack to be launched. It was only with the formation of elite forces such as the commandos and paratroops that night-time assaults became a regular occurrence. Night was usually used just to replenish supplies and position troops ready for a dawn attack. If possible, at dawn the attacking force will always try to come from the east, so that the rising sun is in the enemy's eyes and at dusk they'll try to come from the west.

* * *

Nothing happened for a while and Carter had been tempted to send out another patrol to see what the enemy were doing. He was saved from that by another runner arriving from Able section.

"More troops moving up." The man told him. "Looks like they're reinforcing to company strength."

That made sense. Faced with an enemy equipped with mortars they would assume at least that strength against them. A platoon wouldn't attack a company, but a full strength company might. German military doctrine meant that the formation would have quite a lot of machine guns; The MG 42 that had been introduced the previous year was a versatile weapon and the Germans knew how to use it to best effect. It was belt fed, which meant that it had a higher sustained rate of fire and the barrel was air cooled, so that the gunner didn't have to change barrels as often as a Bren gunner might.

But they still had to deal with well-prepared defences which included reinforced concrete pillboxes. The Germans would have to get close to them to throw grenades through the firing ports and the way the commandos had sited their other defences said the enemy would sustain heavy casualties if they tried it.

The first salvoes were fired from long range; the Germans just trying to force the commandos to retaliate so they could gain some idea of the strength of the defences and how they were arranged. The commandos were under orders not to fire back, however tempting the targets might be.

More mortar bombs were fired from the top of the hill, just to remind the enemy that if they attacked, they would expose themselves.

The attack, when it came, was from the left flank, where the enemy had managed to crawl close using the cover of a drystone wall. Sustained machine gun fire enfiladed the slit trenches and the Bren guns in the pillboxes were unable to aim far enough to the left to defend the attack. On the far side of the river 3 Troop opened up with their Bren guns, firing into the Germans attack, which discouraged any further attempts on that side. Round 1 to the commandos.

After that the Germans restricted themselves to harassing fire. Carter would have liked to have sent out fighting patrols, but he was unable to protect the flanks of any attack, which could result in them being cut off. So the two sides were stuck in a stalemate; the Germans were unable to advance, while the commandos were unable to beat off their attackers.

The stalemate was broken around mid-morning. It was heralded by a plume of dust to the south, followed a short while later by the rumble of a heavy engine and the squeal of tracks. Carter hoped that it was just a half track. The mortars and heavy machine guns sited at the top of the hill would be able to stop that. But he wasn't able to raise himself high enough to see over the cover. The sound changed, with the tracks making more noise as they came onto the tarmacked surface of the road. Carter rose from the slit trench from which he was commanding his front line, clambered over the rear and sprinted back to the pillbox on the bridge. Once inside he was able to look along the road and identify the threat.

It was as he feared. Making its way forward was the bulk of a Tiger tank.

It was another weapon that had been introduced the previous year and was rightly feared by the infantry. If it had arrived in Africa in large enough quantities it might have changed the balance of forces in the area enough for the *Afrika Korps* to hang on for longer. Its 88mm gun meant that anything the Allies had was no match for it, except perhaps for the American Sherman tank. Even then the Sherman had to be pretty close up to penetrate the Tiger's heavily armoured skin.

Carter knew of only one infantry weapon that might be effective against the behemoth that was approaching, the PIAT[1]. Even then it had to be fired from within a few yards and directly into the side of the tank. And the commando didn't have any of them.

The tank ground to a halt and its turret started to turn. Carter held his breath; he knew what the target would be. There were men in that pillbox. He thought about shouting a warning, but it was already too late. The tank fired and the pillbox disappeared under the powerful explosion of the 88mm shell. It was devastating. When the smoke and dust cleared, half the nearside wall of the pillbox was missing and the thick concrete roof was canted down at an angle. No one could have survived the blast.

The turret started to turn again, towards the pillbox that sat closer to the road. This time the occupants knew what was happening. They appeared at the rear entrance and sprinted for the cover of the ravine. The tank's machine gun opened fire. One of the men fell, tumbling over and over before coming to an untidy stop. The second made it, throwing himself over the edge of the ravine and sliding down to the bottom.

This signalled a general withdrawal from the defence on that side of the bridge. Without the pillboxes to provide cover from the Bren guns, the gaps that were created meant the slit trenches became vulnerable to the advances of the paratroops. The tank's machine gun continued to harass the commandos as they rushed towards the ravine and the parapet of the bridge. More men fell; his men. Seeing them sprawl in the dust he felt a personal pain inside himself. At this distance, all wearing the same uniform and their steel helmets, he couldn't identify the individual casualties. He would have to wait for a roll-call to find out who had died and who had made it.

A man clutched at his thigh, Carter thought it might be Arthur Murray. He fell and Carter willed him to get back to his feet before the machine gun sought out his prone frame. He struggled upright again then another commando grabbed him under the arms and helped him towards the ravine, the injured man making headway with huge hops on his good leg. It was like some bizarre three-legged race. They made the edge of the ravine and slid their way to the bottom.

Seeing their enemy in retreat, the German paratroops rose from their cover and attacked, firing rifles and Schmeisser machine pistols from the hip. But the heavy weapons were waiting for them. Mortar bombs peppered the ground around the recently vacated defences and machine guns raked an arc across the landscape. The Germans stopped their advance as suddenly as it had started and hurried back to their cover.

The tank turret turned again as the barrel of the gun was elevated. It fired once more and Carter hurried to the rear firing port of the pillbox to see where the shot had landed. It was well below the top of the ridge, meaning it couldn't silence the heavy weapons. The tank would have to withdraw along the road to create a better angle and if it did that the commandos could return to counterattack. The stalemate had returned.

But the pillboxes on the right-hand side of the road were still intact and the tank turned its attention on those. Ernie Barraclough's men were already retreating, having seen the carnage on the eastern side.

Carter took the opportunity of the tank being otherwise engaged to evacuate the pillbox. "Come on, you two!" he ordered Glass and O'Driscoll. "Get back across the bridge and take cover with 3 Troop."

"I'd better hide my wallet." Glass quipped. Even under fire the commandos resorted to their banter between the men of different troops.

Carter let his men go first, before leaving the pillbox. He knew he had only seconds before he was spotted and the machine guns sought him out. He zigged and zagged his way back across the bridge and then across the open ground to the right, where 3 Troop were dug in. The nearest slit trench was already overcrowded, so Carter headed for the next, a few yards further along. As machine gun rounds started to crack around his head, Carter dived and landed at the bottom of the trench in an untidy heap. He let out a groan as the butt of his Tommy gun crunched against his ribs.

"You OK, Sir?" A voice inquired. Carter looked up to see himself being examined by the grinning face of Sgt Wally Hammond, on of Andrew Fraser's troop sergeants.

"Fine thank you, Sergeant." Carter replied. "Nothing that won't mend." Now that he was in the direct heat of the sun Carter felt thirsty. He drew his water canteen from its pouch and removed the cork, tilting it so that the cool water ran into his mouth.

Careful, he warned himself. They hadn't been able to carry water supplies with them, anticipating refilling their bottles from the river instead. That source of re-supply was now a contested area.

Raising his head, Carter surveyed the ground on the other side of the river. There were three bodies he could see, plus the two men in the wreckage of the pillbox. Five casualties that he knew of. Five men that he had come to know and trust and who had trusted him.

"Any idea what the plan is?" Hammond asked.

"We stay on this side and prevent the Jerries from crossing the bridge." Carter replied.

"With that tank? They can come across any time they like."

Which was puzzling, because the tank was just sitting on the road, burning petrol. Having destroyed the hardened defences on the southern bank, it should be moving forward to take the bridge and allow the paratroops to cross behind it, unmolested. So why was the tank commander not doing that?

"I think they don't know we've disarmed the demolition charges, Wally." Carter mused. "That tank commander thinks that if he starts to cross, we'll blow the bridge and send it, his tank and his crew to Kingdom Come."

"So, what is he doing?"

"Probably waiting for reinforcements, so he can clear this bank and let the paratroops cross the river through the ravine. Once across they can send men under the bridge to check out the demolition charges."

"Which they'll find have already been removed." Wally grinned. He was a cheerful sort, unless you were a slovenly soldier who crossed his path.

"Their lack of knowledge is to our advantage. With any luck, 50th Division will be here soon and they'll have to withdraw."

"No sign of them yet. The plan said they'd be here by now."

"You surely didn't believe that." It was Carter's turn to grin.

"Should have known better, I suppose."

"But in the meantime, our job is to make sure those paratroops don't get across. That bridge is ours."

There was a sudden crack of machine gun bullets above Carter's head. He looked around to see who had been ill advised enough to show themselves and attract the gunner's attention. It saved him from having Andrew Fraser land on top of him as he jumped into the slit trench.

"CO's orders." He said as soon as he had dusted himself off. "We're to withdraw to the top of the hill. It's easier to defend up there. We can keep the enemy at bay and they can do little to get at us. We'll wait out the arrival of 50th Division up there."

"A withdrawal under fire is risky." Carter observed.

"Not as risky as staying here. That Tiger can blast our positions to smithereens and we can't touch him. Better to have some distance between him and us. We're to fire a green flare when we're about to leave and they'll start throwing mortar bombs and machine gun fire down on the paratroops to keep their heads down. That will just leave the tank."

"Which has two machine guns."

"And limited visibility for their gunners. We have to take the chance or we'll end up dying here."

"I guess we have no real choice. OK, these are your trenches, so we'll follow you."

"When do you ever do anything else?" Fraser laughed as he jumped almost vertically out of the trench and sprinted across the road to issue the order to the men on the far side. Machine gun fire followed him but he seemed to have a charmed life, because he made the nearest trenches without being hit.

It was less than five minutes before the green Very flare soared into the sky. Almost immediately Carter heard the distant cough of mortars firing and the Vickers machine guns opening up. Smoke erupted from where the mortar bombs landed, the intent being to provide cover and to distract the machine gunners. The light breeze meant that the smoke spread slowly across the front of the German positions.

One of the mortars changed its point of aim to drop smoke in front of the Tiger tank, giving Carter the cue that it was time to depart. Looking forward over the top of the slit trench he saw a two man MG 42 crew crabbing sideways to get clear of the smoke. But on top of the hill a Bren gunner had been expecting such a move and opened fire, sending the Germans diving for cover.

"Time to go, Wally." Carter said, turning back, only to find that he was on his own. Shaking his head ruefully at being so slow to move, he clambered out of the slit trench and started zig-zagging up the hill.

The smoke bombs were switched to high explosives as the mortar crews tried to pin the Germans in their positions and prevent them running through the smoke to get a better view. It would be a brave man that risked the curtain of shrapnel that was blanketing the German front line.

But the Germans could still fire blind, anticipating what the commandos were trying to do and Carter heard the whip crack of shots passing him by. Something hit his boot, but whether it was a bullet or a stone thrown up by a bullet he didn't know and wasn't stopping to find out. Something else plucked at the sleeve of his shirt and he felt the cooler air against his skin as the gentle breeze penetrated the tear.

His lungs were heaving as he breasted the crest of the hill and forced his way through the hedge into the orchard. All along the edge of the orange grove other commandos were doing the same. Once through they dropped to the ground, turning back to fire at the enemy through the gaps at the base of the hedge.

Carter made his way across to the pillbox, the most prominent feature at the top of the hill and the one the CO had chosen to make his temporary HQ. Slumped on the ground, his back against the wall, lay Arthur Murray. Somehow he had been helped all the way up the hill under fire. It could wait for the moment, but Carter would find out who had helped the officer. There would be an award of some sort for doing it. The man had risked his life.

The CO and the 2IC were deep in conversation.

"What's the plan, Sir?" Carter asked.

"Just to stick it out up here and keep the Germans off the bridge. That Tiger daren't risk crossing without infantry support. It would be too easy for us to get men behind him and jam something in his tracks. If that happens he's stranded. For all they know we've got explosives available and that would mean the end for him. There aren't many weak points on a Tiger, but there are a couple. I've got snipers zeroed in on the end of the bridge and along the edge of the ravine, to stop the infantry from getting across. The Vickers and the mortars are the best defence though."

"Where do you want my men?"

"We're quite well fixed for offensive fire right now, so take your men to the back of the orchard and rest them. I'll rotate you with one of the other troops later, probably after lunch."

Carter checked his watch, surprised to see that it wasn't even mid-morning.

"Any word on when 50th Division will get here?"

"No. We're not getting very good radio reception. We're at the far end of the range for our sets. But I think that artillery fire tells the story."

Carter had grown so used to the sound of the distant guns that he had tuned the noise out. But the CO was right. It told the story. The two sides were still trying to batter each other into submission, which meant that the tanks and infantry couldn't be advancing.

"If you take a look with binoculars you can just about see the town." The CO continued. "There's a lot of smoke from burning buildings. Some of its black smoke though, which suggests vehicles on fire; maybe tanks."

It wasn't a comforting thought, but Carter didn't want to display any signs of pessimism. Commandos were never pessimistic, or so he had been told. He nodded his head in salute and left the CO to his discussions with the 2IC.

Carter spent a few minutes comforting Arthur Murray. The man was in a bad way, having lost a lot of blood. But someone had bandaged his wound tightly and the bleeding seemed to have stopped. Once 50th Division arrived they'd be able to get him proper medical attention.

Spotting Sgt Major Chalk, Carter crossed to him and told him where to assemble the men. "Let them have a brew and something to eat. They'll be replacing one of the troops in the line later. Do you know how many we've lost?"

"Still doing a head count, Sir." He answered. "But I know of five dead and three wounded."

Ten percent of his command. In an ordinary infantry unit they'd regard that as heavy casualties. In the commandos, it was getting off lightly. But the day wasn't over.

---

[1] Projectile, Infantry, Anti-tank (PIAT). This was a new addition to the British Army's armoury, introduced just in time for the Sicily landings. It was the first true ant-tank missile and had a deadly effect on German tanks; the Germans had never seen the like before. For

the first time ever, infantry could tackle tanks on an equal footing and beat them. In Sicily they were only issued to selected Canadian infantry units and the commandos didn't receive them until much later. That early in July 1943 they were still a well-guarded secret, so it is surprising that Carter had heard of them. The missile contained a shaped charge which focused all of the weapon's blast into the armour, expelling a molten metal 'plug' into the interior of the tank. The crew were killed by flying metal fragments rather than by blast, as had been the case with anti-tank artillery rounds. From the outside the tank could appear undamaged, except for the tell-tale hole where the missile had hit. The weapon was mounted on a monopod with a square plate on its foot and was fired like a rifle. However, its barrel was more like a pipe, wide enough to contain the missile, which had a diameter of 3.3 inches. The missile itself weighed less than a mortar bomb. The PIAT was designed by Major Milliss Jefferis (the rank was honorary as he was actually a civilian) of the Special Operations Executive (SOE) for use by SOE agents behind enemy lines, but the army had purchased 115,000 thousand of them by the time they went out of service in 1950. Unfortunately, by the time of the Normandy Landings the Germans had developed a counter to the PIAT in the form of an armoured skirt that forced the premature detonation of the charge, making the weapon less effective. In Normandy only 7% of enemy tanks destroyed were by PIATs, about the same strike rate as rockets launched from aircraft. In the film "A Bridge Too Far" a PIAT is shown in use against a German pillbox on Arnhem Bridge.

8 – Every Man For Himself

Carter had just been told to ready his men to take over in the front line of defence. They would move across the road to hold the right hand flank. But the warning shout of a forward sentry stopped all activity at the top of the hill. Men crawled forward to peer through the hedge to see what new threat was approaching.

It was two more Tiger tanks, still just black blobs at the foot of plumes of dust as they crawled across the coastal plain, heading straight for the bridge. They were only identifiable as tanks because of their long barrelled guns. But the shapes grew and soon the growl of their engines could also be heard.

"O Group!" Henry Finch's parade ground bawl shattered the silence at the top of the hill. The word was passed from mouth to mouth to the more distant outposts.

"Wait for my orders." Fred Chalk was told, as Carter and Barraclough rose to answer the CO's summons. It took a few minutes for all the officers to arrive at the pillbox. From the CO's stern expression nothing could be gleaned with regard to what he had planned.

"The arrival of two more tanks has changed things more than somewhat." He said with a grim smile. "One tank and we were OK, we could have held out for days if necessary, but three tanks means the Germans want this bridge very, very badly; either to re-supply during the night, or to withdraw across it at some point. Whichever it is, they can now push us off this ridge. Two of those Tigers can sit back and blast our positions, keeping our heads down, while the third tank crosses with the support of those paratroops. If we try to move back down the hill to deal with the tank, even if we could deal with it, we'll be cut to ribbons.

As I see it, we have three options. We can fight; we can surrender; or we can withdraw."

Not retreat, Carter noted. Withdraw. There was whole lot of difference in terms of how the commando would view itself after this was all over.

"Now, I'm not going to be the first CO of a commando to lose his entire command by surrendering." Vernon continued, "So I'm ruling that option out. I also don't intend sacrificing men to try to hold a bridge that 50th Division will have to retake anyway, once we're all dead. Has anyone any other suggestions?"

"I say we fight." Ronnie Pickering, said. He was 1 Troop's CO and his arm was in a sling from a wound he had suffered in the fighting the previous evening.

"I admire your spirit, Ronnie, but sane heads have to prevail. We're no use to Montgomery if we're all dead. In the absence of any other options, I'm giving the order 'every man for himself'. We'll break up into groups, no less than four and no more than eight and make our way back to the Allied lines by whatever means we can. We won't all make it, I'm sure, but enough will to keep the commando intact. Aim for the village of Augusta. It sits on a peninsula about two miles south of where we landed last night. If we can make radio contact, we can ask to be lifted off by the Prince Leopold. At the very least it's a very defensible position; we can't be flanked because of the sea. It's also a lot closer to the Allied lines, which means relief shouldn't be long in arriving once 50th Division break through from Lentini."

"Can't we wait here for 50th Division?"

"No. The last word I got was that they're struggling. Those tanks down below seem to be part of an armoured division. No one knew they were here. What should have been a routine advance against infantry has turned into a slugging match between tanks and artillery. I'm guessing that if there's no breakthrough by sunset, the two sides will disengage for the night and resume hostilities in the morning. With the best will in the world, we can't hang on for that long."

Every man for himself. It was an unusual order, but not unheard of. Each man was free to act on his own initiative to save himself. He could even surrender if he thought that was the best way to preserve his own life. No one would think the worse of him for that.

"Brief your men to withdraw down the reverse slope of the hill, out of sight of the enemy. Then head east towards the coast. The coastal defences will still be manned, I should think, so tell the men not to go too far that way. Then they can turn back south and cross the river wherever they can."

"My men are on the other side of the road." Ronnie Pickering pointed out. "It would make more sense for us to go west."

"Mine too." 5 Troop's Co added.

"If you fancy your chances going that way, you can if you wish." Vernon responded. "But you'll have a much greater distance to go to reach Augusta."

"Can we head straight for the Allied lines? The Jerries can't have the whole area swamped with troops."

"You can go whichever way you feel is best." Vernon smiled. "Your way is just as likely to be successful as mine."

"Can we attack the enemy?" The 2IC asked. "You know, harass him, disrupt his operations."

"If you want to, I can't stop you." Vernon said. The 2IC was known to be something of a firebrand. The CO knew that telling him not to engage the enemy would be a waste of time. "My main concern is to save as many men as possible, but they're commandos. They've been trained to take the fight to the enemy and I can't blame them if they decide to do that."

Each man would effectively become his own commanding officer once they left the ridge, free to make his own decisions about what to do and what not to do. If there was an officer or NCO present their orders would have to be obeyed, but for the rest it was a time for freedom from the usual constraints of military discipline.

"Remind the men not to steal from the civilians." Vernon told them. "They've all been given Lira to pay for food. If I hear of any looting or other bad behaviour the culprits will regret it."

"I assume that by bad behaviour you don't include killing the enemy?" The QM asked. That brought a laugh.

"Providing the enemy is armed and fighting back. The men are still bound by the Geneva Convention."

* * *

Carter sat alone at the top of the hill. The men didn't need him to sort themselves into groups. Since the day they had arrived at the training depot at Achnacarry they had worked in pairs, known as 'me and my pal'. If one stood guard, the other cooked the food and brewed the tea. If one had to climb a wall, the other gave him a leg-up or held his weapon. If one had to go through a door, the other provided covering fire. The pairs became inseparable, on and off duty. From that they would team up with other pairs, probably from the same sections. The only question that remained was who would team up with Carter himself. It would probably be with Ernie Barraclough and Fred Chalk. Arthur Murray would have made up the fourth, but he was now too sick to move. He'd be left for the enemy to look after. It was hard decision, but there was no alternative. Vernon couldn't ask men to carry a casualty through enemy occupied territory. The rough handling would probably kill him anyway.

6 Troop were on the left flank, the side nearest to the coast. They would be the first to depart. Each group would wait for 2 minutes for the group ahead to get clear before the next moved off the top of the ridge. It would take time for the whole commando to disperse. 3 Troop were next and 4 Troop after them. 1 and 5 troops, on the other side of the road should then follow, but Carter suspected they were already on the move. The commandos were trained in covert movement and hiding in the minimum amount of cover. They didn't

have to head south. They could hide in the hills until 50th Division arrived. They might not all escape, but enough would.

2 Troop had drawn the short straw. Their job was to keep the mortar tubes and the Vickers machine guns firing, to give the impression that the commando was just about to attack. Even if the Germans didn't believe that, the hail of metal from the top of the hill would keep their heads down for long enough for most of the commando to sneak away. Their last act would be to disable the heavy weapons to put them beyond the use of the enemy. To carry the weapons with them would slow them down. Then 2 Troop could depart.

Once darkness arrived the commandos would have their greatest advantage. They owned the night when it came to moving around without being seen. From the northern most tip of Norway to the thick jungles of Burma they had already proven their skill in that respect.

Carter looked up to see two men approaching. Glass carried his Bren gun across his body, its weight supported by a strap that ran over his shoulder. O'Driscoll was weighed down by the haversacks containing the pre-loaded magazines for the heavier weapon.

"What do you two want?" Asked Carter, already knowing the answer.

"Every man for himself, the order is, Sorr." O'Driscoll answered for them both. "So we thought we'd come over here. You seem a bit bereft of company right now."

"Yeah." Glass continued, "and we didn't want you sneakin' off without us."

"And definitely not without me." A familiar voice came from behind Carter. Prof Green dropped to the ground beside the other two.

"Groups of four to eight." O'Driscoll continued. "This makes us four. If anyone else wants to join us, they'd be welcome."

"Do I get any say in this?" Carter suppressed a smile."

"Well, you don't have to stay wid' us if that's what you mean." O'Driscoll answered. "But every time you turn round you'll find us there, behind you."

"OK, but I'm giving the orders." Carter said.

"No change there then." Green said. he unstoppered his water bottle and drank. But there wasn't much water in it. He took the bottle from his lips and held it upside down. Not a drop ran out.

"Looks like water could be a problem." He said.

"How is everyone else fixed?" Carter asked.

"I've got about a quarter bottle." Glass said, shaking it so that he could hear the contents sloshing about.

"About the same." Said O'Driscoll.

Carter shook his own bottle. He could tell from the noise it made that it was almost empty.

"Looks like we'll have to improvise. There's plenty of lemons on the trees still. We can squeeze them for their juice."

"Lemon juice? Surely they'll dry us out more than hydrate us." Green protested.

"They'll dry out your mouth, that's true. The dryness is caused by ascetic acid, but there's still a lot of water in them. If you've any sugar, you can squeeze the lemons into a mess tin and stir the sugar in to sweeten it. If we have to rely on them, they'll keep us going for a couple of days, anyway."

"You seem to know a lot about lemons, Lucky." Green observed.

"You're not the only one that reads books." Carter grinned. "Actually, it was Lt Barraclough who told me. He used to come to Italy every summer. They have big lemon festivals during the harvest season. Pity it's not winter, though. These orange trees would be giving up their fruit.

"Ah, so that's why me mammy always made marmalade in the winter." O'Driscoll said, realisation hitting him.

"Yes, they ripen from December onwards. There's fruit on them now, as you see, but you'd be hard put to squeeze any juice out of them." Carter jerked his head upwards to indicate the trees under which they were sheltering.

"If life gives you lemons, make lemonade." Green quipped.[1]

"Very profound." Carter chuckled.

The Tiger tanks opened fire on the top of the ridge, preventing further discussion. Great gouts of soil were thrown up every ten seconds or so as the tanks targeted the concealed defences. Shrapnel buzzed through the air, bringing down branches from the orange trees and threatening the lives of any man foolish enough to stand upright. Carter and his men could only hunker down in whatever cover they could find. Carter took his men forward to 2 Troop's positions, where they had dug slit trenches and weapons pits for the mortars and machine guns. They could also see below the slope of the hill in front of them, all the way down to the river and work out what was going on.

The paratroops made another foray forwards, closing on the first Tiger to offer support, but the intensity of the fire from the top of the ridge sent them back again.

"We're getting low on mortar bombs." One of the troopers shouted above the noise of the bombardment, hurrying along the top of the ridge with a bomb in each hand and another tucked under each arm. The ground erupted in front of him as an 88mm shell exploded. When the debris had stopped falling and Carter could raise his head, he saw no sign of the man.

"Time for us to go." Carter said to his three companions.

"But the rest of the troop haven't moved out yet."

"I know, but we aren't going the same way as them. The safest thing for us to do is get off this ridge. We can do that by going straight down the rear. If we stay here much longer we're going to get killed. As soon as the mortars stop firing the Jerries will start moving forward. The Vickers will slow them down, but they won't stop them."

He forestalled any further discussion by duck-walking across the orange grove to the far side, then forcing a passage through the hedge. Prof Green shrugged his shoulders and followed his example.

[1] Although this saying is usually attributed to Dale Carnegie in his 1948 book. "How to Stop Worrying and Start Living", Carnegie himself said he got it from Julius Rosenwald, co-founder of Sears, Roebuck & Company. As Rosenwald died in 1932, the phrase must have been known before the war, though how Green came to be aware of it is another matter.

* * *

They were forced to stop and take cover when the sharp-eyed Danny Glass spotted a figure silhouetted against the skyline of the next ridge. They had travelled about a mile, down into the valley behind the ridge and over the next hill. They were just starting to descend into the next valley when Glass spotted the soldier.

There wasn't much in the way of cover close by, just a single stone wall separating one field from another. They pressed themselves hard against its base, lying prone, gripping their weapons tightly and hoping not to have to use them.

They had no idea how many enemy there might be, but the soldier wouldn't be alone. Typically a patrol would be made up of eight men, but it could be a whole company advancing.

The wait seemed to be interminable, but in reality was only a few minutes. They heard voices chatting as the men approached. They were speaking German, which probably meant they were more of the paratroops that had landed the previous night. They seemed relaxed.

But it only needed one of them to glance over the wall to see what was on the other side for the four commandos to be discovered. The first voices passed, but the tread of feet went on. This was more than an eight man patrol. Carter tried to count the footsteps as they passed, but each man's tread was overlaid onto that of the man in front or behind, making the counting difficult. When the last man had passed, Carter thought he had counted twenty sets of feet. Given the margin of error, that probably meant it was a full-strength platoon; twenty four men under the command of an officer.[1]

They stayed where they were for several more minutes. If the Germans were good soldiers, the last man in the file would be turning around at regular intervals to make sure there was no threat behind them. He might even walk backwards for some of the time. If the commandos stood up too soon, they would be seen.

Satisfied that the threat had finally passed, the four men rose to their feet. "Where do you think they were going?" Green asked.

"To the ridge above the river." Carter said. "Now the Jerries have captured it, they'll want to hold onto it and they don't know if we've withdrawn completely, or are just catching our breath before mounting a counterattack to retake the hill. There'll be patrols like that out all around, trying to locate us. We were lucky we saw that one before they saw us."

Putting the patrol out of his mind, Carter led them on up the slope of the next hill. But that was where the enemy had appeared, so they exercised some caution. About halfway down the other side was a small grove of lemon trees and Carter led them through it. Reaching up he plucked one of the fruit from a tree and sliced it in half with his commando dagger. Tilting his head back he raised half the fruit above his mouth and squeezed hard.

At once it felt as though his tongue had shrivelled up and his cheeks sunk in as the ascetic acid attacked his taste buds. The three troopers did their best to muffle their laughter as they saw a grimace of distaste cross their officer's face.

Working his jaw to try to summon some saliva back into his mouth, Carter spat what remained of the juice out. "Perhaps I'm not quite thirsty enough for lemon juice yet. But it would help if we could find some water."

The last valley had been formed by a stream, but the bed was dry where they had crossed it. July was high summer and there was very little water available from natural sources. Even beneath the shade of the lemon trees the heat was severe. Dehydration could incapacitate them just as severely as a bullet wound.

Glass's nose twitched and he turned to sniff the slight breeze that was coming up the gentle slope. "Do you smell that?"

With his senses still under attack from the lemon juice, Carter couldn't smell anything other than the fruit, but the others could.

"Someone's cooking something." Green said.

"Over there." O'Driscoll pointed down the hill and to one side, where a building stood. The light breeze was blowing straight up the hill from that direction.

"You've got the sharpest eyes, Danny. What do you make of it?" Carter asked.

"Looks like a farmhouse, with a walled garden on one side. The roof looks a bit shabby. There may be a hole in it. I'd say it was deserted, but I think that's where the smell is coming from."

"Can you see anybody? Soldiers or civilians."

"Not from this side. We'd have to get closer to take a look."

"That food smells delicious." O'Driscoll spoke their thoughts aloud. They'd been living on bully beef for almost the whole week, except for the few hours that they'd been on the Prince Leopold on their way to Agnone.

"Delicious enough to risk your life for?" Green asked.

"Delicious enough to risk my life and that of me Ma." The Irishman replied. He turned and gave Carter a pleading look.

"It would do no harm to get a bit closer. If there's enemy there we can still go around them."

The gentle hill looked as though it ended in another dry stream bed and that would give them enough cover to approach the farm. It would be above them on the same side as they were at the moment and the rear of the house would be facing them. A sentry in a rear window might see them. Carter wished he still had his binoculars, but they had been left behind in the slit trench when he made the dash up to the top of the ridge from the river.

Moving from one bit of scrubby cover to the next, they picked a careful path down to the bottom of the hill. It was a pity the quality of the soil wasn't better, then the fields might be thick with crops. As it was, goats would struggle to subsist on the meagre grass and bushes. But they had seen no sign of livestock, either. It seemed that at the first sign of the invading forces, the Sicilians had taken their animals and moved to somewhere they considered to be safer.

The stream had gouged itself a deep channel, strewn along the bottom with water smoothed boulders, some the size of a football. But the steep banks did allow the commandos to approach to within a hundred yards of the farm without being seen. Close up it was clearly a ruin. Great holes perforated the moss covered tiles of the sagging roof and the only window in the rear wall was empty of glass. But it also didn't have a sentry watching.

Glass swapped his Bren gun for Paddy O'Driscoll's rifle and clambered out of the stream bed without waiting to be asked. Carefully he crept up on the rear of the building before edging around the far side. He reappeared a few minutes later and returned to the stream bed.

"Six of them." He reported. "Italians. They're sat around a fire, cooking their lunch and drinking wine, by the look of it. No sign of any sentries."

"Can we take them?" O'Driscoll asked. He was practically drooling, even though they could no longer smell the food now that they were upwind.

"A Girl Guide with a blunt penknife could take them." Glass grinned.

"Well, Sorr?" O'Driscoll had his pleading look back on his face.

"How would you do it?" Carter asked Glass. He was the one who had seen the layout, so he was best placed to suggest a plan of attack.

"There's gate on the far side. It leads onto a track, which I guess joins the farm to the road. Two men can crawl around that side. I go down the top side with Paddy here. When we fire a burst from the

Bren the Ities will panic, then you jump up and threaten them and I'm pretty sure they'll just put their hands up."

"The Bren gun might attract attention if there are any more patrols in the area." Carter objected.

"A short burst wouldn't mean anything to anyone. It could just be a jumpy sentry. If a fire-fight breaks out, that would be different."

"Besides, Sorr," O'Driscoll grinned slyly. "There might be water there as well. After all, whoever lived there before must have drunk something other than just wine."

Carter knew he was beaten. To be truthful, he was just as hungry as them and anything other than bully beef was a treat that couldn't be missed. "OK. We'll take a chance. Prof, we'll go around this side, where the slope of the hill means we can stay below the top of the wall. Give us five minutes, Danny, then let go with that burst from the Bren. But keep it as short as you can."

Glass nodded his agreement. The four of them clambered out of the stream bed and split into pairs, Glass and O'Driscoll going to the left, up the slope, with Green and Carter keeping to the right.

As they got closer, Carter heard the sound of the Italian's voices. They were loud; boisterous. Glass had probably been right about them drinking, Carter thought. A burst of laughter rang out as one of them said something funny; or perhaps rude. Their noise made it easier for the two commandos to creep along the base of the wall.

Reaching the corner, Carter peered around. If there was a sentry, the place he might be was at the gate. But there was no one there. With German patrols roaming the countryside, the Italians seemed to feel secure. They hadn't considered the fact that the patrols were seeking out commandos, who were good at moving without being seen.

They duck walked the last few yards until Carter's face was resting against the mossy wood of the gatepost, driven into the ground where the stone wall ended. The gate itself hung open from the other post, on broken hinges. His thigh muscles screamed in protest at the strain being out on them, but Carter pushed the discomfort from his mind. He had suffered far worse.

Carter checked his watch; about thirty seconds to go, by his reckoning. He eased the safety catch off on his Tommy gun. He hoped he wouldn't have to fire it, but he needed to be ready, just in case.

The sound of the Bren gun split the air and Carter sprang to his feet, feeling Green do the same. He raised his Tommy gun to his shoulder, aiming directly at the group of Italians clustered around the fire. The six of them seemed to freeze in whatever position they had been when the weapon had fired. One even had a bottle half way to his mouth, as though about to take a drink.

Carter saw their rifles, stacked together in two triangular arrangements, their muzzles resting against each other in mutual support. They were several feet away, useless to the Italian soldiers. None of them seemed to be wearing a sidearm.

Slowly, one of the soldiers raised his hands above his head. One by one the others copied him. Carter stepped through the gateway, gesticulating with the muzzle of his gun that the Italians should move away from the fire to the side furthest from their weapons. They complied readily enough.

O'Driscoll and Glass climbed the wall and dropped down on the inside. The Italians eyed them warily. They were the ones who had fired, so they seemed to represent a greater threat in the minds of the Italians. They changed their direction, moving towards the corner formed by the two sides of the wall, further from the two troopers.

Carter used the muzzle of his Tommy gun to indicate that the prisoners should sit down, which they did, huddling together to give themselves the illusion of security. That suited Carter. It made them a bigger target, if they needed to shoot. He doubted they would have to. The Italians were showing no sign that they might resist.

The food was some sort of stew, rich and savoury. Empty tins littered the ground next to the fire, showing the origins of the food. The men got out their mess tins and Carter filled them. They weren't going to be caught like the Italians, though. The four of them took up positions that would allow them to see any approaching threat. They ate their food quickly, knowing that if the alarm had been raised they might have very little time.

The Italians watched the commandos eat what had been their lunch, giving them morose and hostile stares. Carter took pity on them and carried the pot over to their corner, placing it within reach and then withdrawing. The men found spoons in their leather equipment harnesses and took turns to eat.

"What are we going to do with the prisoners?" Green called across. "We can't really take them with us."

Carter hadn't given the matter much consideration, but the corporal was right. Dragging six prisoners around with them would be bound to give them away. Even if they were able to hide, the Italians could cry out at any moment. There really was only one option.

"We strip them of all their gear and send them down the road. They'll be picked up by their own side soon enough."

"They could come back and pick up their weapons and come after us."

"There's a well over this side." Glass chipped in. "We can throw their weapons down that."

"Good idea. We'll top up our canteens first, though. I don't want my water tasting of gun oil."

Finishing their food, Carter went over to the prisoners and mimed removing his clothing. The Italians seemed to get the idea and divested themselves of their equipment before removing jackets, shirts and trousers. Carter let them put their boots back on. Stopping them before they took off their underwear, Carter signed for them to heap the clothing and equipment up near the well.

While they had been doing that, Glass had taken their water canteens across to the well and drawn a bucketful of water up. "Smells fresh enough." He called across. He used the water to wash out his mess tin, then sent the bucket back down to be refilled. This time he used his mess tin to sample the water. "Yeah, tastes fine too."

Filling the canteens, Glass returned to the farmyard. Carter indicated to one of the men, the youngest looking, that he should pick all the gear up and start dropping it down the well. He made three trips before it had all been disposed of.

"Go." Carter said. "*Partire!*" He thought that the word might be French or even Spanish, but it did the trick and the six men headed off down the path, taking nervous looks behind them, suspicious that the commandos might shoot them as they 'tried to escape'. But Carter held his Tommy gun in the crook of his arm, the barrel pointing downwards, while the other three maintained their gaze out over their appointed sectors of the local terrain. The three men rested the butts of their weapons on the ground, the barrels pointing skywards.

Once the six men had disappeared around a bend, screened by a rise in the ground, Carter went over and dismantled one of the rifle stacks and carried the three weapons to the well. He was followed by Prof Green, who held the other three rifles. They dropped them into the well and heard them splash into the water.

Returning to the farmyard he called the others across to him. "I've been thinking …" he started.

"Oh no! He's come up with a new way of getting us killed." O'Driscoll laughed.

"Actually, you might be right." Carter responded with a chuckle. "But what is the job of the commandos?"

"To carry the fight to the enemy." Green said, reciting the lesson from memory.

"To disrupt his operations." Glass added.

"To degrade his ability to make war." O'Driscoll finished.

"Right. And now we have the perfect opportunity to do that. We've been trained to operate behind enemy lines and if we're not behind enemy lines now, we never will be."

"That's true enough. But aren't we supposed to be escaping? Shouldn't we be on our way to that Augusta place?" Green, as usual, was the spokesman for the group.

"The area between the river and the British frontline is crawling with German paratroops and Italians, not to mention Tiger tanks. If we try to get through there we'll probably be caught. I know the CO sounded optimistic when he gave us our orders, but I think that was just to keep up morale. The reality is it will be hard to get through there, especially in daylight."

"It'll be dark in a few hours." O'Driscoll said, glancing towards the sun, which was starting its long slide down the sky towards the western horizon. "The Germans are unlikely to patrol at night. We can just slip past them in the dark."

"Precisely. It will be dark soon. And when it does get dark, the Germans are going to start to use the road to re-supply their front line. We're ideally placed to disrupt that. We wait for their supply vehicles, shoot them up with the Bren gun and then slip away. The Germans will have to stop sending vehicles along the road while they try to hunt us down."

"Surely the Paras at that Primasole place will stop vehicles from going south." Glass said.

"The bridge they're holding, assuming they've held it, is only one of the bridges across the canal up near Catania. The Jerries can bypass the Paras, but they can't bypass our bridge. They have to cross that, build another bridge somewhere else or make a big detour inland and risk bumping into our army's left flank. Well, what do you think?"

There was silence for a few moments while the three troopers considered Carter's argument. They knew he was right about what their job was, but could the four of them do that much damage? Probably. Could they evade capture? At night they probably could. Did they have to do it? Well, it wasn't expected of them and Carter had offered them the chance to say no.

"The 50th Division are north eastern lads." Green said.

"So what?" Glass asked, puzzled.

"The Jarrow marchers were from the north east."

"It's always politics with you, isn't it, Prof?"

"Everything's about politics one way or another. This war is just politics by another means.[2] But this is different. The Jarrow marchers were my comrades, my brothers if you like. I raised money to feed them on the march. Some of those 50th Div lads will have had family members on it. I think I have a duty to help them and if disrupting the Jerry supply lines does that, then I'm in favour."[3]

"Paddy?" Carter looked towards the Irishman.

"Ach, sure, if you put it that way, then I'm OK."

Glass let out a resigned sigh. "You lot are going to get me killed one day, I know it. OK. Count me in as well."

Carter slapped him on the shoulder. "You know what they say, Danny. If you can't take a joke, you shouldn't have joined the army."

"I didn't 'join', I was conscripted." Glass grumped

"But you did volunteer for the commandos and you know we're not the sort to avoid a scrap."

"But we don't always have to go looking for one. It is OK to let the scrap come looking for us from time to time. But you three will only get yourselves killed if you haven't got me with you, so I better come along if only to save your necks."

"Good on yez, Danny." O'Driscoll gave him a playful punch on the arm.

"Right. That's settled. I think the more distance we put between ourselves and this farm the better, so we'll head north west and look for somewhere to mount an ambush before it gets dark.

[1] The author's father, on whose experience this section of the book is based, escaped detection in exactly this manner. It just goes to show how unobservant soldiers can be at times.

² A misquote of 18th century military philosopher Carl von Clauswitz, who actually said "War is the continuation of politics by other means".

³ Green is right to suppose that some of the men might have been from Jarrow. The full name of the division is 50th (Northumberland) Division. Although by that stage of the war it included infantry battalions from other parts of the country, the 161st Brigade was made up of the 6th, 8th and 9th battalions of the Durham Light Infantry. Jarrow and Durham are only eighteen miles apart and the regiment would have recruited from the area. The Jarrow March, also called the Jarrow Crusade, took place in October 1936 as a protest against unemployment and poverty in the north east, especially in the Tyneside area. In 1936 unemployment in the north east was 16.8%, having peaked at 28% in 1932. That was compared to a national average of 13.1% and only 7.3% in the South East, with unemployment in the ship building industry at 33%. The Jarrow march was the longest in a series of 'hunger marches' that had started in the 1920s. The march started with 200 men, of which 168 completed the whole journey, with 12 more coming in as replacements. 1,200 had volunteered to take part, but cost implications limited the numbers who could actually march. The marchers completed the 291 miles in 22 stages, the longest stage being 21 miles from Northampton to Bedford. The marchers were greeted in London by large crowds of supporters. Many commentators regard the Jarrow march as significant in triggering the sorts of social reforms that were to take place after the Second World War.

9 – *Kommandobefehl*

In the open farmland through which the road ran, finding a suitable ambush site wasn't easy, but not impossible. At one point the road ran through a shallow cutting, the banks barely head high to someone standing on the road.

"If we can stop a vehicle there," Carter pointed to the southern end of the cutting, "any other vehicles will be trapped behind until the driver of the rear vehicle works out what's going on and reverses out. If we can wreck the vehicle, the road will be blocked until recovery equipment can be brought up to clear the road. That could take half the night."

They chose the site for the Bren gun, giving it the best line of fire along the road. They didn't really have enough men for a proper ambush; one that would take out an entire convoy in one go. For that they'd have to have many more men, including those acting as "stops" before and after the cutting. The ones before would give advance warning of what was coming. They didn't want to ambush troops, because they would fight back. Cutting off supplies, however, was another matter. The men after the ambush were supposed to give the ambush a second crack of the whip, stopping any vehicle that managed to break through the initial attack.

Four men couldn't achieve that sort of effectiveness. If they managed to stop a single vehicle it would be a victory. Anything more than that would be a triumph.

Looking upwards, Carter tried to gauge how long they had before sunset. Not much more than two hours, he decided. But they couldn't hang around on the side of the road in daylight. They were too visible. "Come on. We'll go and find somewhere to lie up for a couple of hours." He said, leading them into the fields on the opposite side of the road.

They found a corner formed by two of the ubiquitous stone walls. Carter wondered if all they really farmed in the area was rocks, there were so many of them making up the walls that divided the fields.

The walls had crumbled, but their debris was high enough to provide cover, but low enough so that he could lie down behind them and keep watch.

"You three get some sleep. I'll keep watch." Carter ordered.

"Shouldn't we take turns?" Green asked.

"We're only going to be here a couple of hours. Not much point waking people up every half hour to change shifts. No, I'll take the watch and I'll take a nap after we've set up the ambush and we're waiting for something to come along the road."

Carter knew how tired the men must be. They hadn't really had a chance to sleep since they had formed up to march back to the beach at four o'clock the previous morning. Had that been only thirty six or seven hours before? It seemed like a lifetime. Once back on the Prince Leopold, the men had barely had time to clean their weapons and repair their kit before they'd had to start preparing for this operation. Carter himself had snatched barely an hour of fitful sleep between delivering the final briefing and being called up on deck to board the landing craft.

With little to occupy his mind, it turned to thoughts of home. He missed his wife, he realised. It had been nearly eight months since he had last seen her, during the brief time he had been allowed home before they had taken ship for Gibraltar. He had children now; twins born while he had been in Gibraltar, a boy and a girl. Children he had never seen; might never see. A lump formed in his throat as he contemplated that possibility.

Carter shifted his position, removing a stone that was digging into his thigh. He wondered what they were like. Had they started walking yet? At what age did children start to walk? He realised he had no idea. He would have to ask in his next letter home.

The last thing he had done before allowing himself that short nap, had been to write a new 'goodbye letter'. These were letters that some of the soldiers left in the care of the ship's captain, so that if they failed to return, they could be sent to their loved ones. Carter tried to keep his up to date, fresh, so that Fiona would know that he had been thinking of her before he had gone ashore. He took particular care to make sure that it was dated for the day they would fight, rather than the day it had been written. He had added a page for each of the children he might never see, so that when they grew a little, they would know that he was thinking of them.

Which made his mind wander to wondering when the mail might catch up with them. The last letters they'd received were several months old, posted before they'd even left Gibraltar for their new base in Algeria. Since then they'd crossed the whole continent, from west to east and then travelled back to Europe. The mail had yet to catch up with their meandering course.

Carter had hoped to see something of the world when he had joined the army, but he didn't think he'd see quite as much of it as he had in the last few months.

* * *

The prodding in his chest woke Carter, insisting on him paying attention. He groaned, realising that he had committed the biggest sin that a soldier on guard duty could commit. He had fallen asleep. If one of his men had done that he would have been on a charge. He forced his eyes open, when all they really wanted to do was stay closed.

The prodding continued persistently. Carter saw what was doing it; a booted foot. His eyes opened wide in realisation of what he was seeing. That boot had never seen the inside of a British Quarter Master's store. It was a high topped boot, with trousers tucked into the neck. The British wore gaiters to stop their trouser bottoms flapping about and snagging on things. Carter turned his head, continuing to raise his eyes along the body of the man standing over him. Above the trousers was a smock made of some sort of disruptive pattern material, that gave it a camouflaged effect. It was belted in the middle, with the belt attached to a leather equipment harness.

The man was standing in front of the sun, so his face was in darkness, silhouetted against the bright light, but there was no mistaking the shape of the helmet on his head. Carter reached out to pick up his Tommy gun, but realised it wasn't where it should have been. He sat up.

What about his men? Had they escaped. He looked around to see that they hadn't. They, too, had just been woken. Glass rubbed at his eyes, the other two looked bemused. Arrayed around them were German paratroops, all levelling their weapons at the commandos. They must have been unable to believe their luck, finding four of Britain's elite fighting force sleeping like babies, just waiting to be woken up and taken prisoner.

The soldier who had woken Carter took a couple of paces backwards, making room so that Carter couldn't attempt to grab him. He jerked his rifle barrel upwards: Get up!

Carter obeyed, moving slowly so as not to panic the German into pulling the trigger of his rifle.

The paratrooper pulled at his own equipment harness, indicating that Carter should remove his. A wise precaution. Who knew what a commando might be carrying in his kit that could kill a man. Carter did as instructed.

After Carter had dropped his kit on the ground, the paratrooper bent down and pulled Carter's commando dagger from its scabbard, smiling at his prize. It was only natural that he should covet such a trophy, Carter thought. Nestling at the bottom of his own kitbag, back on board the Prince Leopold, was a Luger pistol that Carter had taken from a German officer in Tunisia.

"*Bring seine Ausrüstung hier*!" A voice commanded, changing the paratrooper's smile to a scowl. The man who had spoken was holding a Schmeisser machine pistol, making him an NCO or an officer. NCO probably, Carter concluded from the size of the group. He was pulling rank to claim Carter's dagger. The soldier reluctantly handed over the webbing harness and all its treasures.

The other three commandos were also being divested of their equipement, before being subjected to a search of their pockets. Their weapons and equipment were shared out amongst the eight Germans, spreading the burden around. The NCO gave an order and two of the paratroopers clambered over the wall and started walking back towards the road. One of them carried an MG 42 machine gun, while the other was festooned with ammunition belts. Carter was prodded in the back by the paratroop that had searched him. "*Gehen!*" The soldier shouted.

Carter had no idea what *'gehen'* meant, but it suggested 'go', so he followed the machine gunner and his loader over the wall and started walking towards the road. Behind him the tramp of boots told him the rest of the patrol and their prisoners were following.

They headed south, back towards the river. The pace was unhurried. After about a mile, the leader turned right, onto a side road which led, after about another half mile, to a large house. The house was surrounded by high walls, into which was set outbuildings. Sentries stood alert outside the gate and Carter could see the barrel of a machine gun projecting from an upper window.

They were led inside, attracting curious stares from the sentries. Words were exchanged between them and the new arrivals, with some laughter. Carter had the feeling it was they who were the butt of the joke. This was confirmed when one of their escort made a snoring sound, producing more laughter.

The patrol came to a halt and Green, O'Driscoll and Glass were prodded with rifles, moving them away from Carter. Their destination was one of the outbuildings. But Carter was led forward into the farmhouse itself.

The building was well maintained but empty except for military equipment. Whoever owned the house had removed all their possessions when they had fled the area. In one room Carter could see a soldier crouching over a radio set. Carter was prodded again, urging him to continue forward. He was getting heartily sick of being prodded.

The interior of the house was unlit, giving everything a gloomy air as the sun set and twilight arrived. Carter was pushed into a room that was dominated by a large iron cooking range at one end. A door was lying across some ammunition boxes that were acting as trestles, forming a table on which a map was spread out. To Carter's experienced eye it looked like a road map, rather than one that had been created for military use. Behind the makeshift table stood an officer, recognisable as such only because he wore a holster on his belt. Otherwise he was dressed in the same garb as the rest of the Germans. Seeing Carter being escorted into the room he straightened up.

"Name!" he snapped.

"Carter. Captain." Carter gave the required information. "Do you want my service number?"

"That won't be necessary right now. If you promise not to attempt to escape, I will dismiss your escort."

"I promise." Carter said, not meaning it. If the opportunity arose, he would be off like a shot.

The officer exchanged some words with the paratroopers, obviously some sort of report on the capture of the commandos, then he dismissed the two men who had provided Carter's escort. "I am *Major* Klaus Gerhardt, second in command of the 1st *Fallschirmjäger* Regiment. My Commanding officer sends his apologies, but he is detained elsewhere." Carter doubted the commanding officer even knew of their existence, but it was a courteous thing for the German officer to say. "I have to say, we were rather surprised to find commandos in the area."

"You came as rather surprise to us, as well." Carter replied, a grim smile on his lips. Perhaps if they had engaged the Germans the previous night, they might have avoided the battle for the bridge. But hindsight was such a perfect tool.

The German laughed. "Not as surprised as we are to be here. Until a few days ago we were expecting to go to Sardinia. It seems that Berlin expected your Italian landings to start there. It was only two days ago that our orders were changed. We haven't even got enough maps!" Gerhardt seemed angry, glaring at the sheet of paper spread out across the table.

"We had something of a similar problem." Carter admitted. "We were also surprised to find Tiger tanks here."

The German expression changed and he beamed a smile. "Yes, the Herman Goering *Panzer* Division. I suspect that in keeping them here, *Generalfeldmarschall* Kesselring disobeyed an order. We have to be happy that he did so. Had he, not, your army would already be in Catania. Instead, they are still in Lentini."

"Probably not for long. We have two complete armies in Sicily, one British and one American."

"Of that we are aware. But we don't have to stop you here; we only have to slow you down while we prepare defences in Italy. You will not find it so easy to land there as you did here."

There was little point in debating strategy with the Major. They both knew that in warfare it was numbers that counted and, for the present, the Allies had the necessary numbers.

"I take it that yours is the regiment that is now occupying the bridge." Carter said, more for something to say than because he was really interested.

"Yes. We should really be engaged in Lentini, but now that we know your intentions ..." He didn't need to say anything more. "Your men fought bravely. Can I ask what your orders are now?"

"You know that I can't answer that."

The German laughed "Perhaps you don't have to. Only four of you were captured by my men, and similar numbers have been captured elsewhere. You have dispersed and are now trying to get back to your lines. I must wonder at what you were doing so far north. I don't believe you were lost."

"We were just trying to stay concealed." Carter lied. There was no point in telling the German what they had really intended. "We were going to stay hidden until our relief force arrived. Your men got lucky."

"That is not what I was told. You were all sleeping. I am surprised at that." The note of censure was clear in the German's voice, one professional criticising the actions of another.

Carter decided to say nothing. He felt bad enough as it was, without having to admit his faults to an enemy.

There was the sound of raised voices behind Carter, in the entrance hall of the house. Gerhardt strained to see around Carter and identify the problem. There was the clatter of metal shod heels on the tiled floor and another officer strode into the room. From his uniform Carter knew at once that he wasn't a paratrooper. For a start he was wearing knee length boots. Jackboots as they were sometimes called. In the gloom the colour of his uniform was hard to make out, but it looked like the *Feldgrau*[1] of the army. But his cap gave away his real identity. The cap badge was the skull and crossbones of the *Waffen SS*.

There was an arrogance about the man, Carter noted. He expected everyone to defer to him. But *Major* Gerhardt wasn't about to defer to anyone, least of all an SS officer.

Carter couldn't understand any of the conversation between the two men, but he could tell it was becoming heated. The SS man was the first to start raising his voice, while Gerhardt appeared to remain calm, but whatever was being discussed raised the Major's hackles. When the two men practically bawling at each other, two paratroops hurried into the room. One was the NCO that had commanded the patrol that had captured Carter and his men. He clutched his Schmeisser, not in a threatening manner, but one that made it clear that he might use it if need be.

The SS man fell into a stony-faced silence, glaring at the paratroops, before raising his index finger and pointing it at Carter, while addressing the paratroop officer. He said a few final words then stormed from the room.

"I regret that outburst." The German said, as his two men followed the SS man from the room. Whether they thought there was no further need of their presence, or whether they were making sure the SS man had left, Carter couldn't be sure. Perhaps it was both.

"I take it that was about me?"

"It was. That is *Sturmbannführer* Goessler. He is apparently from the Catania security detachment. He has heard that there are commando prisoners being held in our area and has come to get them. He demanded that I hand you over for execution under the *Kommandobefehl*[2]. You have heard of it?"

"We hear of most things that relate to you *Führer's* opinion of us." Carter answer was non-comital.

"The *Sturmbannführer* is quite determined to take you, but I have refused to allow it. Although he is a member of the SS, we are of equal rank and technically he can't give me orders. However, he has said he will return and when he does I expect him to be in the company of *Feldgendarmerie* and will have a written order from someone who I can't ignore. If that should happen, I won't have any choice but to hand you over. If I fail to do so I will be arrested and will probably be executed alongside you. I am sorry *Hauptman* Carter."

"I understand, *Herr Major*. Will he take my men as well?"

"Perhaps not. He only seemed to be interested in officers. He asked if I had any others and I told him I didn't."

"Do you?"

"I have an *Oberleutnant* who is wounded. He will die, I think because I can't get him to proper medical treatment right now. I would rather he died peacefully here with me than was tied to a post in front of a firing squad."

"May I see him? If he knows I'm here it may give him some comfort."

"Of course. He is in the same accommodation as your men. I was about to ask you to join them anyway, before we were so rudely interrupted." The German extended his hand. "I am truly sorry, *Hauptman* Carter. As one soldier to another I respect you and would wish that we could meet in happier times."

Carter shook the man's hand. It seemed the right thing to do. He was trying to behave in a civilised manner, as required by the rules of war, if there were such things. It wasn't his fault that his country was being run by barbarians.

Gerhardt called out and the NCO returned to collect Carter. He was escorted from the building and across the yard to one of the outbuildings. The door had a sturdy lock, Carter noted, as the NCO opened it. He was shoved inside and the door slammed shut behind him, the key grating in the lock as it was turned once more. The darkness inside was almost total. The sun had set and twilight had become night while he had been inside the house. The inside of the building smelt of manure, suggesting that its former occupants had been four-legged.

"Prof, Paddy, Danny?" Carter called into the darkness.

"Over here, Lucky." Carter recognised Green's voice. The three men were sat with their backs to the exterior wall.

"I'm so sorry, men. I let you down. I fell asleep on guard duty." Carter admitted. It was probably a good thing that they couldn't see the stark expression on his face.

"It happens, Lucky." Green said.

"It's happened to me." O'Driscoll admitted. It didn't make Carter feel any better to know that. Whenever it was that O'Driscoll had fallen asleep, it hadn't resulted in them being captured, or killed.

"You're very quiet, Danny." Carter observed. Such silence from the Londoner was unusual. He had an opinion on just about everything.

"Not much to say, Sir."

The use of his rank at that time didn't bode well, Carter thought.

"You must have something to say. Swear at me. Call me a bastard. Whatever. I deserve it."

"Whatever I say, it won't get us out of here."

Carter wanted to tell him that it could be a lot worse; that the SS wanted to execute him but weren't interested in any of the others.

But that wouldn't help. Trying to make Glass feel guilty about his officer's fate wasn't the answer to anything.

"I was told there's an injured man in here with us."

"Yes, he's over there, to our right, against the side wall." Green told him. "The Jerries have patched him up, but he's in a bad way."

"Do we know who he is?"

There was silence for a second, then O'Driscoll coughed, as though he was having trouble speaking. "Er ... yes Sorr. It's Lt Murray."

Arthur Murray. It wasn't too much of a surprise. The man had been seriously injured the last time he had seen him. But he hadn't appeared to be near death. Carter felt his way across the room, like a child playing blind man's buff[3], until his hands made contact with the wall, then he crouched down, searching the ground by touch, seeking out Murray. He was helped by the sound of Murray's breath rasping in his throat. Carter touched Murray's head, feeling his soaking wet hair, then his face. He was covered in sweat to the point where rivulets were running down the side of his neck.

"Arthur? Can you hear me?" He got a soft groan by way of reply.

"Don't try to speak, Arthur." He continued his examination. Murray's shirt gaped open, his chest also slick with perspiration. Around his stomach was wound a bandage. That was new, Carter realised. Murray's original injury had been to his thigh; painful but not necessarily terminal. A stomach wound was another matter entirely, as all soldiers knew. How Murray has suffered his wound, Carter could only imagine. It might have been shrapnel from one of the 88mm shells, or it could have been a bullet or a bayonet when the paratroops finally assaulted the top of the hill. It made no difference.

Murray grabbed Carter's hand. "Water!" he rasped.

During their first aid training, the commandos had been told not to give water to a man with a stomach wound. Why had never been explained, but it hardly seemed to matter now.

"Have we any water?" Carter asked.

"No. Let's see if we can get some though." Prof Green answered. Carter heard him move towards the door, just a slightly paler line around it showing where it was. A fist thudded against it. "*Wasser! Wasser bitte.*"

"*Schweigen!*" Came a shout from outside. "Silence" it was repeated in English

"Our comrade ... *Kamerad* ... is sick. He needs water. *Wasser bitte.*"

"Wait!" They heard feet crunching their way across the yard. It was only moments before they heard them returning. The key turned in the lock. "Back!" the soldier ordered.

Green backed away from the door, just as it swung open. Something was thrown into the room to land with a heavy thud, then the door was shut and locked once more. Green scrabbled around on the floor until he found the object, then took it across to Carter.

"I think it's one of our own canteens." He observed, as he handed it over.

Carter pulled the cork from the top and bent down over Murray again, tilting the canteen to dribble some water between the injured man's lips. "More." Murray rasped. Carter repeated the dosage. "Thanks." Murray said, slightly more audibly.

"How are you feeling?" Carter asked.

"Apart ..." he struggled to get the word out, "Apart ... from ... a hole ... in my ... thigh and ... another ... in my ... belly ... I'm ... just ... dandy." He finished with what might have been a chuckle but might also have been a cough.

"You'll be OK. You'll pull through, you'll see." Carter tried to reassure him.

"Don't ... lie ... to me ... Lucky." This time he did cough. "I won't ... see the ... sun rise." He coughed again. "More ... water."

Carter fed him some more water. Murray fell silent and it was only the rasping of his breath that told Carter he was still alive.

The silence became oppressive, Carter locked in the misery of what he had allowed to happen, the others because they had nothing to say and Murray too ill to speak anyway.

[1] Although the *Allgemeine* and *Waffen* SS originally wore black uniforms, from 1940 onwards they wore the standard Field Grey, or *Feldgrau*, of the *Wehrmacht*. The last mass wearing of black uniforms by the SS was at the victory parade held in Paris in June 1940.

[2] The infamous Commando Order or *Kommandobefehl* was issued on the instructions of Adolf Hitler on 18th October 1942 and stated that all commandos/special forces personnel who were captured, even those in uniform, were to be executed without trial. Only twelve written copies were produced, which allowed some German officers to avoid implementing it on the grounds that they hadn't seen or heard of it. It is unclear how many men died as a direct consequence of the *Kommandobefehl*, but it is probably over a hundred.

[3] Sometimes called "blind man's bluff", but according to the Encyclopedia Brittanica the correct terminology is "buff".

* * *

The evening wore on, the stifling air inside the outbuilding depressing their spirits. Carter had his own problems to think about but decided not to mention the *Kommandobefehl* to his fellow prisoners. If the SS officer hadn't seemed interested in the other men, there was no point in worrying them about something that might not happen.

For Carter, though, it was a different matter. Would he be able to face death bravely when it came? As a commando he was used to the idea that he might be killed in action, but he had always thought that he would hardly know it had happened. One day he would be charging an enemy position, or the enemy would be charging him and then he'd take a bullet and that would be that. But this would be different. This would be him being stood in front of a firing squad, able to see the enemy soldiers as they marched up to carry out their orders.

He'd heard that a lot of resistance fighters and partisans had been forced to kneel and were shot in the back of the head. Is that how they would deal with him? Would that be a better way to go, unable to see the gun pointing at him?

Despite the warmth of the night, a shiver ran down Carter's spine.

Feet crunched across the farmyard. Probably time to change the sentries, Carter thought. Or was this it? Was the *Sturmbannführer* coming to collect him? Carter heard voices talking. One was firm and commanding, while the other seemed puzzled. Carter wished he knew more German, or any German for that matter. But a conclusion had been reached. Boots marched away, but whose they were couldn't be guessed.

The key grated as it was turned in the lock. Carter expected the door to be swung open and for soldiers to come in and seize him. But the door remained shut. Well, almost shut; its own weight opened it a crack.

"What's going on?" Prof whispered.

"No idea. The door's been unlocked, but I don't know why."

"Hang on, I'll take a look." Green could be heard crossing the room. The thicker line of moonlight was extinguished as his body blocked it out. Then the door opened wider, before closing again.

"I think it might be a trap." Green said. "There's no guard outside the door and I can't see any sentries around the house or the yard. But I bet if we step through the door we'll be shot for trying to escape."

"No, I don't think that will happen." Carter was as puzzled as Green, but he didn't suspect a trap. "I've met the officer in charge here; seems like a decent sort of chap, for a Jerry. He …" Carter was torn about whether to tell them about the SS officer. But it provided an explanation for what seemed to be happening. "You've heard of the *Kommandobefehl*, haven't you?"

"The Hitler Order, you mean?"

"Yes. Well, there was an SS officer here earlier, wanted to take me away to be shot. But the Major in charge wouldn't let him. It wouldn't make any sense for him to now have us all shot for trying to escape."

"So, you think he might be letting us go?"

"The evidence points that way. It keeps his conscience clear. If we get captured again, that's another matter, of course. I doubt if the good Major has given orders for us to be escorted from the area, even if he's happy to see us steal away into the night."

"What about Lt Murray?" Driscoll asked. "We can't just leave him."

"We haven't any option." Carter said, hating having to make the decision. "If we try to move him, he's going to die."

"And if he's here when that SS officer comes back he'll be shot." Glass said.

"If he lasts that long" O'Driscoll muttered, but they heard him anyway.

Arthur Murray made the decision for them. "Go!" he croaked. "I'm … a dead … man anyway … Can't … kill me … twice." The effort was too much for him and he fell silent.

"If we're going, we better go now." Green said, opening the door wide. "If we stay here debating it, the Germans will get bored and lock the door again."

There was no arguing with the logic. Whatever Major Gerhardt had said to persuade his men to turn a blind eye, they couldn't be allowed to think about it for long. It was an offer that would be withdrawn if it wasn't accepted quickly.

"OK. We go now. Prof, Danny; get over to the gate and make sure the road is clear as well. Paddy, you keep watch on the house."

Turning away from the door, Carter felt around until he located Murray in the darkness. He grasped his hand. "Sorry, old chap. I hate leaving you like this."

"Not ... your ... fault." He gasped. "Just the ... fucking ... war."

"The water canteen is right by your hand." Carter pressed Murray's hand to the object, so he could be sure of its location.

"Don't ... think ... I can ... get cork ..."

Carter drew the cork out and then stood the canteen on its narrow base, so that it wouldn't empty itself. He folded Murray's hand around it, but he was barely able to grip. But it was all Carter could do for him.

"Goodbye, Arthur." Carter said.

"Bye ... Lucky."

Maybe it was a tear that rolled down Carter's cheek, but Carter persuaded himself it was sweat. Commandos don't cry. It's in the rule book, he told himself. He straightened up and crossed to the door.

"Come on, Paddy. Let's go."

Sparing time to glance towards the house, Carter could see the faint glimmer of an oil lamp, the shadows it was casting moving in the darkness. But outside the house the sentries were absent. Although the muzzle of the machine gun in the upstairs window was still present, Carter couldn't see the shape of a gunner behind it.

They ran across to the gate, which stood wide open. It was the same story; no sign of guards. Glass and O'Driscoll were crouched in its shadow, waiting.

"I thought you two were never coming." Glass hissed.

"Well, we're here now. We go down the road until we're out of sight of the house, then we cut to the right of the path. That will take us towards our own lines." He led the way, knowing the other three would follow. Without his weapons Carter felt naked. If they were found by another patrol they would have no choice but to surrender again. As they ran along the path they heard noises behind them, like someone trying to break down a door. Major Gerhardt, no doubt, concocting his cover story for their escape.

They heard the sound of engines, at least three vehicles. Carter led them off the road and they crouched behind a scrubby bush. It offered no real concealment, but the night was their real protection.

The first vehicle to pass was a motorcycle combination; typical of the way the *Feldgendarmerie* travelled. The second vehicle was a *Kübelwagen* , a convertible with its canopy down. As well as the driver, there was someone else in the rear. Finally came a small truck, just the right size to carry a single prisoner and his guards. They had escaped just in time, Carter suspected.

They waited until the vehicles were out if sight and then stood up, returned to the road and started to run again. If that was the SS officer, he would order the small force of paratroopers to go and search for the escapees. Carter had no desire to be in the vicinity when that happened. Deciding they had gone far enough, Carter turned off the road and led them into the barren fields. There, progress was slower as they had to negotiate rough ground as well as clamber over walls, but the longer they went without being seen, the more likely it would be that they would escape.

10- Montgomery

Sensing the men were getting tired, Carter brought them to a halt at the bottom of a valley. "I think this next hill is the one that overlooks the river." Carter said as they sat catching their breath. "If there are any Jerry patrols about, that's where they're likely to be."

After ten minutes he led them on, up the hill. They went at a walk, anxious not to make too much noise. The summit of the hill was barren, but below them they could make out the dark scar that marked the ravine through which the Gabriel river ran.

"It's very quiet." Carter whispered, as they paused to search out any sign of the enemy. On the horizon there was the occasional flash of artillery fire, followed by a distant rumble, showing where the battle for Lentini was still being fought. Star shells soared skywards to light up the disputed areas, interspersed with smaller parachute flares where the soldiers in the front line tried to prevent enemy patrols from infiltrating their defences. But the ridge itself was quiet.

"Surely that's a good thing." Green observed.

"It is; but it's also a bit odd. The ravine and this ridge make a natural defence line. Tanks can't cross the ravine except across the bridge and infantry would have a lot of open ground to cover to take this hill. It would be a real bugger. There should be pioneers crawling all over the area, digging trenches and gun pits, ready for the Germans to fall back."

"Looks like they're not going to defend it then."

"They're too thinly stretched to defend it." Carter concluded. "They can defend the bridge, but they can't cover their flanks. Which means that the infantry can cross up and down stream of the bridge and get around behind them. They must be planning to defend somewhere else."

"What about the bridge? Will they be there now?"

"Oh yes. They need that for their withdrawal. Then they'll blow it up as the first units of 50th Div get close."

"All those men killed to take it and hold it. What a waste." O'Driscoll whispered. Carter didn't know if he was meant to hear it, or if it was just Paddy reflecting on what had happened.

"Not wasted. It's what we do. We're expendable, which is why we aren't attached to a division. All those Jerry paratroops that are here, holding that bridge now, should be down in Lentini, making things even tougher for our boys there. It wasn't quite what was planned, but our boys didn't give their lives for nothing."

They heard the sound of engines and made out the shape of half a dozen trucks crossing the river, heading south.

"But they're still getting supplies through." Green observed.

There was an explosion, followed by the chatter of small arms fire and the lead truck came to a stop, causing the second in the convoy to run into the back of it. The other trucks pulled to a more controlled halt, but the four commandos could see the strike of bullets where sparks flashed off metal.

"Not necessarily." Carter chuckled. "It seems some of our lads are still down there making a nuisance of themselves." It was what he had planned to do with the four of them, had he not let them down by falling asleep.

Heavy machine guns opened up from the area in front of the bridge as the Germans tried to lay down covering fire to protect the convoy, but they couldn't use mortars for fear of hitting their own trucks. Carter doubted that the machine guns would do more than scare a few rabbits.

A parachute flare soared skywards as the Germans tried to illuminate their targets, but Carter could see no sign of the attackers. They were commandos, he'd have been disappointed if he had been able to pick them out.

The gunfire around the trucks themselves stopped as the hidden attackers withdrew. Fire licked along the canvass side of the first damaged truck., It wouldn't be delivering whatever was on board. They could hear the laboured engines of the other vehicles as they saw them turn off the road to try to get around the obstruction. More small arms fire opened up as other hidden attackers intervened, helped by the bright light of the flare as it swung beneath its small parachute. It was a classic two stage ambush. The rear truck came to a halt, backed up onto the road and turned to head back towards the bridge. The other three slid to a halt and Carter suspected the crews had been killed in the second ambush.

The flare flickered out but there was still some illumination, because the fire in the truck had taken hold and a column of flame rose into the air. In the distance Carter saw the flash of artillery, then a round exploded close to the burning vehicles.

"They'll hit our lads." O'Driscoll protested loudly.

"Shush!" Carter silenced him. "We can still be heard if there's a listening post close by. The artillery don't even know what caused that fire. All they know is there's something burning so they're giving it a few rounds. They must have forward observers out." It also meant that there was now British artillery within range, suggesting that some progress had been made around Lentini.

The artillery had the stricken trucks bracketed[1] and were raining shells down onto them. One of the trucks exploded, throwing bits of vehicle and burning cargo around the area, spreading more flames, which caught some of the vegetation in the area. Then the artillery ceased firing just as suddenly as it had started.

"The front line must be quite close." Green suggested.

"Not necessarily. If those were twenty five pounders,[2] then they could be seven miles away."

"But the front line will be closer." O'Driscoll said. "You won't find any gunners in the front line." It was an old slur made by the infantry against their colleagues in the Royal Artillery, going all the way back to the Napoleonic wars and earlier.

"It's still far enough away to make it difficult for us to get there." Carter reminded them in a whisper. "The Germans will have patrols out hunting our lads and we could bump into one of them at any time. But so long as it's dark, we still have a chance."

Heavy footsteps sounded from the top of the hill and the commandos fell silent, as they sought out their origins. They were coming from their right, the side furthest from the bridge. Probably a patrol. Quietly they slid backwards, away from the highest point of the ridge.

The patrol crossed in front of them, silhouetted against the stars and the occasional flash of artillery fire. Carter counted them; at least twenty four. A full platoon. If they had been protecting the flank of the bridge against an approach by the British, they should have remained in their positions, which suggested they had been out hunting for the commandos. Carter waited until the sound of their footsteps had faded into the darkness. That had been close.

The Germans had been hurrying, Carter had noted; moving too fast to carry out a proper search of the ridge. Perhaps they had interpreted the artillery barrage as being the prelude to an attack by the British. If that were the case, they wouldn't have wanted to become isolated.

Carter drew his three companions close to him again, so that he could speak in a whisper. "On the far side of the river, the Jerries will probably have listening posts. We need to move to our right a bit more before we try to cross. I think a thousand yards should do it. Once we're over, we'll head straight south until we come to our front lines. That artillery strike on the Jerry trucks means that the artillery must be on this side of the town by now and that means 50th Div are on their way. We'll run into them soon after daybreak, I'd have thought."

"We could just wait here." Glass said.

"We could, but as we just saw, they Jerries have got patrols out. It's what I'd do if we were still on the bridge. We can't risk them finding us up here. Besides, If I were leading an attacking force, I'd bombard this ridge just in case the enemy had dug in. We don't want to risk being blown up by our own guns. Not after all we've been through."

That settled the argument. Carter rose from the ground and led them along the top of the ridge, keeping just below the summit in order not to be seen as a silhouette against the sky.

[1] When artillery is firing accurately onto a small target it is said to have 'bracketed' it, the way that words are confined within brackets to separate them from the rest of the text.

[2] The QF 25 lb Field Gun was the standard medium range artillery piece in use with the Royal Artillery. The "QF" means it is quick firing, having a firing rate of up to 5 rounds per minute for short periods. It had a maximum range of about seven miles. First introduced in 1930, it was produced in large quantities during World War II and remained in use with the British Army until it was replaced by the 105mm Light Gun during the 1960s. The replacement was essentially the same weapon with a metric calibre barrel which made it compatible with the ammunition of its NATO allies. The 25 lb Field Gun still remains in service in some countries around the world and its last known use in combat was by the Kurdish Peshmerga against ISIS positions in Mosul, Iraq, in 2017.

* * *

Their descent into the riverbed presented a challenge. It would have been difficult in daylight, but at night, with no way to see where they were putting their feet, every step offered an opportunity to slip and tumble down the side of the steep slope. At the very least there was the risk of sending a loose rock sliding down, making a noise loud enough to alert the enemy to their presence.

Carter thought they had travelled far enough west to get around any enemy patrols, but he couldn't be sure. They may have left the area covered by the regiment that held the bridge, only to enter the operating area of a different paratroop regiment.

But they reached the bottom without mishap and stopped to take a drink from the shallow river before starting the slow climb up the other side. The hazards were just as tricky. The dry season had made the granules of soil shrink, so they weren't packed so tightly around stones and rocks. Carter placed his foot on one outcropping, which he thought was firm, only to have it roll out from under him to tumble to the bottom of the ravine and land with a splash which seemed to echo for ages. They held their breath, expecting a challenge, but none came.

It nearly happened a second time, but this time Carter was ready. As soon as the stone started to shift he lifted his weight off it and moved it to another, firmer, toe hold.

At last they reached the top, lying on their bellies while they listened to the night time sounds, seeking out any noise that didn't fit. All they heard was the chirp of cicadas and the distant rumbling of artillery fire as the battle for Lentini continued unabated. Montgomery wasn't allowing the German and Italian defenders any time to rest and resupply.

Satisfied that they were still undetected, Carter led the men forward again. They crossed a wall, no doubt placed to prevent animals from wandering into the ravine, then made their way across a series of fields. All were empty, waiting for the autumn rains so that crops could be grown once again, or for the grass to regrow so it could feed the animals. This far south the growing seasons were almost reversed when compared to the damper British climate.

Danny Glass was leading. Carter saw his arm go up to warn them to stop, then he lowered himself to the ground. Carter crept forward to lie beside him.

"Smell that?" Glass breathed into Carter's ear as he lowered himself beside him.

Carter sniffed the air. He caught the scent almost at once: petrol. "Yes, I can smell it." he breathed back

"I'd lay odds there's a tank ahead of us." Glass whispered again. "Maybe more than one."

The burst of a star shell in the distance helped to silhouette a large object. The angular shape in front of them couldn't be anything other than manmade, that was certain. Nature didn't create smooth surfaces and sharp corners like that.

"I'll go." Glass said, raising himself onto his elbows in preparation for crawling forward.

"No. I'll go this time." He didn't need to add that he had a debt to repay and by risking his life he might make some reparation for his failure the previous afternoon. Glass didn't argue. Of the three troopers, he had been the one who was least forgiving.

Carter didn't take any risks, kitten crawling[1] his way towards the target, going around the low bushes and outcroppings of grass, rather than trying to push through them. He used only his toes and forearms to move himself, raising his body off the ground just enough to stop his clothing from scraping the ground. It was a tiring way of moving, but it was also the one that gave him the best chance of approaching his objective without being seen.

The bulk of the tank loomed in front of him, a giant object compared to himself. It was at right angles to his line of approach, but with the turret turned sideways so the barrel of its 88mm gun projecting towards him. He crept closer, until he was touching the vehicle. Once in its shadow he half stood and moved to the front end of the vehicle and peered around it.

There was a second tank, forming an acute angle with the one he was alongside. That one had its front at the far end but, like the first, its gun projected outwards. He retraced his steps, then continued to the rear of the first tank. There was a third, also forming an acute angle with the first. The three Tigers made up the three sides of a triangle, each able to start its engine and move straight off if they were attacked, without risking a collision with its neighbours. Their three guns also provided them with all round protection if they had to defend themselves. Within those protecting sides lay the tanks' crews; Carter could hear the sound of their snoring.

Three tanks, therefore the total number of crew was fifteen men.

He heard the sound of movement. A shadow detached itself from the tank ahead of him and started to move towards him. There was no sound of alarm, no challenge. Just a sentry who had decided it was time to make a circuit of the perimeter of the campsite.

Carter hurried backwards, to the far end of the tank, turned the corner and slid beneath the vehicle, using it for cover. That had been close. He listened as the sound of feet approached and then passed his hiding place.

There would probably be a radio operator awake as well, concealed inside one of the tanks, listening for orders.

It was ironic to think that if they'd still been in possession of their weapons, Carter and his three men could probably have captured the tanks without firing a shot. That would have been some coup. Even if the Germans had woken and fought, the commandos would have had them trapped in a triangular killing zone, unable to escape.

Glass had been in the Royal Tank Regiment. He'd have been bound to have known how to drive one of the behemoths. They probably couldn't have fired the main armament, but they certainly could have used the Tigers' machine guns to defend themselves.

Carter could just imagine the CO's face as he sat on top of the turret, guiding a Tiger through the British front line.

But being unarmed was a different matter entirely.

His flight of fancy was tempting him, though. Was it possible to take the tanks? He could kill the sentry easily enough when he next passed. Thanks to two former Shanghai police officers, all the commandos knew how to snap a man's neck as easily as breaking a twig. That would give him possession of the guard's weapon, probably a Schmeisser machine pistol and that would tip the balance in their favour. One man, wide awake, against 13 men asleep and one cowering inside the hull of his tank. A single short burst from the Schmeisser would probably be enough to get the tank crews to surrender. Then he could call up his three men to disarm the Germans.

Could he do it? Dare he try it? He weighed up the risks.

If he failed, he would be dead, for sure. But his three men would still be out in the dark. Would the Germans go looking for them?

They might simply climb into their tanks and drive away, putting any further danger behind them. Only if his men showed themselves would they be at any risk. Common sense would tell them not to do that.

But common sense didn't always prevail. Prof Green, for one, would probably try to come to Carter's assistance. And if he came, the other two would be almost bound to follow.

No, he couldn't risk their lives in that way. If it had been a single tank crew, that might have been different, but fifteen men, even when thirteen were asleep, was a different kettle of fish. It only needed the guard to make a noise when Carter grabbed him and the whole adventure would be over before it had really begun.

Listening for the sound of footsteps, Carter prepared to return to his men. There was no sound, so presumably the German had completed a full circle and returned to his start point and was now leaning against the side of a tank once again.

Carter crawled out from his hiding place and rose to his hands and knees. Rising a little further he turned the corner, heading away from the tank ... and walked smack into the sentry.

Although Carter was surprised, the sentry was more so, having no idea that anyone other than him was awake.

"*Wer ist es?*" He challenged Carter. It was all he was able to say before Carter slammed his fist into the soldier's midriff, doubling him over, followed by a knee smashed into the German's face. There was the sound of bones being crushed. The man keeled over, unconscious before he hit the ground. Good job German tank crews didn't wear steel helmets[2], Carter thought. The rim would have injured his leg.

Bending over the comatose man, Carter pulled at his equipment harness, buttons flying from the German's epaulettes under the strain. He needed the harness because it had the man's ammunition pouches attached. Without those the man's MP40 would soon run out of bullets; not quite useless, but only one extended burst of fire away from becoming so.

The man groaned, starting to come around from the assault. Carter had no option but to silence him permanently. He grabbed the German around the throat, his thumbs pressing hard either side of his windpipe. Some residual survival instinct made the man grab for Carter's hands, trying to pull them away, but there was no power in his grip. Gurgling, the man breathed his last.

Now armed, Carter reconsidered the possibility of taking on the rest of the sleeping tank crews but dismissed the idea again. The risks were still too high.

There was a squeal of a badly greased hinge and the hatch of the closest tank swung open. A head and shoulders appeared against the night sky.

"*Was gibt W…*" was as much as the man got to say as Carter fired a short burst at him from the Schmeisser. The German jerked back, his head crashing against the tank's hatch, before he slumped out of sight, back down inside the turret.

That'll set the cat amongst the pigeons, Carter thought. Time to go.

He turned and sprinted back into the darkness towards the place he had left his three companions. Behind him he heard voices raised in panic. He almost tripped over his men in the dark.

"Quick, this way!" He hissed at them, as he headed off in a new direction; one that would take them away from the Tigers. The voices could still be heard, demanding to know what had happened. There was the fizzing sound of a parachute flare being fired and the commandos threw themselves onto the ground before it could explode and illuminate them. The flare popped into life, lighting up the farmland around them, but clearly showing up the tanks for the first time.

"Three of the buggers." Glass said.

"Yes. One sentry and a man on radio watch." Carter whispered. "Both dead now."

"You weren't planning in stealing a tank, were you?" Prof Green asked from a few feet away.

"Yes ... No ... I don't know. Maybe. But it doesn't matter now. As soon as that flare goes out, we move again."

The night air was split by the roar of a tank engine starting up, then a second and finally the third. Whatever the Germans thought was happening, they weren't going to hang around waiting for it to happen. The turret of the nearest Tiger started to turn and its secondary armament, a machine gun, started firing. Tracer showed the line of fire, but it was nowhere near the three commandos and getting further away as turret turned.

The first tank lurched away, heading parallel to the line that Carter had tried to take. Behind it the second fell into line. The third, parked pointing away from that line, had to turn first before it could follow. Within minutes the tank engines were just a distant rumble; the flare had already gone out.

"I t'ink we need an explanation, Sorr." Paddy O'Driscoll sad.

"Yes, of course. Well, I got close to the tank, the one Danny saw, but a sentry came around, so I hid underneath. I thought he'd gone, so I started to come back here and ran straight into him. Or maybe it was a different one. Anyway, I had to kill him, but I got his gun." Carter raised the weapon as evidence that he was telling the truth. "Then the man on radio watch stuck his head out and I shot him. The rest you know."

"And you were really t'inking of stealing a tank." O'Driscoll sounded incredulous.

"For a short while. It seemed so simple, if I could only grab a weapon. Then I did have a weapon, but I had to use it too soon, so I'm afraid I just ran."

"And what would you have done with the tank if you had stolen it?" Danny asked.

"The plan was to kill all the crew that were sleeping, then you could drive us back to the British lines, where we'd be welcomed as heroes."

"You'd have got the four of us killed if you had done that. I can't imagine His Majesty's Long Range Snipers[3] letting us within a mile of the front line before throwing everything at us. They certainly wouldn't be polite and give us a chance to explain."

"I must admit, I hadn't thought that far ahead. But it didn't matter because I didn't have a weapon and decided not to take the risk. Bumping into the sentry was just an accident and it didn't really change my mind, even when I had his gun."

"So what do we do now?"

"We get out of here. There could be patrols on their way to find out what the shooting was."

Carter stood up and started to walk southwards again, where the flash of artillery fire and the bright lights of flares continued to show where the battle for Lentini was raging.

[1] This is the technical name for this manoeuvre. It mimics the actions of a kitten when it first starts to move around and is still barely able to see. A faster method of crawling is the leopard crawl, which uses the knees and elbows as well as the toes and hands and raises the body, especially the hips, higher off the ground. Consequently it isn't quite so covert a way of moving as the kitten crawl.

[2] World War II German tank crews originally wore an oversized beret style headdress over a hardened felt liner. This provided a certain amount of protection against soldiers striking their heads against the interior fittings of their tanks. The wearing of helmets had been tried, but they tended to restrict movement, so the Germans decided efficiency was more valuable than protection. From 1940 onwards a black version of the standard M40 field cap (similar to a forage cap) was authorised for use by *Panzer* troops. The M43 cap, also known as the ski cap, is the one usually depicted being worn by the *Afrika Korps* and this was also used by tank crews serving in southern Europe. It looked a bit like a modern baseball cap, but with side flaps that could be folded down to cover the ears.

³ Derogatory slang for the Royal Artillery.

* * *

Every so often they heard gunfire off to their left and right, sometimes behind them, which indicated that there were still commandos taking the fight to the enemy. Or maybe it was just nervous sentries who thought the commandos might be out there still.

At one point, Carter had to bring them to a halt again, to avoid a patrol. They were given plenty of warning of its approach. From their loud voices they could tell that they were Italians, rather than German paratroops. Two were also smoking. Carter was tempted to teach them a hard lesson for their unmilitary behaviour but decided against it. The four of them were still behind enemy lines and it would only take one lucky, or unlucky, shot for them to be left with a casualty to carry. The eight man patrol never knew how close they had been to a sudden death.

As they drew closer to the front line, Carter tried to work out where they might be able to cross. There were plenty of clues. Parachute flares still soared skywards from both sides and were usually followed by bursts of machine gun fire. From that activity Carter was able to identify a stretch of ground about two hundred yards wide where nothing seemed to be happening.

Why that area was so quiet was a question he couldn't answer. It might indicate some sort of natural barrier, such as a lake; but he didn't recall any lakes marked on the maps he had seen. Not in this area, at least. He ruled out swamp or marsh for the same reason. The most likely explanation would be that the enemy were too thinly stretched and had just decided that they couldn't spare the men to protect the area. If that were the case they might have patrols out, keeping the two exposed flanks in touch with each other. That was what Carter would do in those circumstances. He'd also have the area covered by automatic weapons from both flanks, firing just enough ahead of the defensive positions to create a crossfire, but at the same time not risking hitting friendly troops.

After consulting his watch, Carter glanced left, towards the eastern sky. There was just the faintest change of shade, a thin blue area right on the horizon, to indicate that dawn wasn't far off. They had to clear the Axis side of the line before the sun rose. To leave it until later would put them at risk of discovery.

But at the same time it would be dangerous to approach the Allied lines in darkness. It only needed one jumpy sentry to end all the good work they had done that night. It would be far better to approach in daylight, where the colour of their uniforms could be seen.

How far apart were the front lines? He wondered. Both sides would have wanted to keep a safe distance during the night, to stop patrols blundering into the enemy positions. Probably more than the effective range of a rifle, which was around three hundred yards for most infantrymen, but within the effective range for a Bren gun or an MG 42, which was five hundred yards.

As dawn approached, both sides would also start to send artillery and mortar spotters forward, ready to start the day's hostilities with a bang. That would close the gap somewhat. They would close the gap between the two front lines by between fifty and a hundred yards. If they were identified they could be by-passed, but if not, they represented another threat. Not for their own firepower, which was probably minimal, but because of the shit-storm of fire they could call down.

Lowering himself to the ground, Carter waved to his men to close in on him. "We're close now, chaps." He whispered, "But we've got to take things carefully. If any of us get spotted, the others are to go to ground and try to remain undetected. It's better for one of us to get back alive than none of us. Once the sun comes up we'll be easy meat for the Jerry machine gunners, so don't take any risks. At the first sign of trouble, get your hands in the air."

Glass snorted. "After all we've done, you'd have us surrender!" He snarled.

"I'd have you live to fight another day. While it is fine to die for your King and country, it's far better to live for it. And it's just plain stupid to die needlessly. There's nothing we can do here that's going to change the outcome of the fighting. We just have to stay alive."

"I agree with Lucky." Green tried to pacify Glass. "We've come too far to get killed now."

"Personally, I've never been too keen on dying for an English King anyway. I'll die for Ireland if need be, but I'd rather live for her." O'Driscoll chuckled.

"You can say what you like, but I'm not going to surrender." Glass said.

"In that case, you better have this." Sliding the Schmeisser across the ground to him, Carter shrugged out of the German equipment harness and passed that across as well. Carter hoped that Glass wouldn't be stupid enough to use the weapon, but in the mood he was in, anything was possible. Carter could order him to surrender, but he couldn't make him and if he disobeyed the order and ended up dead, there was little Carter could do or say that would make any difference. Short of knocking the man out and carrying him to the British lines, which would slow them all down, Glass could do as he liked. He even had the CO's official sanction: every man for himself.

As Glass pulled the harness on and buckled it up, Carter rose into a crouch and led them forward once again. The line of blue on the horizon was noticeabley broader, going through the shades between the palest eggshell to the deepest indigo directly above their heads. But there were fewer stars visible now that there was more light. They didn't have much time.

It was growing lighter by the minute, Carter could see that. The humps of dried out grass and stunted bushes were more defined in their shapes and other features were becoming visible. Walls were starting to stand out as features, rather than looming out of the darkness to take them by surprise. Hearing movement to his left, Carter dropped to the ground. His men followed suit.

Raising his head to peer over the dry grass, Carter made out the source of the sound. Silhouetted against the pre-dawn light were soldiers, climbing out of defensive positions and heading northwards, away from the British lines. Carter could clearly see the shape of an MG 42 angled over the shoulder of the nearest German as he scrambled over the loose soil of his weapons pit. Beyond him was his gunner, a rifle slung over his back to leave his hands free to handle the box containing the belts of spare ammunition for the gun. There would be other belts wrapped around his body, just in case he dropped the ammunition box, but they weren't yet visible.

There was a general withdrawal in progress, Carter could see that. But there weren't many German troops. All the flares that had been fired and the outbreaks of machinegun fire had just been a bluff, persuading the British that their enemy was stronger than he really was and discouraging a night attack. Judging by the spacing of the gun pits, there could barely be more than a platoon strength spread along two or three hundred yards of ground.

Carter looked to his right, but whatever was on that side was still obscured by the dark background of the Sicilian interior. But he could hear more noises, which suggested more movement. Carter doubted that the Germans there were staying in their positions. This was a pre-planned withdrawal, and no man would be left behind.

"We don't have to stop you here." Carter remembered the German *Fallschirmjäger* officer saying. "We just have to slow you down." And that was what the front line had been doing. But with the arrival of the dawn the British would advance and expose the thinly stretched defences, penetrating the line and isolating the small groups of men.

During the night the Herman Goering Division had no doubt broken contact and slipped away to the west and north. Their self-propelled guns would have withdrawn in stages, keeping up the artillery duel until the range became too long. The Germans wouldn't have used the bridge over the river Gabriel. It was too narrow and would have created a choke point behind which the thousands of men and hundreds of tanks would have become trapped. Inland they wouldn't have suffered that problem, though it would take them longer to reach the next defensive line in front of Catania.

Now the paratroops would withdraw that way, however, keeping the British distracted for a little longer. The three tanks they had encountered during the night were no doubt part of the ruse, providing artillery and machine gun cover for the paras as they withdrew, making the British think they were a more significant force. It was also why no defences had been dug at the top of the ridge. There was nothing to defend. At least there wouldn't be, once the bridge had been blown. And beyond that bridge was the British 1st Parachute Brigade, ten miles away at Primasole, depending on that bridge for 50th Division to advance and relieve them.

But there was still time, if Carter could reach the British front line. An armoured reconnaissance unit could race ahead to the bridge and prevent it from being blown. It was a faint hope, but still a hope. Once there, they could hold it for long enough for heavy armour to arrive, putting the German paratroops in the same position as 15 Cdo had been the previous day.

Was it really only a day since he had seen the sun rise over the bridge? It seemed so much longer.

But first Carter had to reach the British front line. He half rose, experimentally, to try and establish if anyone was interested in them enough to pause the withdrawal and prevent them crossing to the British positions. Nothing happened; no shots rang out, no voices were raised in alarm.

He started to move. "Come on chaps. Looks like the Germans are only interested in getting away now. We need to hurry if we're to prevent the bridge being blown before our advance units can get there."

The men moved tentatively, not as confident as Carter was about the enemy's lack of interest in them. But as soon as they realised that Germans were all facing north, they increased their pace. The sky was turning brighter, another fine day dawning in Sicily as the eastern sky turned blue. The first glimmerings of the sun were just painting the horizon with gold.

There was no more than a couple of hundred yards to go now, Carter estimated and they would be safe.

Something plucked at the sleeve of Carter's shirt, then he heard the distinctive crack of a rifle. He dived for cover, the men behind him cursing as they also went to ground. From which direction had the shot come? In front, he decided. It must have been. A nervous sentry, seeing unidentified figures advancing at speed. It was understandable that he might shoot first and ask questions afterwards.

"British!" Carter shouted, at the top of his voice. He raised himself up on one elbow waved his other arm, calling out again. "We're British commandos. Don't shoot."

"How do I know you aren't Jerries?" a voice shouted back. Carter couldn't make out a word of what had been said. Had he got it wrong? Had they, in fact, stumbled into the rear of the German lines, rather than the front of the British positions? But it didn't really sound like German either.

"Look, we're British." Carter decided to take a chance. He stood up, extending his arms above his head to show he was unarmed.

"OK, I can see you. Come forward one at a time." The voice said some more unintelligible words.

Carter still didn't know what had been said, but the challenger hadn't taken another shot, which must surely be a good sign. He took a step forward. Still no shot. He took another, then another. He could see where the shot had come from now. The stubby nose of the Lee Enfield rifle poked through a V shaped gap in a low wall in front of him; more the tumbled remains of a wall really. The gun's owner was well concealed. Carter couldn't make out any feature to identify the man other than the barrel of the weapon.

He advanced to about halfway, then came to a stop. "Captain Carter; 15 Cdo." He shouted.

"Come on in, Captain." Another voice called. This one was also accented, but far more understandable. He recognised it as northern. Of course, 50th Division were from the northeast. He'd run into a Geordie unit. He'd been told that some of their own officers didn't even understand the men they commanded and the further south their origins the worse the language barrier became. They had a couple of Geordies in the commando and the men said that when they got together for a chat they might as well have been speaking Swahili for all the sense they made.

Now he could make out shapes behind the wall. Two of them. One was the rifleman, a steel helmet pulled down low over his eyes. Next to him was a bareheaded man, no steel helmet so that he could accommodate the headphones that were currently hanging around his neck.

"If you don't mind hurrying up." The man with the headphones said, "Before the Jerries spot us and start dropping mortar bombs on our heads."

"I don't think there's much chance of that." Carter replied, clambering over the wall and lowering himself to the ground on the others side.

"Well, get your fucking head down anyway, just in case." The helmeted man said.

"I'm sorry, what did he say?" Carter asked.

"He said we'd rather not take any chances." Came the more diplomatic reply. Carter could see that the man had a pair of pips on each epaulette, signifying that he was a Lieutenant.

"Jack Milburn." The officer introduced himself, extending his hand to be shaken. "102nd Northumberland Hussars. Also known as the 'Geordie Gunners'. Pleased to meet you, Captain Carter. That's Gunner Armstrong there. He's the one that nearly shot you."

"I forgive him." Carter chuckled. "Please, call me Steven. I take it this is an artillery OP[1]?"

"It is. We're looking for tanks. Seen any?"

"Yes, three Tigers, last night, due north of here. I think they're covering the Jerry paratroops as they withdraw, which they've started to do. I doubt you've got any enemy withing five hundred yards of you right now, with the gap increasing by the minute. Can you get Div HQ on that?" Carter pointed to the radio set nestling against the base of the wall, where it was best protected.

"No, but I can get Battery HQ and they can relay messages."

"OK. Can you tell them that the Jerries are withdrawing across this whole area and if they want to save the Ponte bridge over the River Gabriel they need to send mechanised units forward now, before the Jerries blow it."

"We were told you boys were holding that bridge." Milburn said.

"Yesterday morning we were, but not since then. The Jerries have had plenty of time to replace the demolition charges."

The officer grunted, then put his headset back on before picking up the radio's handset and muttering into it.

"Can I call my men forward?" Carter asked the soldier who was acting as the observer's escort.

"Yes, no problem."

Carter took that as an affirmative. "OK, lads come forward." He called. "Try not to give away this position."

"A bit fucking late for that now." The gunner grumbled, but he got away with his insubordination on the grounds that Carter had no idea he was being insubordinate.

"Any reply from Div HQ?" Carter asked, tapping Milburn on his shoulder to attract his attention.

The man slipped the headset off. "No. Your message has been relayed though. It will take a bit of time. It will have to go through regiment and brigade before it gets to division, then the answer has to come back by the same route."

"Sounds inefficient. What happens if you spot a target?"

"So long as I can positively identify it as a Jerry tank, I can order the guns to engage. We're an anti-tank unit, so we aren't interested in anything other than them at the moment. If Div wants us to target anything else, they'll let us know."

Carter's three companions had joined them behind the wall.

"Nice souvenir." Armstrong said, spotting the Schmeisser that Glass was still carrying.

"What did he say?" Glass asked.

"Any chance of a cup of tea?" O'Driscoll asked.

"What did he say?" Armstrong queried. "I didn't understand a word of that. What language is he speaking?"

"He's speaking with an Irish accent." Milburn translated. "He asked if we have any tea."

"I can get a brew going if you like, Sir."

"Please do, Armstrong. It doesn't look like we're going to be needed for the foreseeable future."

Carter agreed. "I doubt the nearest Jerry tank is within two miles of here. You'd need good eyes to see it from as low down as this."

Armstrong busied himself with his Tommy cooker[2]. Carter found himself salivating at the thought of the simple delights of a cup of tea.

Milburn became alert as Carter heard the crackling of a voice in the man's headphones. There was a brief exchange of messages before the headset was removed again.

"You're wanted at Div HQ, apparently." Milburn explained. "I've to direct you to the forward lines, where you'll be met by someone from the DLI[3]. He'll get you back to their battalion HQ and you'll be passed along the line."

"Have I time for my tea?"

"Not really. But your men are welcome to stay if they want to."

"I have to say, I'd love a cuppa." O'Driscoll interjected, before Carter could ask.

"Me too." Glass added.

"I'll come with you, if I may Lucky." Green said.

"You can if you want." Carter replied, before turning back to talk to Milburn again. "Which way do we go?"

"Follow this wall." Milburn pointed along the line that ran at right angles to the forward edge of the observation post. "When you get to the end, cross into the next field and keep going straight ahead. You'll see an old gnarled olive tree, Just in front of it is the DLI's forward positions. They'll tell you where to go from there."

"Thanks for your hospitality." Carter said, shaking Milburn's hand again. Keeping low, Carter and Green followed the line of the wall as instructed.

"Oh, you'll need the passwords." Milburn said, stopping him from leaving. "The challenge is 'makem' and the reply is 'monkey hanger'.[4]

[1] Observation post.

[2] A small portable stove made from pressed tin, heated by blocks of solid fuel similar to firelighters. One block of fuel provides just enough heat to boil a mess tin full of water or to heat a tin of stew.

[3] Durham Light Infantry. Light infantry regiments on the move 'speed march' at a rate of one hundred and forty paces per minute, compared to the normal infantry pace of one hundred and twenty paces per minute. Light infantry units provide forward reconnaissance units, moving ahead of an infantry Division. To ensure that they are 'light' they don't usually burden themselves with heavy weapons, but otherwise they are capable of fulfilling all regular infantry tasks. In Sicily the three battalions of the DLI that made up 161st Brigade within 50th Division were employed mainly on regular infantry duties.

[4] An interesting choice of passwords, but probably meant half as a bit of banter amongst the men from the North East. 'Makem' is a reference to Sunderland shipyard workers. The origin may be 18th or

19th century with shipbuilders saying "We'll mak' 'em so long as you tak' 'em." (We'll make them so long as you take them.). From that the Wearsiders gained nickname of 'Makems'. The 'monkey hanger' nickname is more derogatory and refers to people from Hartlepool. The story is that during the Napoleonic wars, a monkey was found washed up on shore clinging to some debris. Monkeys were a common pet kept by French sailors. It was assumed that it had either been washed overboard or was the sole survivor of a disaster at sea. The local people who found it had never seen a monkey before. A common newspaper depiction of the French at this time was of someone very monkey like. The monkey was assumed to be a French spy and was hanged. Since then the people of Hartlepool have been referred to as 'monkey hangers'. The story gained popularity thanks to a 19th century music hall song sung by Ned Corvan and called "The Monkey Song", so there may be no truth in it.

* * *

Carter and Green kept as low as possible as they followed the wall towards the rear. There was still the possibility of there being Germans in the area and German snipers were famed for their abilities.

They were challenged as they approached the tree, then allowed through the infantry's positions. Waiting for them was a corporal.

"Follow me, Sir." He said, at once heading off towards the south. They crossed more fields, dodging from cover to cover and passing more infantry, well dug in, as though expecting an attack at any moment.

Battalion HQ was no more than a dug-out protected by the canvass of a tent spread over the top and supported on poles. They weren't even invited inside. An officer was waiting for them.

"Captain Millican, 50th Div." He introduced himself, which explained the red tabs on the collar of his shirt. "If you'd like to follow me, I've got some transport for the next leg."

"Is it far to Div HQ?" Carter asked as they walked.

"That isn't where we're going; new orders. Monty wants to meet you." The Captain gave a broad grin, enjoying the surprise he had inflicted.

"But I can't meet anyone in this state, least of all the most senior British officer in Sicily. Isn't there anywhere that I can tidy myself up and make myself look decent?" There was little Carter could do about his uniform, he knew, but at least he could have a wash and shave before meeting the commander of the 8th Army.

"Sorry, no time. You've got to be debriefed by the Intelligence Corps staff at HQ before seeing Monty. That's why they sent me. I'm Int Corp myself. I'll give you the rundown on what they want to know as we go."

They had reached a Jeep, parked close to a wall so it couldn't be seen easily. Green clambered into the rear, leaving the front seats for Carter and Millican. The latter took the wheel, starting the vehicle and sending them off with spinning wheels and a trail of flying gravel.

The Jeep bounced over the rutted cart track, making Carter feel nauseated by the jerky movements. He clung tightly to his seat; more than one passenger had been thrown out during a rough ride in the low sided vehicles. The turbulance didn't last long and Millican turned the vehicle onto the main road, heading south at speed. On the other side of the road convoys of supply vehicles thundered in the other direction.

"You're the first officer from your mob to make it back to our lines." Millican bellowed. "We've had a few Tommies[1] arrive and we're gathering them together, but the Int staff want an officer's view of what's going on up front. Will you be able to tell them much?"

"A bit. The Germans aren't going to defend the Gabriel River, by the looks of it. Their paratroops are falling back across the bridge, then I assume they'll blow it up."

"What about strength?"

Carter understood what Millican was doing. As he was driving he wasn't able to write anything down, but that wasn't why he was asking questions. He just wanted to get Carter thinking about what he knew, so that his mind would more easily recall the details that the Intelligence Corps staff would want. It would be of enormous use to the Army's commanders to have some idea of what was in front of them and what sort of resistance they might have to deal with.

"One paratroop battalion directly on 50th Div's line of advance, I think. Three Tiger tanks that I know of. Probably the same ones that pushed us off the bridge yesterday. I didn't see any artillery. The Jerry paras are a competent lot. They'll put up a fight if they have to, but it looked to me like their orders were to withdraw. But where they're going, I have no idea."

"Probably to reinforce their pals at Primasole." Millican offered. "The rest of their division seems to have moved up there to deal with our boys."

"How's it going there?"

"No idea really. Like you, they've had to abandon the bridge, but they're hanging on, waiting for us."

Taking a turn far too fast, the Jeep screeched around a corner and onto a side road that led up into the hills. Carter could see an impressive looking villa set into the slope. A Union Flag hung limply from a pole protruding from an upstairs balcony.

"It may be a bit chaotic." Millican shouted. "Monty only moved his HQ from Syracuse during the night. I think he's only been here himself for an hour or so."

Defensive positions were arranged around the area, manned by alert looking guards. Millican slammed the brakes on the Jeep, skidding it to a halt just short of a Dingo armoured car which was parked across the road, its machine gun aimed directly at the Jeep. A soldier held a Tommy gun, also aimed at the Jeep, while another man stepped forward.

"ID!" The soldier demanded, ignoring the ranks of the two officers.

"I'm afraid I've lost mine. I was a prisoner of the Jerries for a short while." Carter explained.

Handing over his own documents, Millican interjected. "I'll vouch for them."

The soldier took his time checking the documentation, then handed it back before snapping into a smart salute and waving the Jeep forward. The armoured car revved its engine and reversed backwards off the road to make way.

At a more sedate pace, Millican drove the Jeep up to the front of the villa and pulled into an empty parking space between two identical vehicles. Jumping down, the Int Corps officer led them up a short flight of marble stairs and into the building. Inside, a Military Police sergeant waited, demanding their ID once again.

A signals trooper backed along the corridor and out of the door, unwinding a telephone cable from a large drum. He disappeared from view down the villa's front steps.

"We're looking for the Int section." Millican explained as the sergeant handed him his documents back.

"Through there, Sir." The policeman said, pointing before he saluted.

The direction indicated was a room to one side of the large reception area. Millican led the way. It turned out that the Int section was a large echoing room containing a single trestle table with a typewriter sat in the centre and a field telephone handset on one side, its cable trailing across the floor and out of the nearest window. A couple of wood and canvass collapsible camp chairs were arranged in front and behind the desk, ready for use. In the corner a corporal was sat in front of a radio, a headset clamped over his ears and talking into a microphone.

Without ending his conversation on the radio, the corporal indicated that the new arrivals should make us of the camp chairs.

"I'll leave you now." Millican said. "Whoever debriefs you will make sure you get to see Monty." The two officers shook hands, then Millican shook hands with Green before turning to leave.

Carter took the chair on what might be assumed to be the visitor's side of the trestle table. Green decided not to take the one on the other side and remained standing.

They weren't kept waiting long. A rather harassed looking Major arrived. "You must be Carter." He said, extending his hand. "I'm Corchorane, on Monty's Intelligence staff." He dropped into the empty canvass chair. "And who might you be, Corporal?" He asked Green.

Green snapped to attention, but as he was bareheaded he didn't salute. "Cpl Green, Sir. I'm with Captain Carter."

"I've had no instructions to debrief you. Tell you what, if you go and see the MP at the main entrance, he'll point you in the right direction to get a spot of breakfast."

"Very good, Sir." If Green was offended by being dismissed, he did a good job of hiding it. He turned on his heel and marched smartly from the room."

"He's a good man. One of the best." Carter's tone suggested that he might have taken offence on Green's behalf.

"I'm sure he is, but I only need your story. If Green's been with you throughout, he probably wouldn't be able to add anything of value. Now, we lost contact with your CO around lunchtime yesterday. Communications had been a bit erratic up to then anyway. Your radio was at about the limit of its range, apparently. I don't know why we lost contact, but we assume that either the radio's battery had died or that the set had been destroyed to stop it falling into the enemy's hands. Do you know which?"

"Not really, Sir. In the late morning the CO gave us the order to disperse, so I assume that he left the bridge area shortly after the rest of us. I doubt he would have wanted to be weighed down by a radio set, so he may have destroyed it."

"Ah, there we have the first bit of the puzzle solved. You were ordered to disperse, giving up the bridge."

"We were, Sir. There were three Tiger tanks threatening us and we had no way of fighting them. If we'd have stayed there, the enemy would have chopped us up piecemeal." Carter knew he sounded defensive, but he also knew how actions in the field could be misinterpreted when it came to allocating blame.

"Don't worry, Carter. I'm not judging the performance of your unit or challenging any of the decisions that anyone made. I just want to know what happened. More importantly I want to know what you can tell us about what the enemy is now up to. Perhaps you had better run me over the story, starting from lunchtime yesterday and finishing when you arrived at the artillery OP."

Starting from the beginning, Carter told of their experiences, leaving out only the tiny detail about him falling asleep while on guard. He made it sound as though they had been surprised by the enemy patrol, rather than being found by them while they were asleep. The words the German major had said, about only delaying the Allies were paid particular attention.

Corchorane asked some more questions, which Carter did his best to answer, then after about half an hour a clerk appeared in the doorway. "Excuse me Major …"

"Yes, Simpkins. We're on our way." The Major replied. "It seems that the General is ready for us, Carter. I'd better take you up."

He rose and Carter also stood, following him out of the office, across the echoing hall and up a long flight of marble stairs to the upper level of the villa. The upstairs was even more chaotic than the lower level, with officers hurrying about with bits of paper in their hands, impromptu meetings taking place in corners and the constant buzz of field telephones demanding to be answered. Carter was guided through the middle of this to a pair of double doors that stood open.

Within this new room there seemed to be officers everywhere, Colonels, Lieutenant Colonels and Majors. Carter felt quite insignificant amongst them. They were standing, sitting and perched on the end of trestle tables. Maps were pinned to the walls. In the middle, sat behind a trestle table with only one buff folder positioned in the middle of it, was the instantly recognisable figure of General Montgomery.

He stood as soon as he saw Corchorane. Alongside his table stood a tall, good looking officer wearing the crown and two pips of a full Colonel, below which were commando shoulder flashes.

Montgomery wasn't tall, but his wiry frame seemed to buzz with energy.

"Thank you Corchorane." Monty replied as Carter came to attention in front of the trestle table. "At ease, Carter. You know Colonel Laycock?"

"Only by reputation, Sir." He turned to face the former commander of Layforce. "Your raid to capture Rommel was the talk of the Mess for weeks."

Laycock smiled modestly. "A failure, I'm afraid." He replied.

"But the very essence of what the commandos were established to do." Carter responded.

"Precisely what we sent you to do." Montgomery interjected, smoothly regaining control over the conversation.

"My apologies, Sir." Carter stuttered. "I'm afraid I haven't had a chance to get myself cleaned up. I wouldn't normally …"

Montgomery gave a dismissive gesture, accompanied by a short, barking laugh. "Ha! Do you think you're the first officer I've greeted that's come straight from the front lines? Or from behind enemy lines in your case. Used to happen all the time in Africa. I wouldn't have it any other way.

I've called you here to give you a personal thank you for what you and your men did at the Gabriel river."

"I'm afraid that operation was a failure." Carter said in a low voice.

"You let me be the judge of that. All night long my radio intercept bods have been hearing reports of commandos attacking German supply convoys, Italian shore defences, patrols and all sorts. You've been creating chaos, which Col Laycock here assured me you would do. OK, you couldn't hold the bridge, but there was no way you could have anticipated encountering Goering's paratroops."

"Actually, we could have held them off, Sir. It was the tanks that forced us off the bridge. We had no idea there was armour in the area."

"Yes." Montgomery exchanged a meaningful glance with Laycock. "I'm afraid we've had a bit of a problem with aerial reconnaissance. With no airfield available on Sicily, the aircraft have to return to their aircraft carriers, or to Malta, to get their films developed. They send the pictures on to us by fast launch, of course, but they're still several hours out of date by the time they arrive. The ones that showed the Herman Goering Division advancing didn't turn up until the early hours of yesterday morning, by which time it was too late to warn you and also too late to revise the plan. It's why we've been stuck in Lentini for so long."

It wasn't exactly an apology; generals didn't apologise to captains, but the explanation was as close to an apology that anyone was going to get.

"If we'd had PIATs we might have stood a chance of holding, Sir."

"PIATS, eh?" He turned and looked across the room. "Terry, tell me about PIATs." He called.

An officer stood up and shuffled through some papers until he found the one he wanted. He crossed the room and handed it to Montgomery.

"We've had very good reports from the units that have them, Sir." He said as Montgomery scanned the paper. "They'll destroy any tank of an earlier mark than the Tiger. With all their frontal armour they're a tough nut to crack. But if you can get a side shot, or a shot from behind, where the armour is thinner, you stand a chance. If you can get a shot at their underside, they're as good as dead."

"Their underside?" An intrigued Carter said. "How do you do that?"

"If a Tiger has to climb over an obstruction, such as a wrecked vehicle or a pile of rubble, it will show its belly for a short time before it tilts downwards. A gutsy man with a steady hand can get a projectile into its underside, which has thinner armour. But you have to be close up, just to get the angle right. It isn't a job for the faint hearted."

Montgomery gave another of his short barking laughs. "I don't think we have to worry about the commandos having faint hearts. Make a note for the evening Sitrep[2]. I want more PIATs as soon as they can be delivered and when we get them, Carter's men can try them out on the Jerries." He turned back to face Carter again, effectively dismissing the officer he had called Terry. "I'm sure you'd fancy having another go at the Tigers, eh?"

"We would like to get our own back, Sir." It was the sort of thing he was expected to say, but he did happen to mean it.

"As I thought. As the first officer to make it back to our lines, you get the accolade, but I'm well aware of what the men of your unit have done and I'll say as much to Colonel Vernon when he gets here."

"I don't suppose there's any word ..."

"No, but I'm sure he'll be OK. Now, I'm afraid I've still got a battle to fight, so I'll leave you in the hands of Colonel Laycock. Once again, thank you and your men for all you've done." Montgomery sat down and picked a file up from his desk, Carter already gone from his mind.

Laycock stretched out his arm to guide Carter away and out of the room.

"So what do you think of Monty?" He smiled as the went down the stairs.

"Quite the live wire, Sir."

"Yes, energy to burn. I don't know how he manages on so little sleep. I saw him down in Syracuse at close to midnight and he was upstairs and running things again before dawn. Now, I've organised a muster centre for your men, back down by the main road. As they come in, that's where they'll be sent. There's a dressing station set up as well as a field kitchen. There's a couple of Int Corps sergeants as well, to debrief them as they come in but we'll try not to make that too much of a chore.

I'm putting you in charge for the moment, as you're the only officer to have made it back so far. As you get enough men together, have the military police flag down one of the lorries coming back from the front lines. There's plenty of them. They're to take the men and drop them at the port in Syracuse. The garrison commander back there has orders to get them sorted out with billets."

"Can we get our kit sent ashore from the Prince Leopold, Sir? Most of the men will have only what they stand up in. Some may not even have weapons, like me."

"I'll arrange that as soon as I get back upstairs. Shouldn't be a problem. The Prince Leopold is anchored offshore right now. I'd billet you on board, but I'm afraid she's off back to Tunisia tomorrow to pick up 49 Cdo. The marines are coming to join us."

"That might create some inter-unit rivalry, Sir."

"I hope it does. The commandos work best when they have a bit of competition."

"Will we be back in action soon?"

"Hold fast now, Carter." Laycock laughed. "There's only about twenty of you accounted for at the moment. And here's you wanting to get back into the fray."

"Sorry, Sir, it's just that we've had to wait months between ops in the past and the men get fidgety if they're not in action"

"I know, Carter. Don't worry. This operation has only just got going in real terms. There will be plenty more for 15 Cdo to do before we complete the capture of the island. And then we've got Italy. I suspect that will be a much harder nut to crack. I think I can assure you that you'll be back in action sooner rather than later. Monty has a few ideas about how he wants to use you, now that he understands your strengths.

Now, if you'll excuse me, I've also got quite a lot to do." He placed his hand on Carter's shoulder. "Monty really was impressed by what your commando has done, you know. It was always going to be a tough job, but it was made a lot tougher by poor intelligence. Monty knows that and the fact that you performed so well has made him see how valuable the commandos can be to him."

Laycock didn't give Carter the chance to reply but turned on his heel and went back into the building. Carter was just wondering where he was expected to go when he turned to find an RASC private standing behind him. "This way, Sir. I'm to drive you down to the muster area."

[1] Many officers still referred to non-commissioned soldiers as Tommies. Shortened from Tommy Atkins, the nickname they were given by the popular press during the First World War, itself taken from a poem by Rudyard Kipling, entitled "Tommy".

[2] Sitrep – situation report. A daily summary of operations sent to higher authority. It will include casualty figures and requests direct from the commanding officer for resources deemed essential for the completion of the mission and which aren't immediately available, hence Montgomery's request for more PIATs.

* * *

The men had been formed into teams to work in the fishing port at Syracuse, unloading stores from the landing craft as they arrived. They grumbled about it, as soldiers often will, but Carter understood why the CO had done it. Without work to keep them occupied the men would be wandering the town, drinking the cheap local wine or beer and getting into trouble. One man had already been threatened with a shotgun because he had tried to talk to a pretty girl and her father had objected. It had only been the intervention of an officer that had prevented bloodshed.

The men were kept out of the main town and its square until after curfew, when the local population had to be off the streets, but selected bars and cafes were allowed to stay open. Even that didn't prevent trouble. Until the arrival of the commandos, the navy and RASC had been cocks of the walk in the town and they resented their turf being invaded by soldiers with a touch of glamour to their reputations. Insults had been traded and fights had broken out.

A couple of burly commandos had been promoted to the acting rank of Sergeant and appointed as Regimental Police, tasked with keeping the commandos out of trouble. If they came into conflict with the military police, it wouldn't have ended well for the redcaps and the CO wished to prevent any of his men being arrested. It would mean them spending time in the glasshouse[1] and Vernon would have no option but to send them back to Blighty[2].

The CO had turned up towards sunset on the 15th July, in company with the QM, the Regimental Sergeant Major and Ecclestone, his clerk and batman. They were in a good mood and Carter suspected that they had been up to some mischief. No stories had yet been told, there would be time for that once the officers had finished trying to rebuild the commando.

In the four days they had been back, over a two hundred and fifty men had returned through the front lines, the last only that morning. That last man had become separated from his group when they had run into a patrol and hadn't realised that not only had the British army caught up with him, but they had passed him by. He was found by an RASC party looking for somewhere to establish a forward ammunition dump. Nearly threequarters of the commando had escaped. Everyone agreed that it was a miracle and a real testament to their commando training. But that final quarter were still listed as missing.

But some had not fared well behind enemy lines and it was clear that their mental state left them unfit for commando duties. Those handful were sent home, an officer amongst them. In the 2IC's opinion, the man had failed to conduct himself in a sufficiently aggressive manner when faced with the enemy. It was the biggest crime an officer could commit, at least in the 2IC's eyes.

Each time Carter went to talk to his men, he received dark looks from Danny Glass. He understood why. Glass was silently accusing him of getting away with his negligence while on guard duty. A trooper who had fallen asleep would have faced some sort of punishment; he would possibly have been sent home in disgrace. But here was Carter still exercising his authority. Carter suspected that Glass felt let down in some way and not just because they had been captured. He had to do something to restore their relationship.

He found Vernon in the small warehouse that the Port Commander was using as an office and had allowed Vernon to use as well.

"Could I have a word, Sir?" Carter said, saluting. "In private." He nodded towards Ecclestone, who was writing something in a buff folder.

"Fetch me a cup of tea, would you Ecclestone. Don't be too quick about it."

Ecclestone hurried off, a curious look on his face. Very little was ever said in the HQ that he wasn't allowed to hear.

"So, what secret is it that you have that is for my ears only?" Vernon smiled indulgently. He indicated a camp chair, but Carter remained standing.

"It's a bit embarrassing really, Sir. I'm afraid I've rather let the side down."

"That doesn't sound like you, Steven. Better tell all."

Carter gave him a potted version of their adventures, paying particular attention to how they had been captured. Vernon's face darkened.

"I'm sure you understand the seriousness of the situation, Steven, otherwise you wouldn't be standing there like a fifth former caught smoking behind the bike sheds." He pursed his lips, deep in thought.

"I'm not going to dismiss you from the commando." He said after a while. "You're a good officer, Steven. If the war goes on much longer, I could envisage you sitting in my chair one day. To send you home would be too great a loss at a time when I need every experienced officer I can lay hands on." He paused for another lengthy period before speaking again.

"Monty has a new operation planned for us. Operation Mad Bugger, or some such … Operation Madrigal, that's it. I'm forming the commando into two troops for it and we're to combine with 49 Royal Marine Cdo when they arrive from Tunis.

It appears that the army has got a bit bogged down around Catania. The Jerries are putting up quite a defence around the airfield there. With the Navy blockading the port, the Jerries will have to evacuate through Messina, to the north. So the plan is to land on the northern coast of the island and advance on Messina, to threaten it. The Jerries will have to withdraw troops from Catania to prevent the town from falling into our hands before they get off the island. At least, that's what they're supposed to think we're up to. It will actually just be a feint. Once the Jerries are on the move northwards, we'll withdraw back to the beaches and will be lifted off by the Navy. But the Jerries can't risk us coming back in larger numbers, so they'll have to stay there to protect the town and its ferry port."

"And you want me to lead one of the Troops, Sir." Carter felt relieved.

"No. I want you to stay behind here. Everyone knows your history and your reputation. To leave you behind will be a clear message that you cocked something up, without me having to explain what it was. Your three men, Green, Glass and O'Driscoll will stay behind as well."

"No Sir!" Vernon looked up at the sound of Carter's suddenly raised voice.

"I'm sorry, I mean, that would be too cruel, Sir. They've done nothing wrong. To leave them behind would be an unjust punishment."

"Well said, Steven. And you're right. I'll tell you what; you can explain the situation to them, without revealing the plan for the operation of course and if they want to go on the operation, they can. It will be their choice."

"Thank you, Sir. May I go?"

Vernon nodded his head and Carter saluted before doing a smart about turn and marching out of the room.

He hurried to find Green, Glass and O'Driscoll, who were taking a break down on the foreshore, their backs resting against the harbour wall and their faces to the sun. He explained about the operation and his punishment. Glass grunted with satisfaction but didn't add any further comment.

"The choice is yours. You can go on the op or you can sit this one out."

"We were all tired." Green said. "Any one of us could have fallen asleep."

"But we didn't." Glass protested. "Only one of us fell asleep when he shouldn't have and it wasn't one of us three." He indicated himself and the other two troopers.

"What I'm saying," Green tried to mollify him, "Is that it's a bit unfair just for Lucky to take the blame. One for all and all for one, eh?"

"You mean like them three moosketeers." O'Driscoll said.

"Yes, just like the three musketeers. I'm for sitting this one out."

"I t'ink I will as well." O'Driscoll agreed. "I'm a bit tired of being shot at."

"Come on Danny. Why get yourself shot at again if you don't have to?"

"If you put it like that … OK, I'll stay behind as well. But it's not because of him." He jabbed a finger towards Carter.

"You can make it for any reason you like." Green was magnanimous in victory. He understood what the word 'solidarity' meant.

Carter returned to HQ. Ecclestone, the clerk, didn't bother to wait to be told. "I'll just go and get myself a bit of lunch, Sir." He said to the CO as he left.

"You do that, Ecclestone. Bring me back a sandwich if you would. Anything except bully beef."

"Fat chance of that, Sir, but I'll do my best."

"Well, Steven?" Vernon asked, when Ecclestone was gone.

"They don't want to go on Operation Madrigal, Sir."

Vernon chuckled. "I suspected that would be the case. But I've also been thinking about what you said. I don't want it to appear as though the three of them are also being punished. So I've had another idea.

The Americans have set up a rest camp down on the southern coast of the island. It's got a cinema, showers, all the comforts of home apparently. There's also a USO[3] show due in a few days' time. I'll send them down there. They'll leave before the commando sets out on the op, so everyone knows they're going."

"They might still refuse, Sir."

"They're going! Even if I have to have them arrested and sent down there with an armed escort." Vernon said firmly.

[1] Military prison. Originates with the first British military prison established at Aldershot in 1844, which had a glazed roof, a bit like a greenhouse.

[2] Originating with the Urdu word *bilāyatī* and was corrupted by the British Army in India. It means "European foreigner" and was used by Indians to describe the British.

[3] United Services Organisations. An American organisation that provided leisure facilities for American troops and entertainment similar to the British ENSA concert parties. Big name stars often appeared in their shows. Perhaps the biggest names of the period was comedian and Hollywood actor Bob Hope and pre-war child star Shirley Temple, though because of her age, she only appeared in shows in the USA. The USO still provides entertainment for

American troops serving overseas and big-name stars still appear in them.

* * *

A convoy of trucks arrived to collect the commando shortly after dawn. The men clambered aboard and they headed northwards.

Operation Madrigal had been cancelled just hours before the commandos had been due to land and no explanation had been given as to why. The commandos had become used to such cancellations, both in Britain and North Africa. Somewhat disgruntled, the men had returned to Syracuse. Now they were being driven north, but with no idea why.

The trucks pulled to a halt a short distance from the bridge that so many men had given their lives to capture and hold. The Germans hadn't blown it up, probably because the lightly armed *Fallschirmjäger* hadn't had sufficient explosives available to do the job.

Sgt Major Finch set about organising the men into three ranks and they were marched onto the bridge. Puzzled glances were given towards a section of the bridge parapet that was covered in what looked like a sheet.

There was a hiatus, the men stood at ease, the officers gathered at one end of the bridge, chatting. As the delay grew longer the men were allowed to fall out for a cigarette, before being recalled as a Jeep approached. The commandos tried to avoid looking at the wreckage of the pillboxes, where they knew that some of their former comrades had met their deaths. A short line of crosses indicated where the bodies of those men had been buried, now properly marked by the graves registration unit.

The CO marched to the end of the bridge to greet the Major General that climbed out of the Jeep, along with a single ADC[1].

The commando was called to attention and presented arms[2] as the General made his way to stand beside the sheet, with Lt Col Vernon taking up a position on the far side.

Vernon shouted the order for the men to stand at ease and there was a crash of feet as the order was obeyed.

"Gather round, men. "The general called, beckoning with his hands to draw the men in from the outer flanks of the parade. "For those of you that don't know me," That's most of the commando, Carter thought, "I am Major-General Sidney Kirkman, the commanding officer of 50th (Northumberland) Division. It was my men who were supposed to relieve you on the 14th of July. I apologise for our late arrival." He paused and there was a polite chuckle, which he seemed to have expected. Carter noted that the laughter wasn't as wholehearted as it was for some other jokes.

"General Montgomery wanted to be here today, but I'm afraid he has been called away on other business, so he has asked me to represent him, which I am very proud to do. Your capture and defence of the bridge on which we are standing, is an achievement for which you must be very proud. Were it not for you, this bridge would now be a heap of rubble and my Division might well still be camped alongside of the river waiting while the bridge was rebuilt. You held it against daunting odds and only left it when you had no other choice. However, not satisfied with just withdrawing, you continued to harass the enemy, causing chaos in the rear of his front line. That action relieved considerable pressure on *my* front line, so I am particularly grateful for what you did.

It therefore gives me great pleasure to unveil this stone, dedicating this bridge to you."

The general pulled the sheet away to reveal a large block of stone that had been inset among the smaller stones that made up the rest of the bridge's parapet. Its bright colour contrasted against the darker stone that had spanned the river for decades. On it were inscribed the words "15 Commando Bridge".

[1] Aide-de-Camp. An assistant or secretary to a senior officer. The military also provides ADCs to members of the Royal Family, usually referred to as Equerries because of their original job of

looking after the monarch's horse. ADC's can be recognised by the gold aiguillettes (braided chords) that are worn on one shoulder. The origin of the aiguillette in military terms was to secure different bits of armour together.

[2] Present arms is a military drill movement which acts as a salute when soldiers are carrying rifles on parade or standing guard. The rifle is held upright in both hands in front of the body, while the right foot is placed at an angle behind the left heel.

This ends the fifth story in the "Carter's Commandos" series.

Historical Notes

The first part of this book is set near the city of Suez, which was close to the location of 3 Cdo's camp at El Ataka. That location doesn't appear on any maps that I could find and has now been subsumed by the suburbs of the city. Sitting at the southern end of the Suez Canal, the city was a hive of activity during World War II and made much of its living catering to the needs of sailors waiting to transit the canal. Like any port city, there were places where polite society never ventured. Or if they did, they didn't tell their wives, though they might have had to tell their doctors.

Camped around the city, mainly on the El Ataka plain, was XIII Corps, part of Montgomery's 8th Army. It was formed by the British 5th Infantry Division, the Canadian 1st Infantry Division and 21st Infantry Brigade Group (an enlarged brigade). Altogether it was made up of more than 30,000 men, including 3 Cdo and 40 (RM) Cdo.

The Salvation Army provided canteens for junior ranks in many locations around the world. Whether or not there was such a canteen in Suez I have no idea, but it is possible, so I have taken the liberty of including one in the plot as an acknowledgement of the excellent work done by that organisation during World War II. The same applies to the Officer's Club, where Carter meets Curshaw. Such clubs were common across the world in places where there were high concentrations of soldiers, especially if the officers' units didn't have Officers' Messes of their own. It would be surprising if the British commander in Suez hadn't established a place where officers could meet and drink in comfort.

My description of El Ataka accords with that of Brigadier Peter Young (see 'further reading'). It wasn't a pleasant place. But it did afford the commandos somewhere to train that was away from the immediate risk of being observed by enemy reconnaissance aircraft.

Piracy was always a problem in the Middle East, long before the troubles in Somalia broke out in the first decade of the 21st century and ushered in a new wave of the crime. Although the governments in the region were able to keep the levels low for most of the time, major upheavals such as World War II, re-focused attention elsewhere and allowed for an upsurge in offending. Piracy was an opportunistic crime which anyone with a boat could try their hand at, so attacks on small coastal craft weren't unusual. I have made piracy sound more organised than it was, but it was an irritant if not an actual problem.

To the best of my knowledge the Royal Navy didn't carry out anti-piracy duties in the Red Sea during World War II, though they had done so in the Far East before the outbreak of World War II and would do so again afterwards. The operations after the war were more of a cover for preventing communist insurgents from moving freely around Hong Kong and along the Indochina and Malay coastlines. At least one operation, code named Bottle, included the involvement of 1 Cdo. The Red Sea Inshore Squadron is my invention and the use of 15 Cdo as part of an anti-piracy operation was mainly to give them something to do in the early part of this book.

Alsourah is a real location on the Red Sea coast of Saudi Arabia. My knowledge of it is limited to what I could glean from the internet. It is now inhabited but the buildings appear to be modern and resulting from recent development so, assuming that the area was uninhabited in 1943, it serves its purpose as the base for my pirates.

15 Cdo's operations in Sicily were carried out by the real life 3 Cdo and took place much as I have described them. Where the needs of my plot have conflicted with actual events, I'm afraid the plot has taken precedence, but any variations are minor. The 3 Cdo landing operations for Operation Husky really were that straight forward. Major John Pooley actually took over from the scouts to speed up the march to the battery. The 2IC's (Maj Peter Young's) attack on the shore defences south of Murro di Porco were also as shambolic as I have described them and they did have to rescue twenty two

men found clinging to a downed glider. The blowing up of the ammunition dump at the Cassibile battery, with potentially disastrous consequences, also really happened. Reports suggest the blast was heard several miles out at sea.

The apparent ease with which the Operation Husky landings were carried out must be attributed, in part, to the success of an earlier disinformation operation, Operation Mincemeat (see the historical notes for Book 2 of the series, Operation Tightrope). That operation persuaded Hitler that the landings in Sicily would be a feint, with the real objectives being Sardinia and Greece. Despite the reservations of the German High Command, Hitler ordered troops and aircraft to be moved out of Sicily to meet what he believed to be the genuine threat. Even on July 10th, the day of the landings, German aircraft were withdrawn from Sicily and sent to Sardinia. Two German panzer divisions and seven infantry divisions were withdrawn from Russia and sent to the Balkans to counter a non-existent threat to Greece.

3 Cdo carried out an attack on Torre Cuba, but I have no first-hand account of the attack and so I have had to invent my own. But a group of British airborne soldiers from a crashed glider was rescued and one of them was killed during the attack, possibly by 'friendly fire'.

Ponte Bridge (Ponte is the Italian word for bridge) is actually Malati Bridge, which crosses the River Leonardo (hence my choice of title for the book) a few miles north of the town of Lentini. There is a new bridge there now, but the old one still stands, complete with its World War II pillbox and a stone in the parapet dedicating the bridge to 3 Cdo, the only honour accorded for the operation. The action doesn't appear among those listed on the Commandos' Standard with their other battle honours. This omission is probably a consequence of the failure of the commando to hold the bridge.

The pillbox built into the parapet of the bridge is still present. For some reason the German tanks didn't target it. Four men remained inside the pillbox, keeping their heads down, until they were taken prisoner when the Germans finally crossed.

The majority of incidents and actions I have described and attributed to Carter and his men really did take place, though they involved several different participants. The description of Carter drinking lemon juice to quench his thirst was real, as told to me by my father and in other contemporary accounts. The incident with the Italians and their lunch also happened.

Carter's capture is partly imaginary, but much of his adventure, including his escape, is based on that of the real-life Lt (later Major) John Erskine. He was an Australian serving with 3 Cdo who was threatened with death under the *Kommandobefehl,* was saved by a German paratroop officer and then escaped when someone left the door to his prison unlocked and unguarded. Whether it was deliberate or accidental, we will never know but Erskine believed it was deliberate.

Like Carter, Erskine was forced to leave a wounded officer, Lt W F Pienaar, behind. It is true that Erskine was more worried about meeting Montgomery in an unshaven state than he was about anything else. The conversation between Carter and Montgomery is a product of my imagination, as are all the other words uttered by Carter. For a full account of John Erskine's time in Sicily, visit **http://www.commandoveterans.org** and search for Erskine's name.

Major Peter Young of 3 Cdo did gather a group of men around him intending to carry out ambushes along the road to Lentini, but he decided to take a nap while he waited for darkness. He did have sentries deployed who stayed awake (unlike Carter) but by the time he woke up the advance units of 50th Div had reached him, so he didn't get the opportunity to create the chaos he had hoped.

The story of Carter's encounter with the three Tiger tanks during his escape is entirely fictional, but the presence of tanks at the bridge was the reason for 3 Cdo's withdrawal.

A stick of British paratroops were dropped into the Agnone area by mistake and were given directions to Primasole Bridge by 3

Cdo's CO. It is likely that the pilot of their aircraft had seen the German paratroops being dropped and thought they were British, decided he was over the British drop zone and made the decision to get rid of his passengers so that he could turn for home. He wasn't the only pilot to miss the correct drop zone, but he was probably the most inaccurate. It isn't known if the men ever made it to their objective.

Primasole Bridge was captured by the 1st Parachute Brigade (Operation Fustian). Like 3 Cdo, they were unable to hold the bridge against superior armoured and parachute forces and were pushed off. However, as they were in Brigade strength and had some light artillery with them, they were able to continue to defend themselves and when 50th Division arrived the paratroops led the attack to recapture the bridge. The Germans had tried to blow the bridge up by rolling lorries loaded with explosives down the road onto the bridge but failed to do any significant damage.

To give a measure of some of the guts and determination of commando officers, here's what happened to the nine that were taken prisoner at Malati Bridge. Lt W F Pienaar, a South African, died of his wounds. As well as Erskine, three other officers escaped while still in Sicily. Roy Westley, Michael Woyodvodsky and Charles Buswell broke out of a train carrying them through the Brenner Pass (the border crossing between Austria and Italy) and made their way six hundred miles back through German occupied territory to re-join the commando in Italy. Peter Long broke out of his prison camp in the middle of Germany and made his way back to Britain through Germany, occupied France, the Pyrenees, Spain and, eventually, Gibraltar. He was back with 3 Cdo in time to take part in the D Day landings.

While no one could anticipate the arrival of German paratroops in Sicily, there can be no doubt that the planners for the operation against Malati Bridge got several things wrong, particularly the presence of armoured units near the bridge. Somehow the presence of the entire Hermann Goering Panzer Division on the island was overlooked, though by the time of the attack on Malati bridge their presence was known, as several British and American units had suffered at their hand. The planners also seriously underestimated the time that both the paratroops at Primasole Bridge and the commandos would have to hold out until the relief force arrived. Whether this was a consequence of hasty planning, a lack of adequate intelligence or just reckless risk taking, we will never know.

A commemorative stone is positioned in the parapet of Malati Bridge, dedicating it to 3 Commando, placed there on the orders of General Montgomery. The action does not appear on the standard that bears the battle honours of the commandos, which is 'laid up' in St Paul's Cathedral.

It is the mark of a great commander that they learn from their mistakes, but Montgomery was to repeat the mistakes of Malati Bridge in Italy (a story to be told in the next episode of Carter's adventures), then on a much bigger scale in The Netherlands in 1944, with Operation Market-Garden, the plan to capture Arnhem Bridge. If anyone ever suggests that Montgomery was a great leader, you can remind them of his failure to learn from his mistakes.

* * *

The Army commandos were established in June 1940 on the direct orders of Winston Churchill. The original concept, a force that could raid across the channel into occupied France, was the brainchild of Col (later Brigadier) Dudley Clarke, a Royal Artillery officer who was a genius at devising deception operations. His suggestion found its way to Churchill's ear and he was taken by it.

It was Churchill who recognised that to maintain the war effort until victory could be achieved, he needed to maintain the morale of the British people following the disaster that had been the evacuation from Dunkirk. The skilful use of propaganda had turned that defeat into a sort of victory, but genuine victories, however small, would be needed if he was to convince the British people that the war could be won.

It would be the commandos that would provide those small victories. Often the targets of their raids were insignificant in military terms but, on occasions, they had a far greater impact than could ever have been imagined. For example, following successive raids on Norway, Adolf Hitler became convinced that they were the prelude to an invasion of that country as a stepping stone for invading Denmark and then Germany itself. No such plan existed, but Hitler ordered 300,000 additional troops to be sent to Norway, where they remained for the rest of the war, along with additional Luftwaffe and naval units. The fact that the invasion of Norway never came about was proof to Hitler that his counter-strategy had worked. Had those troops been available at Stalingrad, El Alamein or in Normandy in 1944, who knows how the outcomes of those battles might have been affected.

15 Commando is a fictitious unit. The Army commandos were numbered 1 to 14 (excluding 13). 50, 51 and 52 commandos were formed in North Africa.

The parachute regiment were formed from No 2 Commando, who had originally been set up to take on the role of paratroops. Even after the establishment of the Parachute Regiment in 1942, the commandos still trained some of their troops in parachuting, though there is no record of them ever having undertaken that role.

No 10 (Inter Allied) Commando was made up of members of the armed forces from occupied countries in Europe who had escaped. There were two French troops, one Norwegian, one Dutch, one Belgian, one Polish, one Yugoslavian and a troop of German speakers, many of whom were Jewish and had escaped from Germany and Austria. They often accompanied other commandos on raids to act as guides and interpreters, as well as carrying out raids of their own.

Achnacarry House is the ancestral home of Clan Cameron and it was taken over by the War Office to become the Commando

Training Centre. The original occupants of the house moved into cottages in the grounds. During the course of World War II over 25,000 commandos were trained there, plus some of their American counterparts, the Rangers, who were modelled on the commandos. Originally each commando was responsible for providing their own training, before the first training centres were set up at Inveraray and Lochailort, in late 1940, before moving to Achnacarry.

The first Royal Marine commandos didn't come into being until 19th February 1942. 40 (RM) Cdo was, like the army commandos, made up of volunteers, but subsequent units (41- 48) were RM battalions who were ordered to convert. For this reason the army commandos tended to look down on their RM counterparts. However, the RM commandos fought bravely and in all theatres of the war. They carried the commando legacy onwards at the end of the war and continue to do so to this day.

If you wish to find out more about the Army commandos there are a number of books on the subject, including my own, which details my father's wartime service; it's called "A Commando's Story". I have provided the titles of some of these books at the end of these notes. These also provided the sources for much of my research for this book.

In the fictional world, Lieutenant Carter and Cpl Green, LCpl Glass and Tpr O'Driscoll have been reunited with 15 Commando, but they are destined, like my father, to have many more adventures before the war comes to an end.

Further Reading.

For firsthand accounts of Commando operations and training at Achnacarry, try the following:

Cubitt, Robert; A Commando's Story; Ex-L-Ence Publishing; 2018.

Durnford-Slater, John, Brigadier: Commando: Memoirs of a Fighting Commando in World War II; Greenhill Books; new edition 2002.

Gilchrist, Donald; Castle Commando; The Highland Council; 3rd revised edition, 1993.

Scott, Stan; Fighting With The Commandos; Pen and Sword Military; 2008.

Young, Peter, Brigadier; Storm from the Sea; Greenhill Books; new edition 2002.

For a more general overview of the commandos and their operations:

Saunders, Hilary St George; The Green Beret; YBS The Book Service Ltd; new edition 1972.

Preview – Operation Terminus

1 – Messina

July drifted into a hot Sicilian August and 15 Cdo settled into a training routine, attempting to get the few available replacements properly bedded into the commando and up to the high standard expected of the men.

Without any idea of what the next operation might bring, the training concentrated on the generics of all operations: armed and unarmed combat, map reading and navigation, radio procedures, cross country marches and sea landings. Catania eventually fell, followed quickly by Messina as the enemy evacuated the last of their troops from the island. The roads became clogged with long crocodiles of German and Italian prisoners who had been cut off or failed to make it onto the last Axis boats off the island. They were marched south, away from where the Allies were massing their forces ready to make the short jump across the sea to Italy.

News of Mussolini's resignation[1] came through, which cheered everyone up, then Catania fell. Everyone knew that the Germans would have to evacuate the island through Messina. It was the shortest crossing to the mainland; only five miles wide in parts. The opposite coast could be seen clearly. The Allies concentrated their efforts on making their departure as difficult as possible.

The commando was told it would move north to Messina to prepare for the invasion of the mainland, just as soon as the Germans were gone. But for the time being they remained in Lo Bello, just outside Syracuse, which might have been a Butlins holiday camp as far as the commando was concerned.

Carter stopped outside the HQ tent and wiped his face with his neck cloth. It was still hot even in the late afternoon and the route march that he had led his troop on had drained him of all his energy.

But the CO's clerk, Ecclestone, had told him that the CO wanted him as a matter of urgency and he shouldn't even stop to take a shower.

Pulling back the tent flap, Carter stepped inside. "CO's with the 2IC, Sir." Ecclestone informed him. "Won't be more than a minute or so, I 'spect."

The tent was dark, but not any cooler than the outside. In fact the lack of air made the interior feel more oppressive. Carter could hear the voices of the 2IC and the CO, screened behind a wall of canvass, but he couldn't make out what they were saying. Probably plotting the next operation, which suggested a reason for Carter having been summoned. Perhaps he was to lead it, or maybe go along with the 2IC as his second in command. The lack of any other officers assembling suggested that whatever it was, it wouldn't involve the whole commando.

There was a rustle of canvass and the 2IC appeared from the back of the tent. Even in the gloom Carter could see that he had a broad grin on his face. "Afternoon, Steven." He said as he passed him. Carter could have been mistaken, but he was sure the 2IC had winked at him. Surely not. The 2IC had many quirks in his personality but winking at a subordinate was a new one on Carter.

"Is Captain Carter here yet, Ecclestone?" The CO's voice called from behind the canvas.

"I'm right here, Sir." Carter replied.

"Come on through." Doing as he was bid, he pushed the canvass screen to one side then let it drop behind him again.

"Take a pew, old chap." Vernon acknowledge Carter's salute with a nod.

Carter sat himself on the camp stool that was the only furniture available other than the trestle table that served as a desk and the camp chair on which the CO himself was sitting. The only adornment to the trestle table was a field telephone sitting in its canvas carrying case. Its cable trailed off the table and disappeared under the side of the tent. Part of the new organisation for the commando was a signals section, made up of commandos who had attended special training while they had still been in Egypt. Their pride and joy was a tiny telephone exchange which had four extensions, one of which sat on the CO's desk. A single telephone line connected it to 8th Army HQ, which was now located in Catania. For the first time in its three year history, the commando was no longer dependent on radios or dispatch riders for its communications with higher authority.

"I've some good news and some bad news, Steven. Which would you like first?"

Whatever the bad news is, get it out of the way first, Carter thought. "The bad news, I think, Sir."

"I thought you might say that. The bad news is that I'm to leave the commando, effective from this evening."

Vernon was right, that was bad news. To most of the men, the CO was the commando, its beating heart and intelligent brain. "I'm sorry to hear that, Sir. Where are you going?"

"Monty wants me to take command of both 15 and 49 commandos. I'll also have an outfit called the Special Raiding Squadron[2] under my wing. It's effectively a Brigade, but it can't be called that, because I'm not a Brigadier. Even Monty hasn't the authority to promote me to that level. He's made me acting Colonel though, which is nice."

"We'll miss you, Sir."

"Don't worry, you can't get rid of me that easily. Wherever you are, you can be sure I won't be far away."

"I take it that the reason that the 2IC was grinning like a Cheshire cat is that he is to replace you."

"Yes, he is. Which brings me to the good news. You are to take over as 2IC, with the acting rank of Major."

"Me ... but ... surely the QM ..." As a substantive major the Quarter Master would be the natural choice to take over as 2IC.

"The QM is coming with me as my Chief of Staff. My only staff in fact, for the moment. So I've had to go looking for the new 2IC amongst the Troop Commanders. You are the natural choice. You have an established reputation and the men think highly of you. I can think of no one better for the job."

"But Angus Fraser, Sir. He has more seniority than ..."

The CO cut him off. "Promotion in the commandos isn't about seniority, it's about suitability and I think you are more suitable. Besides, I want Angus to take over as QM. He seems to have a natural talent as a scrounger."

That was true. Fraser seemed to be able to get his hands on many scarce items and when asked where they came from, the answer was always began "A bloke I know over in ..." and then some other unit would be named. Scrounging was an essential skill for a commando quarter master. The commandos had always been at the tail end of any queue for equipment and sometimes it was only the QM's skills that allowed the men to get anything at all, including essential items of uniform.

"Well, in that case, Sir, all I can say is thank you for your faith in me. After that incident at Ponte Bridge I thought ..."

Vernon waved away Carters reminder about him falling asleep and allowing himself and his men to be captured by a German patrol. "The man who never made a mistake never made anything, Steven.[3] I'm sure it won't happen again. Now, go and find Angus and tell him I want to see him. But don't spoil my fun by telling him why. Oh, and the three of you are buying the drinks tonight."

[1] 25th July 1943. He was replaced by King Emmanuel III, making Marshall Pietro Badoglio his Prime Minister. He was a senior member of the Fascist Party and the Army who had been out of favour since the failed Italian invasion of Greece in 1940. When Italy surrendered in September 1943, it would be Badoglio who would travel to Cassibile in Sicily to sign the Armistice agreement and declare war on Germany. When the Germans disarmed the Italian military, the King, Badoglio and some other senior Party figures escaped from Rome to Brindisi to form a government in exile.

[2] We now know this unit by the much more famous name of the Special Air Service (SAS) but as both Brigadier John Durnford-Slater and Brigadier Peter Young (see *Further Reading*) use this name in their books, we must assume that they were known as the Special Raiding Squadron in Sicily in 1943.

[3] A common misquote of a phrase attributed to Albert Einstein. The correct quote is "A person who never made a mistake never tried anything new." However, the attribution to Einstein is very weak and there are a number of variations on the theme going back as far as 1832, with an anonymous attribution. The earliest version that fits with Vernon's usage is Josh Billings in 1874. Josh Billings was the pen name of American humourist Henry Wheeler Shaw.

* * *

"Back here in an hour." Carter instructed the men in his work party when they reached the dockyard gates. Safely parked up inside was the truck they had arrived in, with its cargo of two long packing cases and another half dozen cube like ones. Carter knew what they contained, which was why Andrew Fraser had asked him to collect them. But he wasn't letting on just yet. The surprise could wait.

"And don't get into any mischief!" he called at their retreating backs as they headed for the Salvation Army canteen. It would do no good. He would no sooner be out of sight and they'd change direction and go looking for something more appealing than tea and sticky buns.

He headed towards the Officer's Club that had been established in one of Catania's better restaurants. With so little food available the place would struggle to survive if the military hadn't commandeered it and kept the staff on, paying them to serve Italian wine and beer, which is all that was available locally.

He had just reached the door when he heard a voice call his name.

"It is you, Steven. I thought it was." Carter looked around to see a tall, elegantly uniformed figure striding across the square towards him.

"Ewan Flamming, as I live and breathe." Carter said, before he spied the three wavy[1] gold rings on the cuffs of the man's uniform and throwing up a salute. "I'm sorry, Commander Flamming that should be."

The man laughed. "Don't stand on ceremony, old chap. After all, it was my little jaunt with you that helped get me the extra thick ring." He tapped the shinier centre ring of the three, which had previously been thinner, denoting the more junior rank of Lieutenant Commander. "And you've gone up in the world as well; a Major now. Last time I saw you, you were still just a Lieutenant. Come, on, let me buy you a drink and you can tell me all about it." He pushed the door of the club open, then stood to one side to allow Carter to enter first.

"Not much to tell, really. I got my third pip through dead men's shoes, quite literally. But my crown[2] came about because my CO was promoted and everyone moved up one rank to fill the gap."

"Honfleur or Tunisia; for the dead men's shoes I mean."

"Have you been keeping tabs on me?" Carter laughed. "Honfleur actually. We lost a lot of good men there. Tunisia was a walk in the park by comparison." They had reached the bar and looked around to find a table. Spotting one at the back of the room, away from the few other customers, they made their way across to it. The club was quiet at that time of the day; most officers had duties to attend to. Carter had only agreed to take a break before returning to Messina because it was so hot and his men were thirsty after the journey and loading the vehicle.

"I have to admit, I do take an interest in what your unit has been up to. You're quite famous these days. You're attracting a lot of attention in London. I hear you added to your lustre by capturing a bridge a few miles from here." Flamming raised his finger to attract the eye of a waiter and one appeared at their table as though summoned by magic. Some people had a knack for that, Carter noted and Flamming was one of them. His easy manner spoke of jazz clubs, expensive cocktails and women who were generous with their favours. Those sorts of people weren't usually Carter's type, but he knew that under Flamming's louche exterior there was a core of steel.

"*Vino rosso, per favore.*" Flamming said to the waiter. "What about you, Steven?"

"Just a beer for me."

Flamming placed the order and the waiter scurried away.

"The wine isn't up to much." Carter advised him.

"I know, but until we get the French vineyards back from the Germans it will have to do. And I doubt that chap would know how to make a decent vodka martini." Carter had to acknowledge that the unshaven and rather scruffy Italian hadn't looked like a cocktail barman. But then, with soap and razor blades in short supply for the civilian population, looks could be deceiving. He might have been the Maître D' at the restaurant before it became the Officer's Club, for all either of them knew.

"So, where are you based these days?" Carter asked. He had a tingling in the nape of his neck that told him that his meeting with Flamming hadn't come about by chance.

"Still based in London. I'm out here trying to put together an operation. I was in Malta for the invasion and I've only just arrived here this week. But it is fortunate that I've bumped into you."

Bingo! Carter thought. He is after something. Flamming had previously tried to recruit him into a new unit he was forming and Carter wondered if this was just another attempt to do the same.

"Look, I'm 2IC of the commando now. I have responsibilities. I can't just swan off …"

"Nothing could be further from my mind, old chap." Flamming hurried to reassure him. "I just need a bit of advice."

Carter doubted that, but it would be churlish to refuse to offer advice if it was sought. "Well, just to be clear, that's all. Now, what can I advise you on?"

Flamming leant in closer to Carter and lowered his voice. "You mustn't breath a word of this to anyone. Is that understood?"

"I think you can rely on my discretion." Carter was a little bit miffed that Flamming should need to remind him about the need for secrecy.

"Sorry, but lives are at stake here. OK. My operation is to bring somebody out of Italy. They have vital information that will be of use to the Allies. But I haven't been allocated any resources for the job. Let's just say that if it goes wrong, people don't want their names associated with it, so they've dropped it on my shoulders and told me to get on with it as best I can. No doubt if the operation is a success then my part will be forgotten as the big-wigs in Whitehall all scrap over whose idea it was, but that's for later."

"Why not use 30 Commando[2]?" Carter asked. "After all, you set them up."

"Partly true. I was involved with them being established, but only as part of a bigger team. But they're massively overworked right now. As well as hunting for intelligence here on Sicily, they're still sifting through the mountain of stuff they've already gathered. And as soon as we cross the Straits, they'll be tied up in Italy doing the same. Besides, they're not parachute trained."

"Is that an essential?" Carter asked.

"The target is too far inland for a seaborne operation alone. There's almost no chance of a ground force getting all the way to the target without being discovered and the target can't get closer to the sea; at least, not without arousing suspicion. So, the force would have to drop by parachute, grab the target and then hope to escape across country to be picked up on the coast. So, we need a second force to take and hold the beach where they'll be evacuated from."

"You aren't asking for much then." Irony was heavy in Carter's tone. "Paratroops, aircraft, commandos and ships to extract them."

"I know I'm asking a lot. Which is why I thought you might be able to suggest a unit I might be able to use."

"The parachute insertion might be a job for the Special Raiding Squadron. They were set up in North Africa by a former commando by the name of David Stirling. He's still their CO. They're currently under the command of our former CO, Col Vernon. They're all parachute trained. In fact, it sounds like it might be right up their street, so to speak. The extraction could be done by any commando unit, I suppose."

"How many commandos would it need?"

"That depends. If the beach is undefended, a troop could probably do it, though if it was me I'd want a floating reserve out at sea to come to my rescue if things got sticky. If it's a heavily defended beach, then it might need a whole commando."

"Could you do the job?"

"I told you, I'm too busy right now."

"But what about your unit, 15 Commando?"

"That's our bread and butter work, so we could certainly do it, but getting us released to do the job wouldn't be easy. We're no longer in the free and easy days just after we were set up and anyone could suggest a raid and Combined Ops might rubber stamp it.

Everything's much more structured now, with a full chain of command going all the way to the very top. Officially we're part of XIII Corps, but our tasking comes direct from 8th Army HQ. Brigadier Laycock is the man to speak to."

"Isn't he the chap that tried to kidnap Rommel[4]?"

"Yes. In fact, this sort of operation might appeal to him. But he'd still have to convince Monty. Given his focus on conventional soldiering, he might take some persuading. He's only just started to appreciate what we commandos have to offer, so madcap schemes involving parachuting behind enemy lines might not appeal to him, unless it can be linked directly to the needs of his strategy."

"That would be a tough idea to sell him. Our target is high value, but more in political terms than military."

"In that case you would need someone in the War Office, or even in the War Cabinet, to influence him. Out here, Monty is Lord of all he surveys. Nobody can give him orders. Even Eisenhower[5] has to ask nicely." Carter swallowed the last of his beer and stood to leave. "Now, if you'll excuse me, I have some rather important equipment to get back to camp."

"Of course. Well, it was nice seeing you again, Steven." Flamming extended his hand to be shaken. "Perhaps we'll run into each other again."

Carter hoped not. Anything that Flamming was involved in was likely to be dangerous. Not that it bothered Carter; he was a commando after all and 'dangerous' was what they did. But he didn't fancy getting involved in any harebrained[6] schemes either. But he didn't say that. Instead he shook Flamming's hand, thanked him for the drink and said some polite words of farewell.

[1] Wavy golf braid rings on the sleeves or epaulettes of the of Royal Navy officers indicates that the holder of the rank is a reservist, rather than a regular. Of the three armed services in the UK, the Royal Navy is the only one to make that distinction between the badges of rank of regular and reserve officers.

[2] The badge of rank for a Major is a crown.

[3] 30 Cdo were established in 1942 as an intelligence gathering unit capable of going ahead of an assault to try to capture documents and other intelligence assets before the enemy had time to destroy them.

[4] This was Operation Flipper, carried out in Libya between 10th and 18th November 1941. It failed because Rommel wasn't at the location where he was expected to be. He had actually left there several weeks earlier. Soldiers from 11 Commando, part of

Layforce, carried out the raid and it was led by Colonel (as he was at the time) Laycock in person.

[5] General Dwight D Eisenhower was the Supreme Allied Commander in the Mediterranean theatre and commanded the Allied armies for the invasion of Sicily and Italy. He would later take command of the Allied forces for the invasion of France. After the war he went into politics as a Republican and became the 34th President of the USA.

[6] Sometimes written as "hairbrained" but its original usage was meant to indicate that the idea had been thought up by a hare, which isn't considered to be the most intelligent animal and is also seen as rather skittish in its behaviour.

* * *

The following morning saw Carter standing in front of a group of a dozen members of 2 Troop, the designated heavy weapons troop. Beside him stood Giles Gulliver, their OC. To his other side stood a sergeant with the maple leaf badge of the Canadian army on the sleeve of his shirt.

At Carter's feet lay the two long packing cases that had been unloaded from the truck on its return to the camp the previous evening. Behind him were the dozen cube like boxes that had accompanied them. It was time to open his surprise.

"Good morning gentlemen. I am pleased to inform you that you have two new additions to the heavy weapons inventory." He stretched out his hand, which contained two screwdrivers. "Collins, MacIntyre, if you would do the honours."

The two named troopers took the screwdrivers and set to work on the top case, It was the work of several minutes to remove the screws and lift the lid off the box. Nestled into cradles of horsehair padding were two long, tube like weapons. Each had a wooden butt like that of a rifle, but the working parts and barrel looked more like lengths of drainpipe, with a cavity cut into each at the end nearest the trigger.

"May I introduce you to the projectile, infantry, anti-tank, otherwise known as the PIAT." This produced a buzz of conversation through the dozen men, pleasing Carter that he had managed to surprise men who thought that little could surprise them after all they had experienced. They had heard of this new wonder-weapon, but none of them had so far seen one, let alone used it.

"Sgt McLean here," Carter indicated the Canadian soldier, "Is on loan to us for a couple of days to teach you how to use these weapons. He has real combat experience using them, so he knows what he is talking about. How many tanks did you say you had stopped using these weapons?"

McLean seemed to swell with pride. "Three, Sir. Two Mk III *Panzers* and one Tiger."

"Thank you. Now, you will be taken a few miles north to where there are some German and Italian tanks that have already been introduced to these, to their cost." There was a ripple of laughter. "And there you will be trained in their use. You will be trained in teams of two, an operator and a loader. Sadly, we have a limited amount of ammunition available, so most of the training will be dry runs using dummy projectiles. But each team will be allowed to fire one live projectile each at one of the dead tanks. You will be taught the best firing positions for each tank, with emphasis on the Tiger, as they are the hardest to disable. Any questions?"

The men muttered some comments to each other, but no one had any questions to ask at that point. "Very well. I'll leave you with Capt Gulliver and Sgt McLean."

As he marched away, Carter heard the men push forward to examine their new acquisitions. He smiled again. Soldiers loved new hardware, especially something that gave them an advantage over a weapon as fearsome as a Tiger tank. After their experiences at Ponte Bridge, they were itching to get their revenge on the German behemoths.

But Carter had other concerns to occupy his mind. The 2IC held the additional role of training officer. His main responsibility while in camp was to improve the skills of the commando and make sure they were prepared for whatever operation they were next engaged on. The problem was that no one had any idea what that operation might be. The crossing of the Straits of Messina was the next obvious move for the Allies, but no one knew what part the commando might take in that. A sea landing was pretty obvious, but against what sort of terrain with what sort of defences? And what would the commando's objective be?

Another artillery battery perhaps? Or perhaps the clearing of beach defences. They had done both in Sicily. Or maybe it would be another bridge.

Reaching the HQ tent, Carter sat down behind the trestle table that he used as a desk, He drew a sheet of paper from the stack that sat on one corner of the table and started to write a list of possible targets. He then numbered them in order of likelihood, in terms of the commando being used to attack them. To the three he had already considered, he added a fourth, triggered by his conversation with Flamming the previous day: relief of parachute forces. But he made it the lowest priority.

Examining each item on the list, he then considered the unique skills the commando would need to have to attack each type of target. The list was similar for each, but each also had its differences. From that he was able to draw up a prioritised list of training activity, supplemented by the normal routine of physical fitness training, small arms skills and unarmed combat.

That gave him the 'what' of his training plan, but not the how. For that he would need resources. He started work on a list of equipment that he would need Angus Fraser to provide and thought of the amused laughter he would get at some of his requests. But none of them would be dismissed. If Fraser could get his hands on the stuff, it would appear.

Top of his list of other resources was sea transport. He would need one of the commando carrying ships, because each training task started much the same way: a run into shore in landing craft, under the cover of darkness. Unless they sprouted wings and flew, there was no way of getting to Italy without crossing the short expanse of water that separated Sicily from Italy.

The other unknown was how much time they might have. It was already early August and it was certain that Monty would want to establish himself in Italy before the autumn rains started and clogged the roads with mud. He had to assume that their next operation was imminent. He studied his list of training tasks again and wondered how many the whole commando would manage to complete. He started cutting out those which he knew added the least value, or which the commandos were already proficient at. More training in them would be beneficial; no training was ever wasted; but some skills were more important than others.

* * *

"Colonel Vernon." Ecclestone, the guardian of the tent flap, said loudly to alert the rest of the tent's occupants to the fact that they had a senior ranking visitor. Carter and Fraser, the other two occupants, sprang to their feet and stood to attention.

"As you were, chaps. Carry on." Vernon grinned at them.

"Welcome back, Sir." Fraser said. "We weren't expecting you."

"I told you I would never be far away." Vernon smiled. "Is Col Cousins in?"

"I'm right here." The CO appeared from behind the canvas screen that offered him a modicum of privacy in the corner of the tent.

"Ah, Charlie. Settled into your new role, eh?"

"Getting used to it, Sir."

"Good, good. I need a word with you. Steven, Angus, you may as well hear this as well. Your input would be valuable."

"Bring your chairs through, please." Charlie instructed. "Ecclestone, a pot of tea if you will."

Everyone had been surprised when Vernon had elected to leave his trusted clerk and batman behind when he took up his new job, but Ecclestone didn't seem to mind. "It's not like I'll get to do any proper soldiering if I go with the Colonel." Ecclestone had confided to Carter after his old boss had departed. It was typical of a commando not to seek out a 'cushy billet'.

The two majors carried their camp chairs through to what Charlie Cousins called his cubbyhole and they settled down, an air of anticipation present as they waited for Vernon to explain the purpose of his visit. Was this when they would find out about their next operation? It was certain that Vernon hadn't arrived just to inquire about their wellbeing.

Vernon didn't keep them waiting. "I've had a request from 8th Army HQ to examine a proposal for a small operation." He explained. "It isn't related to our impending invasion of Italy, but apparently it's quite important."

A little bell started to jingle in Carter's mind. It might be a coincidence, but it was only a few days since he had run into Ewan Flamming. That would have allowed him time to exchange communications with London and make a few requests for assistance and the exerting of influence.

"There's a plan to drop some parachutists into Italy to bring out some big-wig who wants to change sides. I don't have the details yet. But it's been suggested that the SRS do the drop and either yourselves or 49 cover the extraction from a beach. What do you think?"

"Does the name Flamming have anything to do with this?" Carter asked. "He's a Navy chap, a Commander."

Vernon gave Carter a look of curiosity. "What do you know of Cdr Flamming, Steven?"

"We met on one of those secret jobs I did when we were based in Troon. I bumped into him last week in Catania and we discussed something just like this. He asked for my advice. There didn't seem to be any harm in helping the chap."

"You may not feel that way if you get tasked with doing the job, but that is hypothetical for the moment. At the end of the day we do as we're ordered and it does sound like a job for commandos. And yes, Flamming's name did crop up during the conversation. So, what did you advise him?"

Carter told them of the content of his conversation. "And that's just about it. He didn't share any details with me about location or the target. It was just the practicalities of getting in and out of Italy with him."

"I must say I haven't been told a great deal more." Vernon replied. "I can tell you that the intended location isn't anywhere near our planned landing beaches for the invasion, so there would be a bit of a sea voyage involved. Monty wouldn't tolerate any action on the other side of the Strait that might raise the enemy's level of preparedness any higher than it already is. I've already spoken to David Stirling about how his men would reach the target. How would you do the extraction, if 15 Cdo were given the job?"

"Steven, you seem to have given this some thought. Would you like to answer?" The CO deferred.

"I'd set up two teams, each made up of half a troop. One team would stay on the beach, or very close to it, just to defend it in case any Italian patrol turned up unannounced. The other team I'd take about half a mile to a mile inland to wait for the paratroops. If they're being chased they can offer fire support and then close up behind them and act as a rear guard until they reach the beach. I'd also want some naval gunfire available. There's nothing like a bombardment to slow the gallop of a pursuing enemy. With our own mortars and Vickers guns in reserve, I think we could hold off anything less than a battalion strength."

"Andrew, what would you need in terms of additional supplies?"

"We're short on Bangalore torpedoes[1], for a start. They're essential for a beach landing. I'd also want more three-oh-three ammunition and mortar bombs and more PIAT rounds."

"I don't think the enemy would have time to mobilise armour …" Carter started to say, before falling silent as Fraser gave him a warning look. Col Vernon spotted it and gave a laugh.

"Well done Angus. I can see where you're coming from."

"I'm sorry, have I missed something?" Carter's voice told of his puzzlement.

Vernon was the one to reply. "Angus has spotted that this would be an opportunity to ask for materials that are in short supply in the commando, even if you aren't going to need them for the op. It's a chance to fill up his stores with scare items. The ability to spot opportunities such as this is one of the reasons I appointed him QM. And I'll pretend I didn't hear your objection, Steven"

Carter felt himself blushing. He should have spotted the opportunity as well.

"I've been told that the nearest troops are about five kilometres away in a fishing village. They're a platoon strength of Italian garrison troops who spend most of their days drinking wine and most of their nights fornicating with the wives of the fishermen who are at sea or in the army. If the alarm is raised, they'll be ordered out to intercept. The next nearest enemy force is a company strength of Italians about ten kilometres further north. You could expect them to be mobilised as well. Could you deal with them?"

"It depends on whether they head inland to try to intercept the intruder force before they reach the coast, or if they decided to get between the intruders and the sea and lie in wait for them. The first case we couldn't do anything about because we wouldn't know where to look for them, but in the second case we could probably ambush them before they could set up any defensive positions. If we can drive them off, the Navy could keep their heads down with gunfire. The main problem would be to stop the two forces from joining up. But even then, with the SRS on one side and us on the other, they'd be in a far worse fix than we would be."

"OK., Final question. If you were offered this operation to undertake, would you accept it willingly or would you be reluctant to risk your command?"

"From the commando's perspective, I'd rate it as reasonably low risk. We would hold the beach and the means of escape, so I'd accept it willingly. It's the SRS that would have the hard work."

"And they've said they'd love to take it on." Vernon stood up and pushed his beret onto his head. "OK, gentlemen, thank you for your input. I've got to go up to Catania to discuss this with the Brigadier but be on standby to come up for a planning session. If you are happy for Steven to take the lead on this, Charlie," Vernon addressed the CO, "Then there's no need for you to come, but Angus will need to be there, so he can add his two-penn'orth."

[1] A Bangalore torpedo is a hollow tube filled with explosives which can be slid underneath barbed wire entanglements to blow a hole in them. The tubes are about 5 ft in length and can be extended by joining them to empty tubes to provide additional reach. Modern versions are still in use with the British army.

* * *

The summons came the following morning, creating a rush to get to Catania over the damaged roads and through the choking transport. Fraser and Carter shared a Jeep borrowed from a neighbouring infantry unit because, despite pleas to XIII Corps, they still couldn't get transport allocated to them. It was a perennial complaint from the commandos, having to go cap in hand to beg for something so basic.

The roads were choked with lines of prisoners snaking along them under the guard of infantrymen using bayonet tipped rifles. Most of them seemed to be Italian, from what Carter could see. The Germans were mainly fighting the Americans. It was a fluke of how the Axis had organised the defence of the island. But the Germans had put up a stout defence of Catania, delaying the capture of the port and airfield and delaying the British advance.

They were the last to arrive. Brigadier Laycock was chairing the meeting as he would be the one to go to the Commander in Chief to get the go-ahead for any operation. His advice would be crucial to getting the mission agreed. Carter recognised Flamming, of course and introduced him to Fraser. There was a good looking Major that Carter had recognised from the Officer's Club in Syracuse. The man introduced himself as David Stirling of the Special Raiding Squadron. Also present was a Commander by the name of Hanning, representing the Navy, who would have to provide the ships and an RAF Squadron Leader.

"Gilchrist," the RAF man introduced himself. "7 MORU[1]." He saw the puzzlement on Carter's face. "We're the chaps who support the air force in the field."

Carter really was none the wiser but decided that life was too short to ask questions. All he had to worry about was whether he got the fighter cover he needed for the withdrawal phase of the operation and he assumed that the RAF man was the right person to make that happen for him. Besides, Laycock was tapping his fingernails on the table, impatient to get started.

"OK, chaps. Some of you may be wondering why you have been invited here today, others will already know what this is all about. We're calling this Operation Manchester. That name is Restricted, but all the detail behind it is classified Top Secret and mustn't be discussed outside this room until the operation is mounted and you can brief your personnel in a secure environment. Is that understood?"

There were mutterings of agreement. "OK, we'll go around the room and introduce ourselves and then Cdr Flamming will tell you what this is about."

As the introductions were made, Flamming got to his feet and turned over a chalk board to reveal a sketch map of a stretch of coast. It could have been in any country in the world. "I'm sorry to be so secretive about this, but a man's life and that of his family depends on no one knowing this operation has even been discussed.

If we don't get the go-ahead for the operation, then his identity has to be protected and even a tiny detail such as the town in which he lives cannot slip out. Which is why this map uses only code names. I can tell you that the map is a stretch of coastline and is on the west coast, somewhere between here and Rome."

He paused and started to point out the features on the map. "The objective for the airborne element, that's David Stirling and his men, is a town approximately 10 kilometres inland from the coast. Is everyone happy with me talking in kilometres?" There were nods of assent. "Thank you, it's just that the maps we're using are all metric, so for consistency I'd like to keep it that way for the entire operation. Now, the town is codenamed Albert. Once the target is located, the airborne element will take him and his family to the beach, to be met by Major Carter and his commandos, who will secure the beach."

"I didn't realise that the target would have his family with him." Stirling interjected. "How many people are we talking about?"

"There's the target, his wife and two children, aged nine and ten. Is that a problem?"

"Not the children. If the worst comes to the worst we can carry them, piggy-back style. No, it's the woman. She'll have to be properly dressed. I've seen these Italian fashions. She wouldn't make it across the fields in the sort of shoes they wear."

"OK, we can talk about that later." Flamming was anxious not to get side-tracked into detail at this stage of the briefing. There would be time for that later. "What about reaching the target after you've made the drop?"

"We need to be able to move through the streets without being spotted; That's for sure. Could we mount a bombing raid to coincide with the drop?"

"Won't that put your men at risk?" the RAF man asked.

"You don't have to bomb the town itself, just close enough to the town for the population to stay in their shelters. But it would need to be sustained over a period of time; say thirty to forty minutes. If the all clear is sounded while we're still in the town we're likely to be spotted and we'll be no better off."

The Sqn Ldr looked dubious. "Keeping aircraft loitering over a target for that length of time is dangerous. It would give the Jerries time to direct night fighters into the area."

"Could you send them in singly over the time period?" Andrew Fraser suggested.

"It won't stop the night fighters, but it will reduce the target size, so it might work." The airman conceded.

"OK, that's settled." Flamming closed down the discussion before it could get bogged down. The Sqn Ldr made some notes on a pad but didn't make any further objections.

"Now, in terms of getting onto the beach, the Italians haven't considered it important enough to defend. It is formed by a dip in the cliffs on either side, about a hundred metres long. Inland there's sand dunes for about five hundred metres, then the coast road. On the other side, which the SRS will approach from, is open farmland criss-crossed by cart tracks. The beach is nicknamed Victoria. Aerial reconnaissance shows no habitation, and no defences other than barbed wire."

He pointed to the southern side of the map, where a dot had been marked on the coast, with the letter B next to it. "Here we have the nearest town, well it's no more than a village. It has a small garrison, no more than a platoon strength. They have trucks though, so if the alarm is raised, they can be expected to respond. That village is nicknamed Bertie. To the north," he moved his pointer, "About ten kilometres from the beach and two kilometres inland, is a small town, which I've nicknamed Consort. There's a company of Italian troops there.

Now, there's no direct road from Bertie to Albert, which means that any attempt to intercept from there would have to go via Consort, so they don't represent a risk for you, David. However, they could stumble across your commandos, Steven. The garrison at Consort, however, is connected to Albert by road and could move inland to intercept the SRS or along the coast to meet up with the troops from Bertie."

"They could also split their force and do both." Stirling interjected.

"They could, but there's no way of knowing which they will do until they do it, so you'll have to be prepared for all eventualities."

"We always are, old chap." Stirling drawled.

"What I'd like to do now, is go through each of the four phases of the operation with David and Steven taking the lead as appropriate and explaining how you plan to go about each phase, what you need in terms of support, etc. The phases I see are the insertion followed by the extraction, which are both a matter for the SRS; then the securing of the beach and the evacuation, which is where Steven comes in."

"There's also the withdrawal." Carter said. "Once we're off the beach and in the landing craft, we're in the hands of the Navy and, as we discovered the last time we had an operation that involved a return sea journey, the operation isn't complete until we all get safely back home."

"OK, Steven; point taken. That makes it five phases then. The way we'll tackle this is for each of you to say how you want to complete each phase and what resources you will need to make that happen. Aircraft, landing craft, ships etc. Then our colleagues from the RAF and the Navy can tell us what they can do to meet your needs. Don't worry about whether or not your lords and masters are willing to provide those resources …" that brought a chuckle, "… it will be Monty who is asking for the whatever is needed, so the arguments can take place at his level, not ours." That brought more laughter, though Carter knew that if either the RAF or Navy officers suggested that something couldn't be done, their 'lords and masters' would probably also take that view.

"So, David, tell us how you intend getting your men to the target." Flamming sat down, raised his pen above his note pad and prepared to write.

[1] MORU – Mobile Operations Room Unit. A mobile RAF organisation that liaises with army commanders in the field to ensure that air support is provided as required. They provide the same functions as a Group Headquarters would have done in Bomber Command or Fighter Command. A MORU operated out of 3 Ton lorries that had been converted into mobile offices and communications centres.

End of Extract

And Now

Both the author Robert Cubitt and Selfishgenie Publishing hope that you have enjoyed reading this story.

Please tell people about this book, write a review on Amazon or mention it on your favourite social networking site. Word of mouth is an author's best friend and is much appreciated. Thank you.

Find Robert Cubitt on Facebook at https://www.facebook.com/robertocubitt and 'like' his page; follow him on Twitter **@Robert_Cubitt**

For further titles that may be of interest to you please visit our website at **selfishgenie.com** where you can optionally join our information list.

Printed in Great Britain
by Amazon